Return
of the
SPIDER

Why everyone loves James Patterson and Alex Cross

'It's no mystery why James Patterson is the world's most popular thriller writer. Simply put: **nobody does it better**.'
Jeffery Deaver

'No one gets this big without **amazing natural storytelling** talent – which is what Jim has, in spades. The Alex Cross series proves it.'
Lee Child

'James Patterson is the **gold standard** by which all others are judged.'
Steve Berry

'Alex Cross is one of the **best-written heroes** in American fiction.'
Lisa Scottoline

'Twenty years after the first Alex Cross story, he has become one of the **greatest fictional detectives** of all time, a character for the ages.'
Douglas Preston & Lincoln Child

'Alex Cross is a **legend**.'
Harlan Coben

'Patterson boils a scene down to the single, telling detail, the element that **defines a character** or moves a plot along. It's what fires off the movie projector in the reader's mind.'
Michael Connelly

'James Patterson is **The Boss**. End of.'
Ian Rankin

WHO IS ALEX CROSS?

PHYSICAL DESCRIPTION:

Alex Cross is 6 foot 3 inches (190cm), and weighs 196 lbs (89 kg). He is African American, with an athletic build.

RECORDED - 105
INDEXED - 105

FAMILY HISTORY:

Cross was raised by his grandmother, Regina Cross Hope - known as Nana Mama - following the death of his mother and his father's subsequent descent into alcoholism. He moved to D.C. from Winston-Salem, North Carolina, to live with Nana Mama when he was ten.

RELATIONSHIP HISTORY:

Cross was previously married to Maria, mother to his children Damon and Janelle, however she was tragically killed in a drive-by shooting. Cross has another son, Alex Jr., with Christine Johnson.

EDUCATION:

Cross has a PhD in psychology from Johns Hopkins University in Baltimore, Maryland, with a special concentration in the field of abnormal psychology and forensic psychology.

EMPLOYMENT:

Cross works as a psychologist in a private practice, based in his home. He also consults for the Major Case Squad of the Metro Police Department, where he previously worked as a psychologist for the Homicide and Major Crimes team.

PROFILE

A loving father, Cross is never happier than when spending time with his family. He is also a dedicated member of his community and often volunteers at his local parish and soup kitchen. When not working in the practice or consulting for MPD, he enjoys playing classical music on the piano, reading, and teaching his children how to box.

5 - Bureau
3 - New Haven
2 - New York
COPIES DESTROYED

THIS CONFIDENTIAL REPORT AND ITS CONTENTS ARE LOANED TO YOU AND ARE NOT TO BE DISTRIBUTED OUTSIDE OF THE AGENCY TO WHICH LOANED

Central Washington

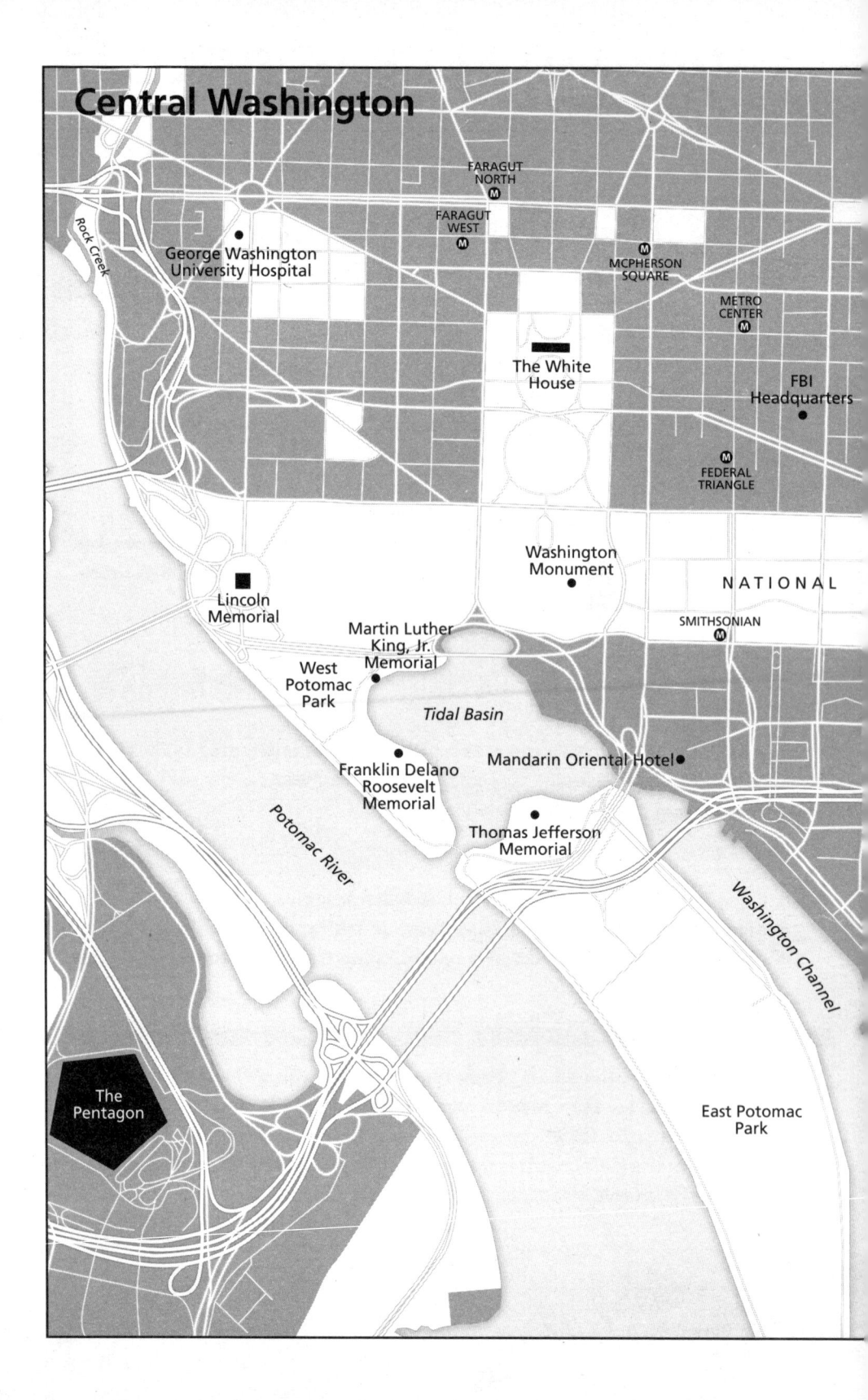

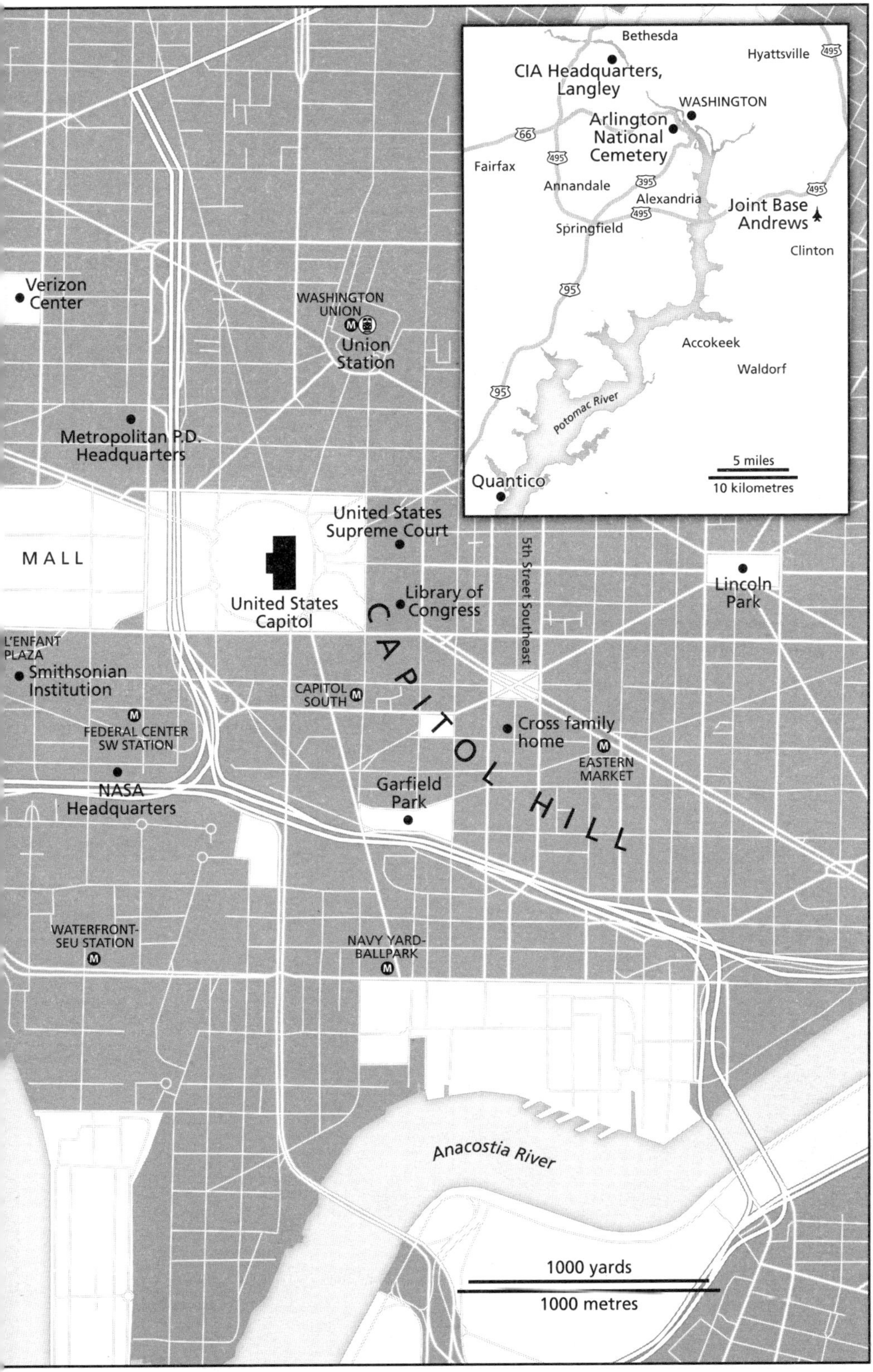

Bethesda
Hyattsville
495
CIA Headquarters, Langley
WASHINGTON
Arlington National Cemetery
66
495
Fairfax
Annandale
395
Alexandria
495
Joint Base Andrews
495
Springfield
Clinton
95
Accokeek
Waldorf
95
Potomac River
5 miles
10 kilometres
Quantico
Verizon Center
WASHINGTON UNION
Union Station
Metropolitan P.D. Headquarters
United States Supreme Court
5th Street Southeast
MALL
United States Capitol
Library of Congress
Lincoln Park
L'ENFANT PLAZA
Smithsonian Institution
CAPITOL SOUTH
CAPITOL HILL
FEDERAL CENTER SW STATION
Cross family home
EASTERN MARKET
NASA Headquarters
Garfield Park
WATERFRONT-SEU STATION
NAVY YARD-BALLPARK
Anacostia River
1000 yards
1000 metres

A list of titles by James Patterson appears
at the back of this book

Return
of the
SPIDER

JAMES PATTERSON

C
CENTURY

CENTURY

UK | USA | Canada | Ireland | Australia
India | New Zealand | South Africa

Century is part of the Penguin Random House group of companies
whose addresses can be found at global.penguinrandomhouse.com

Penguin Random House UK,
One Embassy Gardens, 8 Viaduct Gardens, London SW11 7BW

penguin.co.uk
global.penguinrandomhouse.com

Penguin Random House UK

First published 2025
001

Copyright © James Patterson, 2025

The moral right of the author has been asserted

Penguin Random House values and supports copyright. Copyright fuels
creativity, encourages diverse voices, promotes freedom of expression
and supports a vibrant culture. Thank you for purchasing an authorised
edition of this book and for respecting intellectual property laws by not reproducing,
scanning or distributing any part of it by any means without permission. You are
supporting authors and enabling Penguin Random House to continue to publish
books for everyone. No part of this book may be used or reproduced in any
manner for the purpose of training artificial intelligence technologies or systems.
In accordance with Article 4(3) of the DSM Directive 2019/790, Penguin Random House
expressly reserves this work from the text and data mining exception.

Printed and bound in Great Britain by Clays Ltd, Elcograf S.p.A.

The authorised representative in the EEA is Penguin Random House Ireland,
Morrison Chambers, 32 Nassau Street, Dublin D02 YH68

A CIP catalogue record for this book is available from the British Library

ISBN: 978–1–529–92217–2 (hardback)
ISBN: 978–1–529–92218–9 (trade paperback)

Penguin Random House is committed to a sustainable future
for our business, our readers and our planet. This book is made
from Forest Stewardship Council® certified paper.

Return of the SPIDER

PROLOGUE

The Nest

Present Day

1

MY NAME IS ALEX CROSS.

I have been a criminal psychologist for the FBI's Behavioral Science Unit and am currently working—for the second time in my life—as a homicide detective with the Washington, DC, Metropolitan Police.

In my decades of investigative and profiling work, I've had to interview many people with vicious and violent minds. The worst of them, the psychopaths and sociopaths, the ones who loved to kill—they all had one thing in common: They lied beautifully. So beautifully that I was always left wondering how much of what they told me was truth and how much was spun out of thin air the way a spider crafts a web on a dewy morning.

One sweltering day in May, all that changed. One sweltering day in May, someone put a sledgehammer through rotten drywall and showed me where one of the first spiders I ever encountered had built his secret nest.

There'd been a thunderstorm earlier that afternoon, and despite the lingering heat, an evening breeze had picked up enough to cool the sunporch at our home on Fifth Street in Southeast Washington, DC, where I was trying to play Gershwin after dinner. Caught up in case after case, I had not sat down at the keys for well over a year. The piano was perpetually a bit out of tune, and I was rusty, but I tried to coax the melody of *An American in Paris* out of it.

Gershwin probably wouldn't have appreciated my rendition, but I didn't care. I was sitting at the instrument after a long hiatus, and all thoughts of my hectic life slipped away until there was nothing but the music for almost twenty blissful minutes.

At a quarter past eight, my cell phone blared with the ringtone I reserved for John Sampson, my oldest friend.

"You home?" he asked.

"At the piano on the sunporch. Training to be a lounge lizard."

"Break training—I'm on my way to your place, ETA in three minutes. The Alphonso brothers have surfaced."

"Where?" I said, getting up from the piano bench. I opened the sliding glass door and went into the kitchen.

"Right in District Heights, their mom's old house," Sampson said. I rushed through the darkened kitchen, hearing the television in the front room.

"You mean their aunt's place?"

"Right. She inherited it. SWAT has already been alerted and will meet us there."

"I'll be out front." I hung up and went into the front room.

Nana Mama, my ninety-something grandmother, was on the

couch watching *Yellowstone* with my wife, Bree; she saw me rush in and hit pause on John Dutton riding a horse toward an impossible Montana sunset.

"Gotta go," I said. "The Alphonso brothers just surfaced."

"The meth-head bank robbers?" Nana Mama said.

"The same." I went to the hall closet and retrieved my chest armor and service weapon, a Glock 19.

Bree came out into the hall, clearly worried. "Those guys shoot first and ask questions later, Alex."

"Which is why there's an entire SWAT team on its way to surround them," I said. "John and I are merely witnesses at this point."

"Stay that way," Bree said. She kissed me, and I went out to the sidewalk in front of our home.

Sampson pulled up in an unmarked squad car thirty seconds later. I got in and we sped away. John explained that an informant for the regional drug task force had seen Nicky and Trevor Alphonso — armed robbers of twelve banks and killers of six innocent people in the span of four months — shortly after sundown, heading toward their childhood home on Foster Street in District Heights.

"Their aunt there?"

"The informant says she's out of town, visiting her brother in Chicago."

"Good," I said. "Let's end this. Get these guys behind bars so bank tellers in four states can sleep easier."

Sampson put a bubble on the roof, lit it up, and hit the siren.

2

SAMPSON SHUT DOWN THE siren and the bubble a good four blocks back from the small brick house with double dormers and a bare-grass lawn where the Alphonso brothers had grown up.

We reached the perimeter and parked behind the SWAT van, the rear of which was open. A Black female officer with a headset sat in the back talking to someone as we got out.

"Good, it's Knight," Sampson said.

"The best of the bunch," I said.

Captain Nyla Knight saw us come to the rear of the van, nodded, and pulled her headset to one side. "We have four snipers in position. The breach team is on its way. You can watch it all here."

We climbed into the van and saw a small bank of screens showing feeds from various members of the SWAT team. "How many total SWAT on scene?" I asked.

"Twelve," she said. "Taking no chances with these two."

The plan was for the eight-man breaching team to get flash-bang grenades into the little house from the sides and then use the battering rams on the front and rear doors. We watched the team break into two groups of four. One man from each sub team darted across the lawn to the scraggly bushes below the side windows, where lights glowed behind drawn shades.

"Someone's home," I said.

"Four someones," Knight said. "We ran infrared and —"

The shade on the east side of the house flew up. The window sash was already raised. The muzzle of an automatic weapon stuck out and someone fired, hitting the officer running in to deliver the flash-bang. He fell.

A second gunman opened fire from a window on the opposite side of the house, but the targeted officer managed to take cover.

"Officer down!" Captain Knight bellowed into her headset.

The breach team's commander came back over the radio: "Affirmative, Belmont down! Belmont down!"

A sniper positioned on the roof of a house a block away said over the comms, "Got Trevor, Cap. Permission to fire?"

"Take him," Knight said.

It was hard to see from our angle, but the sniper shot through the open window and hit Trevor Alphonso in the chest, killing him instantly. Members of the breach team raced forward to retrieve the fallen Officer Belmont.

"Once he's clear, put a flash-bang in that open window!" Knight said.

"Roger that, Cap."

The shooting paused. The SWAT captain changed frequencies and called to a support helicopter circling overhead, "Give me infrared on that house."

"Two in the west front room. Another moving to the rear exit."

She switched back to SWAT comms and called her snipers. "Aubrey, watch that back door now."

"On it, Cap," Officer Aubrey said a second before the rear door of the house flew open and Nicky Alphonso surged out, gun up, spraying bullets in an arc and screaming in rage, "This is my house! Welcome to my house!"

Knight said, "Take him, Aubrey."

Amid the bursts of rapid fire from the younger Alphonso brother, I didn't hear the single shot exit Officer Aubrey's rifle, but I saw Nicky crumple, shot through the throat. Lights out.

Frantic radio traffic ensued as the breaching teams readied to attack the house again. The front door opened. Two terrified, sobbing young women stepped out with their arms held high.

Captain Knight breathed a sigh of relief, then looked at us. "That could have gone a whole lot better."

I said, "Not like you had a lot of choice. They went all Scarface on you."

Sampson nodded, said, "Look at it this way, Captain. You cleaned the streets of some serious bad guys, and you just saved the government's justice system a whole lot of time and money."

3

I GOT HOME AROUND two a.m. My phone started ringing less than five hours later, at six forty.

"Cross," I grumbled.

"It's Kane," the caller said. "I just got off the phone with New Jersey state police captain Alexander Barthalis."

"I know Alexander," I said to my chief of detectives. I got out of bed and padded into the bathroom so as not to wake Bree.

Chief Kane said, "Which is why Captain Barthalis wants you and Sampson to meet him in Batsto, New Jersey, ASAP. Got a pen?"

I shut the bathroom door. "Not handy. Text it to me. Can you tell me what—"

The line went dead. Kane had hung up on me in mid-sentence, as he often did.

As I showered and shaved, I tried not to stew over Kane's rudeness. After I'd dressed and snuck out of my bedroom, Bree still snoozing, I saw that he'd texted me and Sampson an unfamiliar address in the Pine Barrens.

John called a minute later. "I don't recognize it. You?"

"Never even heard of Batsto. But Alexander Barthalis requested us personally."

Over the years, we had collaborated with Barthalis several times, including on an investigation into a serial rapist who worked the I-95 corridor between Newark and DC.

"Oh. I like Alexander. Good cop. I'll pick you up in twenty."

Ali, my youngest child, was already up and eating granola and bananas at the kitchen island, scrolling on his iPad while Nana Mama sat at the table drinking coffee and reading the newspaper in her nightgown and robe, her sparse gray hair looking like silk lace above her ageless face.

"Eggs?" she asked when she saw me.

"Toast and coffee will be fine," I said. "John and I have to drive to the Pine Barrens in New Jersey."

"Egg sandwiches for the both of you, then," Nana Mama said, getting to her feet and starting toward the stove.

"How was *Hamilton*?" I asked Ali. He'd seen the play on a school trip.

He beamed at me. "Greater than great! I'd go again tomorrow."

"I would too, actually," I said, pouring myself coffee from the pot.

Ali said, "Did you see the Alphonso brothers getting shot, Dad? It's on the *Washington Post* website."

"It was hard to see," I said. "But we were there. Given their history and their actions last night, they gave the SWAT team no choice."

"World's better off without brothers like that," Nana Mama said, frying eggs.

"I'd rather have seen them brought to trial."

She said nothing in reply as she made two egg sandwiches on sourdough bread, with jack cheese and her special mustard.

I heard a honk out front, so I kissed Ali and Nana Mama goodbye, grabbed the sandwiches, and hurried outside.

When I got in the car and handed Sampson his breakfast, he smiled and moaned. "Did she put the special mustard in there?"

"Twice as much as usual, just the way you like it."

Three hours later, after devouring breakfast and stopping twice for coffee, we were in a desolate area of New Jersey on a two-lane highway flanked by dense pines. We didn't need the exact address in the end.

North of Batsto, we saw FBI vehicles, coroner's office vans, and New Jersey state police patrol cars parked on both sides of a rutted gravel driveway that snaked uphill and into the pines. We got out of the car and walked over to two young FBI agents standing at the end of the driveway.

"Captain Barthalis called us in," I said, showing them my credentials. "Who's in charge?"

"Agent Mahoney," one of them said. "He just arrived on scene."

Ned Mahoney's presence meant this was a very high-profile case. It helped that he'd been my partner back when we both worked in the FBI's Behavioral Science Unit.

"This way?" Sampson asked, gesturing up the driveway.

"Yeah, they're up there."

We climbed the steep driveway in the oppressive heat. I could hear dogs barking in the woods as we broke into a clearing and saw a cabin with a small porch and a shed, both of which looked like they were about to rot away and collapse at any minute.

Moss grew on the roof. The shake shingles had not been stained in years. Most were curling upward, and many were missing. Paint hung in spirals from the eaves.

Ned Mahoney, a short, lean man with gray-flecked sandy hair, stood near the cabin talking to Alexander Barthalis.

Mahoney nodded at us. "I was going to call you two, but Alexander beat me to it."

Barthalis, a burly, florid-faced guy wearing gray suit pants but no jacket, a shoulder holster with a weapon, and dark Terminator sunglasses, said, "Well, who else would I call? Been a long time."

"Five years?" I said, reaching out to shake Barthalis's hand. "Good to see you, Captain."

Barthalis pumped my hand. "Always Alexander to you and Detective Sampson, Dr. Cross."

"It's Alex, Alexander," I said.

"And John," Sampson said, shaking Alexander's hand. "So, bring us up to speed. What's going on?"

Barthalis turned all business. "Four bodies have been found by the cadaver dogs, all of them in the woods right around here. There are probably more."

Mahoney said, "But we think you're going to be more interested in what was found behind a false wall in the cabin's basement. That's what got us to bring in the dogs and the FBI."

He and Mahoney started toward the sagging front porch; Sampson and I followed. "Who's the owner?" I asked.

"Guy named Adam Brenner. He bought it last month when the county auctioned off the property because the owner of record—a Delaware company called MKM Holdings—was decades behind on taxes and unreachable, having gone out of business years ago," Barthalis said. "We know this because Mr.

Brenner had a title search done on the property before making his bid. Here's where it gets interesting."

He stopped on the porch. "MKM's address was a post office box in Camden, and a long-dead lawyer was listed as treasurer. The president was given as M. K. Murphy, and his address was a different post office box in Camden."

I frowned. "Okay?"

"Who sold M. K. Murphy the property?" Sampson asked.

Barthalis pointed at Sampson. "Smart man. The property was sold to MKM by one Gary Murphy shortly after he inherited it from his uncle."

4

GARY MURPHY. MY FIRST spider, now long dead. As was Gary Soneji. Both had inhabited the same body—one mind split by dissociative identity disorder.

Murphy's Soneji side was obsessed with fame, serial killing—and kidnapping the children of the rich and powerful.

Sampson and I caught him and sent him to prison—but things didn't end there. Soneji had been abused repeatedly as a child, traumatic events that damaged his psyche. In prison, he contracted HIV and developed AIDS. Finding out he was terminally ill sent him into a violent rage; he escaped and went on a killing spree that began with a mass murder in a DC Metro station.

I caught up to him in New York City and chased him into a Grand Central Station train tunnel. During a shoot-out, he fell, and the makeshift bomb in his jacket detonated, engulfing him in flames.

Only then was he finally stopped.

But that was years ago, long before Alexander Barthalis called us to the moldering cabin in the Pine Barrens near Batsto.

"You seen inside yet, Ned?" I asked.

The FBI agent shook his head. We followed Barthalis into the cabin, now gutted to the studs.

As we went through the kitchen to the basement stairs, Sampson asked, "Alexander, what alerted you?"

Climbing down the rickety stairs, Barthalis said, "There's a secret room down here, and a notebook with Gary Soneji's name on it. The second I realized this was all *his* doing, I backed out and called your boss and Mahoney's. I brought in the dogs as a precaution, and they almost immediately struck on the east side. It's him."

I reserved judgment.

As on the floor above, much of the old drywall had been torn out, leaving just the studs on three walls. The fourth wall had a ragged gaping hole in it from the floor to the ceiling.

Barthalis reached over and pulled a string. A light bulb went on, revealing a six-foot-by-four-foot space with plain pine shelves on three interior sides and a small stool in the corner.

Mahoney gestured to the hole. "You knew more about him than anyone, Alex."

I put on surgical gloves and stepped inside the hole with my phone out and the camera on, recording what I was seeing.

There were multiple dusty weapons on the shelves to the left. An Ithaca pump-action twelve-gauge shotgun, a .308 hunting rifle, and several pistols of different calibers, including a Charter Arms .44-caliber snub-nosed, blue-barreled revolver. A sliver of white athletic tape on the rosewood grip had the letters *SOS* on it in black ink.

Beside it on the shelf was a .22-caliber semiautomatic handgun, also with white athletic tape on the grip. The letters inked there were *NS*.

A nine-millimeter Beretta beside that was marked *ZK*.

A .45 Remington Model 1911 was labeled *GRK*.

There were several knives on the shelf below the guns, including a black stiletto switchblade also marked *NS*. Beside it was a length of white nylon rope tagged *TBS*. On the bottom shelf lay handcuffs and a coiled length of steel wire, both marked *JWG*.

I took in the shelves on the back wall, which held Polaroid snapshots of various men and women (some clearly dead, some alive), a necklace, several rings, and at least a dozen locks of hair tied with ribbons of various colors.

Gesturing at them, I said, "Trophies. We'll need DNA analysis on all of it."

Mahoney said, "I have crime techs from Quantico on their way as we speak."

"Good," I said. "If these came from long-missing people, we might be able to give their families some kind of closure."

The shelves on the wall to the right of the entrance were wider, and the lower ones held six large clear-plastic lidded storage bins. Left to right in black ink, they were labeled *NS, SOS, ZK, TBS, JWG,* and *GRK*.

On the shelf immediately above the boxes were notebooks of different colors, each with initials matching those on one of the bins below. I reached for a black leather-bound notebook on the highest shelf.

There was a plastic sleeve dead center on the cover. A file card had been put in it.

"'*Profiles in Homicidal Genius,* by Gary Soneji,'" I read aloud from the scrawl on the card. "It has his twisted humor."

I heard a female voice call, "Mr. Mahoney? Captain Barthalis? The dogs are hitting north of the house now. It might be another grave."

"Jesus," Ned said. "Alex, can I leave you to this?"

"Sure," I said, opening the notebook.

Sampson said, "Too small in that hole for me to help. I'll give Barthalis and Mahoney a hand outside."

The three of them left. I looked down at the first page of the notebook, covered in Soneji's distinctive scrawl, and read.

Time and again, history says, "Do not reinvent the wheel. Study what works, or worked. Study who works, or worked."

Art students study the masters. Young athletes study the skills of geniuses older than themselves. So do singers and musicians.

In essence, one art or another, one skill or another, it's all the same. Don't reinvent the wheel. Study the masters.

And so I shall study the masters of murder, the geniuses of homicide.

I lifted my head from the page and gazed at the initials on the bins. Standing in Soneji's secret room holding his murder diary in my hands, I wanted to puke and cry at the same time because my gut was telling me that the bins on the shelves held murder kits, very specific murder kits, and my brain was telling me that a long time ago, Sampson and I might have made a terrible mistake.

In my mind, I saw a big man in prison proclaiming his innocence to me and Sampson before he died.

Deep in the pit of my stomach, doubt and fear grew, as did the strange sense that I was being haunted by a ghost from my long-ago past.

I sat there, frozen by that idea, not wanting to push on in Soneji's notebook but knowing I had to. With shaking fingers, I turned the page and fell back in time.

PART ONE

Profiles in Murder

Twenty Years Earlier

CHAPTER 1

Alexandria, Virginia

GARY SONEJI PULLED HIS black 1985 Saab into the faculty lot of the Charles School, a private college-prep academy.

Before getting out, he paused to assess himself in the rearview mirror.

The balding dark brown wig flawlessly covered his naturally curly blond hair, which he'd cut short. His mustache was darkened with brown wax and shaped into a droop that swallowed his upper lip. Green-colored contacts, English-schoolboy glasses, and facial prosthetics he'd bought from a movie makeup artist completed a disguise that made him look at least ten years older.

Soneji smiled. His own dear wife, Missy, would not have recognized him.

His real name was Gary Murphy. But he had taken on a new identity—Gary Soneji—who so far lived only in his mind.

He stepped out of the Saab, opened the back door, and

retrieved a faded blue blazer. He put it on over his blue button-down dress shirt and adjusted the knot of his blue and red rep tie to make himself look even more disheveled.

He slung his canvas messenger bag over one shoulder and checked his watch. Seven forty. Classes did not start at the Charles School until eight.

Twenty minutes. A chance to practice.

Soneji scanned the faculty parking lot. Two teachers were climbing the stone staircase to the verdant main campus. He spotted a tan Dodge sedan, empty, with a vacant spot next to it.

He walked in a loop until the Dodge was three rows in front of him, took another look around, saw the teachers were gone, and prepared his final stalk. Soneji imagined himself at night and studied the driver's-side mirror until he had calculated how to come at it through a blind spot.

Then he crouched, hurried forward to the next row, and peered through the back window of the tan sedan to the rearview mirror, making certain he would not be seen. When he was sure, he checked all around once more.

Convinced he was unseen, Soneji moved quickly to the left rear corner of the empty parking space. He walked to within five feet of the sedan, raised his hand like a pistol, aimed it where a driver would be, and said, slowly and deliberately, "Bang. Bang."

Not bad, he thought as he turned and headed toward the staircase to campus. He'd practice again later. And then he'd repeat it until he was sure.

A white Jeep Grand Wagoneer pulled into a space by the stairs.

Headmistress Jenny Wolcott.

Soneji cursed his luck. He didn't like Wolcott. She was — well, nosy.

He pasted a plastic smile on his lips as he passed the Jeep and started to climb the stairs, hoping she'd have some rearranging to do before getting out. But her door opened behind him.

"Is that you again, Mr. Murphy, on this fine October day?" Jenny Wolcott called.

Soneji tried not to stiffen as he stopped on the stairs and looked back, smiling and thinking how very much he would like to throttle her. He said, "Me again, Headmistress. It seems Ms. Porter has a world-class flu."

A tiny dynamo of a woman in her late forties, Wolcott had taught English before turning to administration. "What does she have you covering today?"

"'The Lagoon,'" he said.

"Ah, Joseph Conrad. I know you went to Penn, but your degree is in computer science. You feel up to this?"

He managed a smile and said, "I reread it last night. At first the tale seems incoherent, like a dream, but then you start seeing what the author does with light and darkness when the white guy goes up the canal into the jungle lagoon, and then it becomes a nightmare when the one Malay boy abandons his brother to the raja's men hunting them."

"To save his dying girlfriend," the headmistress said. "It's a moral-quandary story that suggests many of the themes later amplified in *Heart of Darkness*."

"That's how I plan to teach it," Soneji replied. "A sketch for them to consider before *Heart of Darkness*."

"Let me know how it goes," Wolcott said as they reached the top of the stairs. She headed toward the administration offices.

"I will," Soneji said, and he turned toward Fowler Hall on the quadrangle, thinking once again how deeply satisfying it would be to snuff out her sanctimonious life.

The halls of Fowler were bustling with teenagers in school uniforms, clutching books, heading toward their first-period classes. Ms. Porter's classroom was on the second floor.

Soneji loved taking on a substitute-teaching role from time to time. It was a break from his boring real job, selling heating oil. A chance to be someone else, someone who by necessity was surrounded by youth. And here at the Charles School, they were the youth of privilege, though not of super-wealth or super-power.

Still, these were elite youth, and they interested Soneji very much. So much promise to be toyed with. So much potential to—

He reached the second floor and spotted seventeen-year-old Abby Howard leaning back against the wall, laughing with Conrad Talbot, who wore his Charles School lacrosse captain jacket and stood very close to her.

Soneji had met Abby in class two days ago, and she reminded him of Joyce Adams, a freshman at Princeton who'd mysteriously vanished years ago. He had fond memories of Joyce, how long and lean she'd been, the first to sate a particular craving in him. But now, years later, the hunger was coming again. Every time he glanced at Abby, he thought of Joyce and how wonderful it would be to repeat that sweet episode.

A knot of students came down the hall, causing Soneji to take a few steps to his right. He stopped with his back almost to Conrad and Abby, close enough to overhear them.

"C'mon, Abs," the boy said. "I've got my brother's Bronco for the week."

"You know my mom doesn't let me go out on school nights."

"Tomorrow morning everyone's doing SAT prep, but we don't need to retake them, so we don't have to be here until noon."

"I did score well already," Abby said.

"You scored through the roof, and so did I. C'mon, Abs, we'll get something to eat in Georgetown and then go to this place my brother told me about on Bear Island, off the canal bicycle path."

"On our bikes?" she asked skeptically.

"No, in the Bronco," he said.

"Is that, like, legal?"

"Nah. But it's okay if you go late enough that no one's there and you drive with just your running lights across the bridge and down the wide dirt path there. My brother's done it a bunch of times. Bet we don't even need the lights tonight. There's a full moon and there's this cutoff to a maintenance road that goes right above the river. You can see Little Falls from there. We'll look at the falls and the moon."

"No, we won't," Abby said playfully. "At least I hope not."

"No moon-gazing, then," Conrad said and laughed.

Soneji wanted to linger, longed to hear more. But he had a class to teach.

He moved on, thinking about the young lovers, thinking about Joyce Adams, and wondering how the genius he'd been studying might handle the situation.

CHAPTER

2

Washington, DC

I WAS A ROOKIE homicide detective on that fine October day, standing in front of St. Anthony's Catholic Church in Southeast DC, listening to organ music, and taking the first case of my new job hard.

John Sampson put his hand on my shoulder. "First one's tough."

Sampson and I had been friends since childhood, but he'd joined the DC Metropolitan Police Department long before me and had been a detective with their major-crimes unit for more than a year. I graduated from Johns Hopkins with a PhD in psychology and started a private practice, but recently I'd left it to join the same investigative unit as Sampson, and this was my first case.

Profiling was all the rage in law enforcement circles at the time. Though I was green as a street investigator in those days, I was experienced as a researcher. Over the course of writing my dissertation, I had interviewed hundreds of hardened murderers in prisons across the country as well as the families of their victims and even a few people who'd been attacked but had managed to survive.

Struggling with my emotions, I cleared my throat and looked at my oldest friend. "Chief Pittman said I would be expected to offer you and the other guys insight into the minds of possible perpetrators, John. But I honestly don't know how the mind of someone who's willing to kill like this works."

Four nights earlier, my friend and I had had to inform Maxine Miller that the body of her fourteen-year-old son, Tony, had been found floating in the Potomac, stabbed multiple times, his face beaten to a pulp.

Sampson squeezed my shoulder. "You will, Alex. Today, it's not all about grief. Maxine wants this to be a celebration of Tony's life. Afterward, you can get clinical about it and point us in the right direction."

I nodded without conviction, then saw my grandmother coming down the sidewalk, dressed in black. Nana Mama worked as a vice principal at Tony's high school.

She and I hugged. She and Sampson hugged. "A sad, sad day," she said.

"We'll find his killer. We're doing everything we can with limited resources," John said.

Her expression hardened. "You mean because of his color, there are limited resources."

"I'm telling you, Nana, Tony Miller won't be forgotten. We will find who did this."

My grandmother nodded and let her shoulders relax. "I

know, John. It's just hard when you've known a boy since kindergarten."

"We understand, Nana," I said. "How are the kids at school holding up?"

"We're bringing in counselors," Nana Mama said. "A lot of students will be here. He was well liked. How's Maria doing?" she asked me, changing the subject. "What is she, six months along now?"

"That's right. Baby's kicking a lot, but otherwise, Maria's great."

"And my great-grandson?"

"Damon was toddling around the kitchen when I left."

A hearse pulled up, followed by the funeral home's limousine. Dressed in black, Maxine Miller got out of the back of the limo with the help of her older son, Thomas.

She saw us and walked over, smiling weakly. "Thank you for coming, Detectives. And you too, Mrs. Cross. It means a lot."

Nana Mama hugged Maxine, and we all walked into the church. The place was packed with students, family, and community members.

Thomas and five other young men carried the casket from the hearse to the front of the church.

Father Nathan Barry, an old family friend of ours, had also known Tony Miller. He was visibly moved as he began the service. He talked about how Tony had lived in one of the toughest, most gang-infested neighborhoods in the nation's capital, the parts the tourists rarely saw; about how Tony's mother worked two jobs; about how he'd tried to resist the gangs and had spoken out against them.

"We don't know who killed this brave young man," Father

Barry said. "But we know who his enemies were. We know because he told us. The gangs did this because he would not join them. The gangs did this because he was their vocal opponent."

Sitting in the pews surrounded by almost a hundred people, I saw the priest's stare and knew he was talking directly to me and Sampson, asking us to find Tony's killer.

CHAPTER 3

AT TEN THAT EVENING, the full moon brilliant overhead, Gary Soneji was four vehicles behind the old red-and-black Ford Bronco carrying Conrad Talbot and Abby Howard north on the Canal Road from Georgetown through the Palisades area of the District of Columbia.

Soneji was not driving his Saab; he drove a white utility van full of junk and trash on the floor in the back.

He wore leather gloves, a brown workman's jumpsuit, and a black ball cap pulled down low. The green contacts were in their storage case back in the Saab. The wig was packed away there as well, along with the round wire-rimmed glasses and facial prosthetics. The sometime substitute teacher was now just some doughy blond guy with a mustache.

Before donning the jumpsuit, Soneji had sat at the counter of the Georgetown café where Abby and Conrad were eating dessert. They'd had no idea who he was. Abby had walked by Soneji twice on her way to the bathroom and hadn't given him a second glance.

The Bronco approached the traffic lights where the Chain Bridge from Virginia met the Canal Road. The light turned yellow and the Bronco sped through, leaving Soneji three cars behind as the light turned red. He watched the Bronco's taillights vanish north on the Clara Barton Parkway.

It didn't matter. Soneji knew exactly where they were headed. He'd looked it up in an atlas of national parks in the school library.

North of the bridge, on the Maryland side of the parkway, there was a pull-off at lock five of the old Chesapeake and Ohio Canal that allowed canoers and kayakers access to the Potomac River.

Bikers, hikers, National Park Service vehicles and equipment, and, evidently, the odd Bronco could cross the top of the lock and take a short bridge to Bear Island and the old towpath heading south.

Roughly a mile south on the towpath, still on Bear Island but back in the District of Columbia, was a maintenance road of sorts that ran down to a large concrete platform above the Potomac River. Little Falls and the rapids were right upstream.

Most of the traffic was heading across the Chain Bridge to Virginia; there were few cars north of the Maryland state line. Soneji checked his rearview and saw no one behind him. Headlights came at him as he neared the pull-out for lock five.

Soneji slowed, put on his blinker, lowered the visor, and let the car go by, which left the road ahead empty. He turned into the parking lot at lock five, deserted at that hour. His headlights revealed trees and the entrance to the wide top of the lock.

There were signs warning that only pedestrians, bikes, and official vehicles were allowed to cross. But there was no gate.

With no cars coming in either direction behind him, Soneji turned off his headlights, waited several seconds to let his eyes adjust, then drove slowly over the top of the lock. It was a tight squeeze, but he made it. Conrad had been right—there was more than enough light from the moon to see, and he never touched the wooden rails.

Once he reached the other side, he glanced to his left and saw headlights flickering on the parkway. He crossed the second bridge much quicker and again without touching the rails.

Soneji was on the actual towpath now, which was easily wide enough to drive on, heading south. A broken line of trees and kudzu to his left partially blocked his view of the river and the parkway beyond. Feeling safe, he took a chance and briefly flicked the van's fog lights on and off.

He smiled. The fog lights had revealed the Bronco's big tire tracks on the gravel and dirt ahead.

As the map had shown and as Talbot's tracks confirmed, a maintenance road branched off from the main trail and headed at an angle across the island toward the Potomac's west branch.

Soneji pulled over just inside the road entry. He turned the van off, sat there a moment listening to the ticking of the engine, and climbed out.

It was a cool October night. The bright moon filtered through the trees, making the way forward much clearer than he'd expected.

Walking around to the back of the van, Soneji flashed on several memories of Joyce Adams in the basement of his uncle's old cabin in the Pine Barrens. The images were all of one flavor: her eyes lit up with terror, his feeling of absolute control over her. He craved that feeling, the power of holding someone captive.

But he had much to learn before he took that kind of chance again. *Stay focused,* he told himself. *You're here to study.*

He opened the van's rear doors, eager now to find out what worked and what didn't. The mechanics. The potential pitfalls of this particular modus operandi.

Soneji turned on a small penlight and put the back end of it in his mouth. His heart rate quickened as he opened a duffel bag he'd stowed there. He pulled out heavy wool socks and a black balaclava and stuffed them in the inner pockets of the jumpsuit.

Shining the light back into the duffel, he picked up a snub-nosed .44-caliber pistol in a quart-size plastic bag and slid it deep into the front right pocket of the coverall. Soneji shut the doors quietly, turned off the light, and started down the shadowed path to the west side of the island.

He tried to see the gun not as his salvation but as a tool. *Focus on the gun,* he told himself. *You can bring a city to its knees with a gun like this. It's been done before.*

CHAPTER 4

GRAVEL CRUNCHED BENEATH Gary Soneji's sneakers. When he saw the woods open ahead, he put the wool socks on over his sneakers and the balaclava over his curly blond hair.

He took a few steps into the clearing and spotted the old Bronco about forty yards away on a concrete pad above the river. It was parked facing away from him toward Little Falls. The moonlight had turned the scene a dusky blue.

Soneji felt a thrill shoot through him.

It wasn't a Joyce scenario, but his heart was suddenly booming. He got out the weapon, breathless at the solid weight of the pistol in his hand.

After gauging where the moon would throw his shadow and locating the blind spot of the Bronco's side-view mirror, Soneji padded forward. He heard the low roar of the nearby rapids and the distant wail of a siren somewhere on the Virginia side of the river.

Feeling the blood pound in his temples, he watched for movement in the car as he closed the distance. At five yards, he could see the silhouettes of the jock and his girlfriend in the moonlight and the glow of the radio, which was playing the intro to Springsteen's "Tenth Avenue Freeze-Out."

At two feet away, he saw they were both topless and entwined in a kiss.

He flashed on an image of Joyce freed of her shirt and bra, then shook the memory off.

Soneji lifted the gun. He aimed through the side window at the back of the lacrosse captain's head, thinking beyond what the genius had done, trying for two dead with one shot. A split second before the gun went off, however, the girl moved her head.

The shot was much louder than he'd expected. Soneji looked at the spiderwebbed window and felt an overwhelming urge to flee the scene. So he did.

He took off, running back toward the spur road and into the darkened woods. He tripped and almost fell, stuck the pistol back in his pocket, and got out the penlight.

He sprinted to the back of the van, meaning to return the pistol, the balaclava, and the socks to the duffel bag, reached for the door handle, and froze.

Someone had scrawled with a finger across the two dirty back doors *Bike trail, asshole. Reporting you to police.*

For two or three beats, Soneji stood there, his mind unable to process the ramifications of the message. Then his survival instinct, honed over years of abuse as a child, kicked in.

He looked at the ground and saw the bike's thin track. The bicyclist must have come from the south, seen the van, stopped to write the note, then looped right and continued north.

Soneji jumped into the van, started it, and rammed it into reverse. He spun the van around, then smashed it into drive. He figured he'd been gone no more than fifteen minutes. The bicyclist had a head start, but how much of a head start? If he'd seen the van right away, he could be across the lock and up on the parkway by now. But if the bicyclist had spotted the van a few minutes later, he might still be on the towpath. And he might have heard the gunshot.

Soneji turned on the fog lights and sped up.

For almost a minute, he felt nothing but anxiety and uncertainty. Then, four hundred yards short of the bridge off the island, he saw a bicycle taillight about a hundred yards away, blinking red, and the bright reflectors of a safety vest.

He floored the gas pedal. When he was fifty yards away and closing, the bicyclist turned, revealing a headlamp and the concerned face of a bearded man.

When Soneji was twenty-five yards from him, the man tried to pull over to his left to let Soneji pass. He was facing away from the van and had not come to a full stop when the van's left front bumper plowed into him, launching both rider and bike off the path and into the darkness of the woods.

CHAPTER

5

SAMPSON AND I WERE assigned to the Tony Miller murder case, but we were pretty far down in the hierarchy at Metro, so the day after Tony's funeral, we also took a six a.m. call from Dispatch.

An angler had found two bodies in an old Ford Bronco out on Bear Island, within District lines, which made the killings Metro's responsibility. It was misty and foggy when we got to lock five. A National Park Service vehicle was blocking the way across, its lights flashing.

A Bethesda Police cruiser was parked beside it, its lights flashing as well. A police officer was turning away angry bikers who were trying to get on the towpath heading to Georgetown.

Ranger Carrie Mulberry saw us, came over, and said, "We've closed off the island, and I've got rangers blocking access at the north and south ends. All went in by bike."

"You been to the vehicle yourself?" Sampson asked.

Mulberry made a sour face and said in a soft voice, "After hearing what Mr. Quirk saw, we decided to hang back and not mess up any evidence for you. He says there are large vehicle tracks all over the towpath leading to the scene."

"Mr. Quirk is the fisherman who found the bodies?"

"Dudley Quirk the Fourth," Gene Lamont, the Bethesda officer, said to us after turning away another bicyclist. "One of those."

"One of those?" I asked.

"One of those people who's gotta tell you they're the Fourth. Lack of naming imagination in the family if you ask me."

"No one did," Sampson said shortly. We looked over at the fisherman, who was sitting on a rock wall.

"He doesn't hear that well," Mulberry warned us before turning to stop a pack of four bicyclists.

We walked up to Quirk, showed him our badges.

Quirk nodded. "I don't usually bring my hearing aids when I'm going to fish. I dropped one in the drink last year and they're awful expensive," he explained, then launched into his story. "I come here on my bike in the dark a couple mornings a week, and I ride over to the other side of the island, close to where you can see the falls upstream, and I fish as the sun rises.

"I got there and saw the Bronco sitting there, and I got angry because you're not supposed to be in here with a rig, you know? I walked up and saw the bullet hole through the side window. And then the boy lying on top of the girl. I turned around and rode back here just as the ranger was pulling into the parking lot. End of story."

"Thank you," I said, exaggerating my lip movements to be clear.

He shrugged. "A prime fishing dawn ruined. But it could have been worse. I could have been in the car with them."

Quirk told us he'd seen two sets of big tire tracks traveling the towpath south to the cutoff toward the west branch of the Potomac, then only the Bronco's tracks heading down the cutoff and another vehicle's coming back the other way.

"You an expert on tire tracks?" Sampson asked.

"Hard not to see them," Quirk said.

We left him, went back to Ranger Mulberry. "Can you drive us to within a hundred yards of that cutoff?" I asked.

"We'll be driving over their tracks," she said.

"They'll be the same tracks down there," Sampson said. "We'll have forensics take samples over there."

"Your jurisdiction, your call," the ranger said.

We crossed the lock and the bridge and headed south on the towpath. Quirk had been right—it was hard to miss the tire tracks in most places.

A few hundred yards south of the bridge, I noticed something on the towpath and said, "Stop."

The ranger stopped. Sampson and I got out and saw shards of clear and red plastic on the path. John said, "Looks like pieces of a headlight and blinker."

Almost as soon as he said that, we heard "Ahh" coming from the woods to our right. We went toward the sound and saw a man lying by a tree stump, a good thirty feet from the path. He was on his side, facing us, entangled in a bicycle frame that was bent like a V.

"Call an ambulance!" I shouted to the ranger and followed Sampson into the woods. The closer we got, the more blood we saw on the biker's bearded face and the more unnatural the angles of his legs and arms looked.

"Sir, can you hear us?"

"Ahh," he wheezed. "Hepp."

"Help's coming," I said.

"Who hit you?" Sampson said.

He wheezed again. His jaw looked swollen.

"Sir?"

But he'd closed his eyes. Mulberry ran up. "Ambulance is ten minutes out. Jesus, what happened to him?"

I said, "Wild guess, I bet he was in the wrong place at the wrong time and got hit by whoever was fleeing."

John said, "We have to treat this part of the path as its own crime scene."

"Agreed," I said. "I think we should call for a backup team to treat this as an attempted murder, and we'll go to the primary scene on foot."

"You go on ahead," the ranger said. "I'll stay with the vic."

Sampson said, "Once the EMTs get here and stabilize him, go through his pack there, see if he's got identification."

The bicyclist wheezed again. Mulberry went to him, said, "Just hang on a little bit longer and we'll get you to a hospital."

We left the two of them and walked in the weeds next to the towpath all the way to the cutoff. As Quirk had said, there was a single set of tracks there heading to the west fork.

It was nearly eight a.m. when we reached the opening above the river and saw the Bronco. Sampson walked toward the SUV, looking for footprints in the soil.

He stopped, squatted, and said, "These are something, but I can't see a tread, and there're little strands of fabric in the prints."

"He's wearing wool socks," I said.

"So he can come in silent and not leave an identifiable trace," John said. "This is premeditation."

Sampson set his police radio on the roof, and we put on gloves and opened the Bronco's front doors. The victims were both Caucasian, topless, and in their teens.

The male victim had been shot through the back of the head at close range. The round had blown a ragged exit hole in his forehead and hit the female victim.

There was so much blood and brain matter on her face, it was hard to tell exactly where she'd been hit—until she groaned and rolled her head to one side, revealing a large scalp wound.

"She's alive!" I shouted.

John grabbed his radio off the roof of the Bronco. "Dispatch, this is Sampson at the one-four-zero on Bear Island. We need a medevac helicopter here right now!"

CHAPTER

6

TWENTY MINUTES LATER, WE watched the helicopter lift off the island carrying a gravely injured but very much alive seventeen-year-old Abigail Howard to the trauma team at George Washington University Hospital.

But there was no such miracle for Conrad Talbot, also seventeen. We knew who they were because we'd found his school ID in his wallet and hers in a small bookbag.

The District's medical examiner was working on the scene, and as we waited for his report, a familiar figure emerged from the woods.

"Here we go," Sampson sighed as the chief of detectives approached us.

George Pittman walked over while unwrapping a stick of gum. "I'm trying to quit smoking, so this is all I get."

"Better than smoking," I said.

Chief Pittman grunted noncommittally and chewed the gum for a moment.

"One dead, one alive?" he asked.

"Correct," I said.

"Who are they?"

"Students at the Charles School in Alexandria," I said.

"Private school. They come from cash, then, right?"

I squinted. "I suppose you can assume that. Why?"

"Because this is going to get a lot of media attention, that's why," the chief said, and chewed a few more times. Sampson and I filled him in on what we'd learned so far. I was surprised when Pittman recognized one of the kids' names.

"The dead one, Talbot. I saw a story about him in the *Post* last spring. Captain of the lacrosse team. Good-looking too. And it turns out that guy on the bike is some Senate aide. We are going to need more manpower here."

I thought about Tony Miller's funeral the day before. Where was Pittman then? But this was only my second homicide case. I wasn't going to turn down help.

The chief went on. "So, gentlemen, I'm bringing in Diehl and Kurtz to take the lead on this."

Sampson grimaced. "Chief, we can —"

"No, Detective," Pittman said flatly. "I can't have two junior members of my team running an investigation like this. I'm sorry. The two of you will work with Diehl and Kurtz, and hopefully you'll both learn something."

I could tell John wanted to counter that with something snarky, but he held his tongue. Well, almost.

"Yes, sir," he said. "Do you want us to notify the families? Or should we leave it to the dynamic duo?"

The chief stopped chewing, and his eyes narrowed. "You and Cross can do it. After that, report to Diehl and Kurtz and me in my office downtown, bring us up to speed. We'll figure out what's next."

"Right away, Chief," Sampson said.

Our boss studied him a moment, searching for evidence of sarcasm. After a beat, he glanced at me and said, "I'll wait here for Diehl and Kurtz."

We nodded and walked away. When we were back in the trees and out of earshot, Sampson said, "You know what that was really about, right?"

"He doesn't want two Black junior detectives being the faces of an investigation into the murder of a rich white kid and the attempted murder of the kid's girlfriend and a Senate aide."

"Nah," John said. "More like he doesn't want two Black junior detectives getting the credit if they *solve* the murder of a rich white kid and the attempted murder of his girlfriend and a Senate aide."

CHAPTER

7

BEFORE WE DROVE OVER to Alexandria, Virginia, to meet with Conrad Talbot's family, I got Abby Howard's number from Dispatch and called her house. I spoke to her mother, Lisa Howard, and informed her that her daughter had been injured and was en route to GWU Hospital. I said we'd meet her at the hospital later this morning.

When Sampson and I got back in the car, he said, "FYI, you should have asked the mother not to call Conrad's parents."

"Oh," I said. "I didn't think of that. Does it matter? Why do you think she would?"

"Well, I'm assuming Abby's mother knew her daughter was out with Conrad last night, and she must have called his family when her daughter didn't come home, so maybe she'll call them now to give them an update. But I'd rather inform the family in person. Especially in cases like this, when it's the death of a kid with his whole life ahead of him. I see it as part of the job. Our responsibility."

"I didn't tell her Conrad was dead."

"I know," he said. "But you get the point."

"Learning."

"Every day."

The Talbot family lived in a sprawling red-brick Colonial on a shaded cul-de-sac in Alexandria about two miles from the Charles School. It was ten minutes to nine when we knocked on the front door with our badges out.

We could hear raised voices inside.

A teenage girl came and looked out the side window. She was dressed all in black, from her Doc Martens to her cardigan, and wore dark eye makeup and a couple of nose rings.

I waved my badge and smiled. She rolled her eyes and opened the front door.

A man yelled, "How the hell should I know where he'd go all night in Geoff's Bronco, Sue Ann? Am I supposed to be psychic?"

"Will, stop being dramatic! I'm on hold with the Fairfax sheriff and—"

Conrad's mother appeared in the front hallway in a robe, her hair up in curlers, a cordless phone pressed to her ear. She took one look at us and scurried away.

The girl snorted.

"Will!" we heard the mother call. "There are two big Black men at the front door."

"They're the police, Mom!" the teen yelled. "They've got badges and everything!"

There was a brief silence, then the loud beep of the phone being clicked off. Will Talbot, a lanky blond man in his forties, came to the door. He wore tennis shorts, a Harvard Business School sweatshirt, and flip-flops. He squinted at us as we held up our badges and identified ourselves.

"Dad, I let them in," the teenage girl said.

"And I'm glad you did," her father said, attempting to smile at us. "What's this all about, Officers?"

"Mr. Talbot, is there somewhere we can talk privately with you and your wife?" I asked.

The phone rang in the hallway. We heard Sue Ann Talbot answer it.

Will Talbot's expression turned from defensive to uncertain. He looked at his daughter. "Stella, why don't you go finish breakfast and ask Mom to come to my office for a second." He turned to us and gestured to a room on his right. "We can talk in here."

Before we could go into the office, his wife reappeared, looking stricken. "That was Lisa Howard. Abby's in critical condition at GWU Hospital."

I wished to God right then I had told Abby's mother not to call Conrad's family, but I nodded. "Yes, she is, ma'am."

The implications registered with both the parents and their daughter at the same time.

"Conrad?" Will Talbot said in a voice that still held hope.

But Sue Ann knew even before I said, "I'm sorry." Conrad's mother looked stunned. She staggered, crashed against the wall, and slid down it, moaning, "No. No. No. No."

Equally stunned, her husband looked past us and whispered, "Little Condor?"

Stella lost her sullen expression and started to cry, and right in front of our eyes, an innocent family crumbled and collapsed.

CHAPTER

8

I SHIFTED QUICKLY INTO support mode. During my years at Johns Hopkins, I'd spent as much time working in a counseling clinic as I had researching criminal behavior, so I listened in respectful silence as the Talbots, now sitting in the father's office, poured out their grief and bewilderment.

"Car crash?" Will Talbot said between clenched teeth. "That damned piece-of-crap Bronco?"

Sampson shook his head. "I'm sorry to say your son was murdered, Mr. Talbot. Shot at close range."

That further crushed their souls.

"Why?" Sue Ann sobbed as she held tight to Stella, who'd curled up in her arms.

"We don't know, ma'am," I said. "We're trying to figure that out."

"Where did this happen?" the father asked, his breathing choppy.

Sampson and I sat down and told him what we knew.

"What was he doing out there?" Stella asked.

"We think he took Abby there to be romantic," I said softly.

Conrad's mother shook her head, weeping. "And — what? Someone just walked up to them, way out on that island, and shot them?"

"Yes, ma'am," John said. "It appears that way. One shot. Abby was wounded and is in critical condition, but it appears your son was blocking her. He slowed the bullet down and redirected it, which probably saved her life."

That set them off all over again.

We waited until they could answer questions and then asked the most pressing ones as quickly and sensitively as we could so we'd better understand their son.

Conrad was their middle child. He'd been smart, athletic, and likable from a very young age. Schoolwork came easily to him. So did lacrosse, his first love.

Abby had entered his life the year before.

"She played lacrosse too. They were good together," Sue Ann said, nodding. "Perfect for each other."

"If you like that perfect type," Stella said.

"No drugs?" Sampson asked.

The girl shook her head. "No way."

Her father said, "They both wanted to play for Division One programs. They were focused. Conrad was so determined that he'd make it…" He choked up. "Just so unfair."

"No enemies?" I asked.

His wife shook her head. "Conrad? He might have made a lot of people frustrated on the lacrosse field, but he didn't have a negative bone in his body. Like Will said, people just liked our son."

Even his sister agreed. "Conrad always just seemed to cartwheel through life. It was like nothing ever touched him."

"He soared through it," Will added. "That's why I called him Condor. They're the biggest birds on earth, built to soar."

At that, the dead boy's father broke down, and his wife and daughter went over to console him.

It felt like time to leave. After again expressing our condolences, we stood up.

Sue Ann said, "Can we call the rest of our family?"

Her husband said, "Conrad's older brother, Geoff?"

"You can call anyone and everyone you want," I said. "This is a time to be surrounded by the people who mean the most to you."

Will Talbot asked, "When can we see him? Won't someone have to identify him?"

"When the medical examiner's work is complete," Sampson said.

I said, "We'll let you know as soon as that happens."

"Detectives?" Stella said with misty red eyes. "Catch whoever did this."

"Count on it," Sampson said, and we left.

CHAPTER

9

"**COUNT ON IT?**" I asked Sampson when we were back in the car.

"Yeah, I probably shouldn't have said it that way."

"We're both learning."

"Every day, brother," Sampson said.

We talked on the drive to GWU Hospital, agreeing that unless we found a third party in a love triangle, we might be dealing with a random incident, some sort of thrill kill.

Lisa Howard and her father were in the waiting room outside the OR where surgeons were working on Abby. Abby's father, a judge advocate general for the U.S. Marine Corps, was in the air, coming home from San Diego. We introduced ourselves and asked how they were holding up.

Lisa Howard wiped at tears. "We were doing okay until I heard about Conrad."

"An out-and-out tragedy," her father said. "Who does something like this?"

"And how are we going to tell Abby?"

"Trust me," I said, "you will know how when the time is right."

That seemed to calm the wounded girl's mom enough for her and her father to answer our questions. Their version of Abby was the same as the Talbots'—she was filled with life and genuinely interested in both academics and athletics.

"When she met Conrad, it was like everything clicked. She's the only girl in a family of boys, and her brothers are athletes, but not like Conrad. Her brothers are funny, but not like Conrad. Her dad is a guy's guy, and Conrad had him charmed, I guess you'd call it, within minutes."

Abby's grandfather said, "That boy had it all, but he did not lord it over people, you know? No arrogance that I saw."

"None," Lisa said. "We were so impressed by that." She paused, her lip quivering.

Sampson said, "Did any other boys show interest in Abby?"

"Interest? I'm sure they did, but honestly, she only had eyes for Conrad."

"No exes? No stalkers? Nobody angry at her?"

To our surprise, Mrs. Howard started sobbing. "Other than me?"

"Ma'am?" I said.

Lisa's father said, "She got angry at Abby yesterday over something."

"Laundry!" the girl's mother said. "I got angry and yelled at her over nothing, and it could have been the last thing I ever said to her."

"But it won't be," her dad said, hugging her. "You heard the surgeon before he went in. She got lucky. She's in for a tough road, but she got lucky."

After asking them to keep us updated on Abby's condition, we left. It turned out that Carl Dennis, the injured Senate aide, was also at GW and also in the OR; surgeons were stabilizing his femur, tibia, ulna, and humerus fractures. In addition to the broken bones, he had sustained a head injury despite the fact that he'd been wearing a helmet.

We spoke with his wife, Kathleen, who was in the waiting room. She said her husband often used the Route 50 bicycle path to commute from their Bethesda home to Capitol Hill.

"He loved it," she said, sniffling. "The ride gave him space."

"He rode at night?"

"Sometimes," she said. "He had all the gear to make you safe, and he was on a designated bike path. You don't expect to get run over there."

We gave her our cards and told her we'd talk to her husband when he was up to it.

Back in our squad car, I said, "Downtown? Talk to the chief and the dynamic duo?"

"We can brief them at the end of the day," Sampson said. "Or at least after we cover all our bases. Let's talk to Conrad's teachers and coaches at the Charles School."

"Abby's too," I said. "Maybe a teacher saw something the parents didn't."

"Or one of their friends or teammates did," Sampson said.

"Seems like the best way forward."

"We're in the rainforest phase of the investigation. Sometimes you just got to grab a machete, pick a direction, and start chopping a path."

"Based on clues."

"Based on evidence. Based on the verifiable facts at hand. Those're your best guides."

CHAPTER 10

AT THE BEGINNING OF the noon break at the Charles School, nine members of the teaching staff filed into a conference room, several vocally irritated at having their lunches interrupted.

Jenny Wolcott, the headmistress, stood near me and Sampson, looking slightly stunned. She waited until the last teacher—a tall, balding, somewhat disheveled man with an untrimmed mustache and round glasses—had closed the door behind him.

Then she smiled grimly.

"I'm afraid I have some tough news to share. These men are homicide detectives with Metro PD," she said, indicating me and John. "Conrad Talbot was murdered last night."

The gasps and groans were deep and real.

"No!" a man in his thirties said. He looked like he'd been kneed in the groin and began to cry. "Jesus, this is awful."

"Abby Howard was also gravely injured, and is currently in the ICU," Wolcott continued.

"That poor girl," said an older woman. "Those two were joined at the hip."

I said, "Abby was hit by the same bullet that killed Conrad, but surgeons are telling her family that she will recover."

Sampson held up his hands. "I know you all had Conrad and Abby in your classes. We need to know if there was any friction between them and their classmates. Or their teammates."

"No one on the lacrosse team," said the sobbing man.

The other teachers all shook their heads. The guy with the round glasses shrugged.

"Sir?" I said. "Was there something you noticed?"

"Not at all," he said, avoiding my gaze. "I'm just a short-term substitute. I barely know who Abby and Conrad are, so I can't comment on their social situations."

"Gary's been here for only a few days," the headmistress explained. "Lucy Porter, the regular instructor, has been out with a nasty flu, but I'll call her and see if she saw anything before her illness."

Sampson said, "That would help."

"On another note," I said, "you might want to call in grief counselors for the student body. When do you want to share the news?"

Wolcott thought, looked at her watch, then said, "The sooner the better, I think. I don't want rumors of this to trickle out. Schoolwide assembly in the gymnasium at one p.m., followed by early dismissal. After-school meetings and athletic practices are canceled. The entire staff is expected to be here, and I will call in counselors as soon as I can."

I had to hand it to the headmistress—she was an organizational dynamo. Within minutes she had the entire event arranged. At a quarter to one, she made an announcement about the assembly over the PA system.

Teachers stood outside classroom buildings and directed students returning from lunch to the gymnasium. Sampson and I went in and stayed off to the side as the students funneled in and took seats on the risers.

A kid wearing a Charles School lacrosse hoodie gestured at the man who'd cried in the meeting and asked, "What's with Coach Eric?"

"What do you mean?" asked the kid in line behind him.

"Looks like he lost his best friend. Eyes are all puffy and red, man."

"Who the hell knows, turd-head? Keep moving."

Sampson and I shared a glance, then turned our attention to the headmistress. She picked up a microphone, marched out to the middle of the gym, and, in a soft voice, told the six hundred students gathered there about Conrad Talbot's death and Abby Howard's injuries.

There were shouts of disbelief, shocked faces, students and faculty crying; the entire school banded together in collective mourning. Eventually someone shouted, "How did it happen?"

Wolcott nodded to us. We came out onto the hardwood floor, and John took the microphone. "I'm Detective Sampson. This is Detective Cross. We're sad to tell you that Conrad and Abby were both shot."

That news set off another eruption of disbelief and shock.

"We need your help," Sampson said after the reaction had died down, although several girls were still crying. "We're establishing an anonymous tip line, a phone number that will be given to you all by tomorrow morning. If you think of anything you believe we should know, do not hesitate to call and leave us a message. Please. Any one of you might have the information we need to find Conrad's killer."

CHAPTER 11

AT HALF PAST ONE we left the school and started driving to Metro PD's downtown Washington, DC, headquarters.

"How do we set up a tip line?" I asked.

Sampson shrugged. "They'll handle that in the office. But I wouldn't hold out much hope for an answer coming from the school. My gut says this was random."

"Or there's a psycho involved who's running under the radar."

"You're Mr. Happy these days."

"Just giving you the spectrum of possibilities."

"Based on your PhD research, Dr. Cross?"

"That's correct. And you probably shouldn't refer to me as Dr. Cross."

"Why not?" John said, taking the ramp for the Fourteenth

Street Bridge. "You have a doctorate. And it adds a little mystery that might unsettle someone we're talking to."

"What, you think it'll make people think I can read their minds?"

"That would help," he said and chuckled. "Can you imagine?"

"Walking around with even more voices in my head? Pass."

The radio squawked. It was Chief Pittman's assistant, ordering us to meet the chief at the ME's office. The ME had put a rush on Conrad Talbot's autopsy.

"Meaning Chief Pittman pressured the ME to put a rush on it," Sampson commented after I hung up.

"Could be."

We entered the offices of the medical examiner twenty minutes later. Chief Pittman was already there waiting, along with Detectives Corina Straub Diehl and Edgar Kurtz.

"You were supposed to come to my office right after you notified the families," Pittman growled. "The three of us were waiting."

Sampson got that look in his eye that I knew meant he might be about to say the wrong thing, so I jumped in first. "Apologies, Chief. After we spoke to the families, we went to the Charles School so we could talk to students and staff before the media got hold of the story."

The chief of detectives said, "The media *has* gotten hold of the story. They're already teasing it for the evening news."

Kurtz, a tree stump of a man with a shiny bald head, squinted and asked, "What did you learn about Talbot from his family and friends?"

I said, "Conrad was the all-around good guy, seemed to cartwheel and soar through life. No public beefs. Started dating

Abby Howard about a year ago. It will all be in our reports by the end of the day."

Sampson said, "One thing. Although I believe this shooting is most likely a random event, we told the student body there would be an anonymous tip line established for information about Conrad and Abby."

Pittman's eyebrows rose. "A tip line specifically for the school?" We nodded.

Detective Corina Diehl said, "It's not a bad idea. Kids might open up to us."

Pittman's nostrils flared as he studied us both. "Do it. Contact tech as soon as this autopsy's done."

At that moment, Emily Chin, the chief medical examiner, came through the autopsy suite's double doors and said, "Okay, we're ready for you, Chief."

The chief of detectives looked over at me. "You've seen a few of these, Cross?"

"Only one so far," I said.

"Rookie," Kurtz said. "Just don't leave your lunch near me."

"Promise," I said, and I followed Sampson and Dr. Chin through the double doors and into a hallway that reeked of antiseptic.

She took us through the first door on the left into an autopsy room. The corpse lay beneath a green cloth on a stainless-steel table.

"His clothes are there," Chin said, gesturing to evidence bags on a counter.

"You stripped him already?" Diehl said. "We usually like to be there for that."

"My bad," Chin said. "Everything's been bagged, logged, and

witnessed for evidence under my signature. Clothes, wallet, two condoms—that was it."

"Anything else we should know?" Detective Kurtz asked.

"I can only tell you what the body tells me," the medical examiner said. She drew back the green cloth, revealing Conrad Talbot's body. His young face looked serene from the eyebrows down, now that the gore had been cleaned away.

At the center of his forehead, an ugly exit wound gaped.

CHAPTER 12

THE AUTOPSY UNFOLDED QUICKLY, with most of the attention paid to the path the bullet had taken after it struck Conrad's occipital protuberance, low and square at the back of his skull.

Dr. Chin noted that the bullet must have been slowed by the window it was shot through and the thick bone of Conrad's skull. It had entered at a slightly upward angle.

Dr. Chin cut a cap of bone off the victim's skull. Studying the brain, she said, "The bullet was fragmented, and although it slowed down considerably, it continued its forward progress. There's a lot of trauma and blood here, but I'd say the remaining energy from the bullet fragments liquefied and cut channels through the brain at a rising angle. I'm eyeballing it at thirty degrees upward tilt. But we'll check."

I steeled my stomach as she removed the brain in its entirety, set it aside for further dissection, reoriented the light over the open skull, and peered inside. "Make that thirty-two degrees rise."

I said, "Can you translate that for a new guy, Dr. Chin?"

The medical examiner said, "I believe it means your shooter was crouched and aiming slightly upward into the cab of the Bronco."

Sampson said, "Or maybe the shooter is unfamiliar with the gun and yanks on the trigger, causing the gun barrel to rise at the shot."

The medical examiner nodded. "That would do it as well."

"Which means what?" Chief Pittman said impatiently.

Detective Kurtz said, "We have either a short assailant who knows how to use a gun or a taller one with limited firearms experience."

"Doesn't exactly limit the fish in the fish pond, does it?" Diehl said.

"Not yet."

Chief Pittman looked frustrated when we left the autopsy suite forty minutes later. "I was hoping for more."

"More, sir?" Detective Kurtz said.

"More to say to the media. More to tell the public so they'll know that the Metro PD is out front on this case and making damn sure the person who took this kid's life will be brought to justice!"

I was surprised at how worked up Pittman was. It showed me that, whatever his motives, the chief of detectives actually cared about his job and truly didn't know what to say to the media and the public.

Sampson picked up on that too and said, "The story you should be telling, Chief, is that at the moment, given the evidence we have, we believe this to be a random act of violence."

Detective Diehl said, "And that in any case, the Metro PD is committed to solving this crime."

Kurtz added, "Which is why the four of us are going to go back to the crime scene and canvass the neighborhood personally. Maybe someone in one of those apartments across the parkway heard something. A gunshot that made them look out the window."

Chief Pittman chewed on that for several moments, then nodded. "That story works. Thank you, Detectives. Good hunting."

"You too, sir," Diehl said and watched him until he'd left the building.

Kurtz nodded at Sampson. "That was impressive, the way you handled Pittman."

Sampson said, "I didn't realize I'd handled him."

"You gotta handle all the big swinging clowns," Diehl said. "Otherwise you'll never get what you need when you need it to close a case."

"Which is what we're all about, understand?" Kurtz said. "Together, Diehl and I have forty years on the street. Neither of us give a damn about moving up, becoming more of a suit than we already are. We like being detectives—being out, asking questions. It's what we're good at. It's all we want to be."

"Same here," Sampson said.

"I'm not happy behind a desk," I said.

"Good," Diehl said. "Then keep us informed, let us take the lead when it needs to be taken, and trust our decisions when we make them."

Kurtz said, "Other than that, have at it. Run down every lead you want. You won't be stepping on anyone's toes as long as you tell us where you're focusing."

"And above all, stay on target," Diehl said. "We are not here to chase glory. We represent the dead, and we work on their behalf."

"Clear?" Kurtz said.

"Clear," Sampson said.

"Loud and clear," I said.

"We'll see you back at the crime scene, then," Diehl said, and they left.

When we got in our squad car, Sampson said, "Diehl and Kurtz. Who knew?"

"Learning."

"Every day, brother."

CHAPTER 13

SEVEN HOURS LATER, WITH little to show for our investigations into the Talbot murder, I pressed the buzzer to the bottom-floor flat in a small two-story house on Fourth Street.

A woman's voice whispered, "Who's there?"

"Tony," I said.

"Mmm," she said, and then, putting on a Hispanic accent, "If it's Tony, he's gotta sing."

I looked around, saw no one, and sang the line from *West Side Story:* "'Maria, I just met a girl named Maria.'"

She laughed. "Not bad. But you started in the middle of the song."

"Best part."

"Sing the next verse, and Maria will know you're her Tony."

"But no dancing."

"Promise."

So I sang, "'I just kissed a girl named Maria!'"

The door buzzed open. I went inside and found my wife, Maria, waiting at the door, barefoot but still in her work clothes, all five foot two inches of her; she shot me the most beautiful smile. Her hands rested on her belly—she was six months pregnant with our second child.

"Babysitter just left, and Damon's conked out," she whispered. I bent my six-foot-two frame over and kissed her hello, then followed her inside.

I whispered, "You know, if you get shorter when we get older, I'm going to throw out my back every time we kiss."

"One of the hurdles you have to face if you want to keep this goddess happy," Maria said with a wink. She gestured down at her belly and laughed again.

"Bring on the bad back, baby doll. Can I look in on Damon?"

"Give it a little bit," she said. "He woke up a while ago and just went back down again. I'm reheating dinner."

"Your mom's sauce?"

"Not tonight."

I sighed. "Still cracks me up that your mother has a secret spaghetti sauce."

Maria stirred a pot on the stove with a wooden spoon. "How many times have I told you my mother's godmother was Sicilian?"

"I know, I know. She helped raise your mother, taught her to cook."

"And me," Maria said. She turned and smiled, and I fell in love all over again.

It had been like that since the beginning. Maria was a social worker at St. Anthony's Hospital in DC, and the first time I saw her, I knew that, despite her small stature, she had one of the biggest spirits I'd ever encountered.

I'd been talking with a couple of cops in the ER at St. Anthony's when Maria Simpson came in with Hector Munoz, a nineteen-year-old gangbanger who'd been shot in a drive-by.

Munoz had a through-and-through bullet wound to his abdomen, but he basically refused to talk to anyone. After the docs gave him morphine for the pain, he relaxed quite a bit but maintained his silence with the Metro patrol officers who were trying to interview him.

Things changed when a young woman walked over to the cops who were talking to Hector. She was wearing high heels and a snug navy-blue dress that flattered her compact gymnast's build. Her features were elegant, as if a higher power had decided to emphasize her large almond eyes and high cheekbones.

As soon as I saw this angel, I wanted to know everything about her. I took a step toward her and saw the name on the badge she wore on a lanyard around her neck: MARIA SIMPSON.

She glanced at me shyly, nodded, then turned to Hector and rattled off a series of questions. Munoz seemed as taken by Maria's beauty as I was. He talked to her slowly and lazily, as if he were flirting with her. She took it in stride and joked and teased information out of him.

Munoz claimed not to know who shot him. He said he'd been out for a walk with some friends and a guy on a motorcycle drove by with a gunman riding on the back.

Maria told the cops, "He says to go back to his neighborhood. Maybe someone saw the shooter. Hector just got shot and went down."

A nurse arrived. "There's an OR opening up for Mr. Munoz in fifteen minutes. I have to take him for prep."

Maria smiled at all of us. "Sorry I couldn't have been more help."

I was honestly so dazzled to have her looking at me that I couldn't say a word.

"Well," she said, "tell whoever is investigating this that if they have questions, I'm available in social services."

She walked off, and I stared dumbly after her, then felt compelled to follow.

"Excuse me, Ms. Simpson?" I managed. "I have some questions."

She turned and looked at me. I felt like melting when she asked, "Who are you?"

"Uh, I'm Alex Cross. I have a PhD in psychology from Johns Hopkins with a focus on violent criminality and its ripple effects."

"Nice to meet you, Alex Cross, PhD," she said, holding out her small, delicate hand. "And I know a thing or two about the ripple effects of violent crime."

"I bet you do," I said. "Could I buy you a cup of coffee? Pick your brain?"

"I'll have to take a rain check on that, I'm afraid," she said.

CHAPTER 14

IN OUR APARTMENT NOW, Maria pivoted from the stove holding a plate of baked chicken thighs, rice, and broccoli spears.

"What are you smiling at, Alex Cross?" she asked in that soft, teasing voice I loved. "You're that hungry?"

"Just remembering how you blew me off the first time I asked you out."

"Asked me out? Blew you off?" she said in mild protest. "You asked if I wanted to grab coffee so you could pick my brain, and I said I'd take a rain check on the coffee."

"But you didn't say no to a glass of wine."

"No, sir," Maria said, sitting down as I began to eat. "I was going against my mom's voice in my head saying, 'You don't know him at all.' But I did say yes to wine."

"Happy you did," I said, raising my beer.

My wife clinked her glass of water against my bottle, beaming back at me.

"Did you know right away?" I knew the answer but still enjoyed hearing her reply.

"I knew that night. I've told you that."

"What was it?"

"It wasn't one thing. More like a bunch of things at once. I guess first was how you really listened to me, how intent you were about wanting to know what I thought."

"You were an expert on some topics in psychology."

"It was more than that, I think," she said.

"I was shocked by your beauty."

"Aww," she said and smiled. "Tell me more."

"Hector Munoz was too. He was hitting on you, and you used it against him."

"Of course I did. The power of the feminine has always been my secret weapon."

"Thank God," I said and laughed. "We did talk for hours that night."

"They kicked us out of the bar."

"I asked you if anyone had ever told you that you were the most charming, intelligent, and beautiful woman they'd ever met."

"Don't forget 'inside and out,'" she said. "That's what you said. 'Has anyone ever told you that you're the most charming, intelligent, and beautiful woman, inside and out, that they'd ever met?'"

I acted crestfallen. "And you said, 'Yes. A couple of times, actually.'"

She raised her eyebrows. "I wasn't being arrogant. Just truthful. And I didn't leave you hanging there, did I?"

"No. You said, 'But I have never been told that I was charming, intelligent, and beautiful by someone as tall, well-spoken, and handsome as you.'"

Maria laughed and ran her hands over her belly. "Good line off-the-cuff, huh?"

"Provoked the beginning of my bad back when I bent over to kiss you. That's when I knew for certain."

"Because your back went out, you knew you loved me?"

"No. It was when we kissed that first time. I just knew. There was before that kiss and afterward, and I had not a second of doubt about who you were."

"Me too," she said and blew me a kiss across the table. "To change subjects, you haven't told me about your day."

My smile faded. "I caught another murder case today. Kid from the Charles School in Alexandria."

"I saw that on the news," she said. "They think it's a random thing?"

"Sampson and the chief are leaning that way."

"You're not?"

I shrugged. "I've just got this odd feeling that it was more than random."

"You think the shooter knew the victim?"

"Either that or the shooter knew it was a place where young couples go."

"And what? Took advantage of the time and place to kill a teenager in cold blood?"

"Bad either way. But I don't know which one is right."

"You sound frustrated."

"I am," I said. "I feel like I haven't had enough police training."

CHAPTER 15

MARIA FROWNED, SET DOWN her glass. "You went through the academy, Alex. You rode patrol."

"For two months before I was moved to major cases. There's a lot that I don't know about investigations, and there are times, a lot of times, where I feel like I'm playing catchup."

"You are playing catchup," Maria said. "But that's to be expected. They did not hire you for your years on the street. They hired you because you have unique insight into how bad guys think, a mindset taught to you by bad guys."

"True."

"Give them insight, then. Do that tomorrow and the day after that."

I laughed and saluted her. "Yes, ma'am."

"At ease, or whatever," she said. "And one more thing to think about."

I held up my palms. "Swing away."

"Use your imagination, but make sure it's imagination rooted in experience and reality. My mother taught me that was what being creative was—learning a skill well enough that you can use your imagination to improve it."

"Like she did with her pottery."

"Like she did with her pottery."

"Message heard. I will take the facts as I find them, then use my imagination to explore reasons to explain them."

She threw her arms wide and cackled. "And the student becomes the master!"

I couldn't help myself. I got up, went over, and kissed her.

"I want more of those," Maria said.

"Me too. I'm going to take up yoga for my back."

"I want to be there for that first class."

"I thought you'd be more supportive."

"I support anything that promotes more kissing."

I remembered something my grandmother said after she'd met Maria and repeated it—with an addition of my own. "You really are an old soul…in a wondrous body."

"Don't start any of that now," Maria said, wagging her finger as she got up from the table and cleared my plate. "Or you won't be able to get up and chase bad guys in the morning."

I made a mournful face, then said, "Can I at least look in on Damon?"

She looked up at the clock and nodded. "I'll do the dishes."

"No, you will not," I said. "I'll take a quick peek and be right back."

Maria smiled. "Then I'm going to put my feet up and watch TV. Volume on low."

I'd squirted the hinges of the door of my little boy's room with WD-40, so it opened without a sound. A slat of weak light cut the gloom inside, revealing Damon in his crib along the far wall, his blankets kicked off, as usual.

He lay on his back, right leg over his left, left hand on his forehead, left elbow held high to form a triangle. How in God's name Damon found the position comfortable, I didn't know, but it was one of his favorite positions to "conk out in," as Maria put it. I quietly crossed the room, looked down at my son, and, as I'd done every day since the miracle of his birth, gave thanks for the second-greatest gift I'd been given in this life.

PART TWO
Master Class

CHAPTER 16

I TRIED TO FOLLOW Maria's suggestion about looking at my work from a different perspective, spending time with the cold hard facts, the proven clues, then trying to extrapolate possibilities from them.

We also searched for evidence from other sources, including the FBI. From my research days, I knew a special agent over there, Ellen Bovers, whom I had interviewed several times.

I called Ellen and asked if there was a security camera overlooking the intersection where the Chain Bridge met the Canal Road. She checked, said there were CCTV cameras on both ends of the bridge and indeed on all the other bridges connecting the District to Virginia and Maryland.

I gave her a six-hour time frame and asked if she could get me video footage from the Chain Bridge camera on the Washington side. Bovers told me she'd try.

Despite that effort and others, it wasn't until six days after Conrad Talbot's body was found that we started to break through. That morning, Abby Howard's doctors gave me and Sampson the okay to ask her a few questions.

Her mother, Lisa, and her father, U.S. Marine colonel and judge advocate general Marc Howard, met us in the visitors' area at the hospital. They had told Abby about Conrad's death the day before, and it had not gone well.

"We should have waited," Colonel Howard said, sighing. "That's on me. But I didn't want her to find out from anyone but us, you know?"

"I can appreciate that," I said.

"Either of you detectives have kids?"

"I do," I said. "A toddler and another one on the way. I promise we will be extra-sensitive with your daughter."

We found Abby on her side, her back to the door, monitors beeping, her head wrapped up like a swami's.

"Abby?" I said when I reached the foot of her bed.

"Go 'way," she said, her voice slightly slurred due to the painkillers.

"Abby, I'm with the police. Detective Alex Cross. I'm here with Detective John Sampson. We're trying to find whoever shot you and Conrad."

She shrugged. "Done, no matter who did it."

Sampson said, "You loved Conrad."

Abby nodded, then began weeping.

I waited until her crying eased before I said, "Abby, we were the ones who found you."

"Should have left me to die."

I said, "In my view, you lived for a reason. I think you lived in part to help us find Conrad's killer. You loved him—don't you owe it to his memory to help us find out who killed him and why?"

She rolled over and glared at us. "If I could, I would. I have no idea who killed Conrad. I don't know who would even think of it. Everyone loved Conrad. Even my dad!"

"I know they did, Abby," Sampson said. "Conrad was one of a kind. But what we're interested in today is what you remember from the night you were both shot."

She shrugged, closed her eyes. "Bronco."

"Conrad's brother's Bronco."

"C loved that thing. Kept talking about it. All night."

"And not paying attention to you?"

Abby opened her eyes, stared at me. "That's right. How did you know that?"

"I get people," I said. "He kept talking about the Bronco?"

"Until we, like, parked by that canal and...I don't know."

"Close your eyes again, Abby. Try to see yourself in the Bronco with Conrad."

She shut her eyes, lay still for several moments, then got tense.

I'd anticipated that. "We are not here to judge you, Abby. We do not care what you and Conrad were doing. We just want to know if you saw or heard anything by the canal."

Eyes still closed, she said, "All I can see is Conrad."

Before I could respond, she said, "Wait. There's a...like...a shadow."

"Where are you seeing the shadow?"

"Out of the corner of my left eye, like, to the side."

"In your peripheral vision?"

She nodded slightly.

"The shadow's at the back of the SUV?" I asked.

"No, like, back left along the—"

She breathed in sharply, her face gripped by terror. "He was there," she whispered. "I saw him there. Right by Conrad's window."

I glanced at Sampson. He drew circles in the air: *Keep her talking.* "What else, Abby?"

"I'm not believing he's there. And then he takes another step and he's got some kind of hood or mask on, and his arm is coming up. He has a pistol. I can see it in the moonlight. I want to scream. I open my mouth to scream and then, like…nothing." Abby opened her eyes. "I still feel like that. Nothing. No reason to go on."

"That's understandable, Abby," I said. "But you believe that Conrad loved you, correct?"

"I know Conrad loved me."

"Good. Good. For today and tomorrow and for the next week or so, I want you to get through your day by remembering Conrad and letting his love for you fill you up. I want you to use his love to give you the strength to start getting better. Just for the next week. Okay?"

She gazed at me, tears seeping from her eyes, and nodded.

"We'll see you soon, Abby," I said, and we left. We thanked her parents and told them she'd been a big help.

In the elevator, Sampson said, "Where'd you get all that stuff?"

"What stuff?"

"Telling her to rely on Conrad's love—that stuff. That from psychology school?"

I thought about it. "Not really. It just felt like the right thing to say at the time."

I looked over and found my oldest friend studying me. "What?"

He laughed. "I've known you since we were nine, Alex Cross, and you're still showing me sides of you I've never seen."

"It's called evolution, man."

"I've heard of that concept," he said as the elevator door opened. "Guess I'm one of the less evolved."

"And judging from your tone, being one of the less evolved makes you happy."

Sampson thought about that, then grinned. "Yeah, I guess it does. All warm and happy."

CHAPTER 17

BEFORE WE LEFT THE hospital, we learned that Carl Dennis, the injured Senate aide, had been transferred to a rehab facility in Bowie, Maryland.

The less-evolved detective had a dentist appointment, so he dropped me off at Metro PD headquarters shortly after noon. Before I could get to my desk, Chief Pittman leaned out of his office and motioned me in.

"Tell me something I don't know about Conrad Talbot," he said once I was there.

"Abby Howard got a glimpse of the killer before he fired the gun."

"Okay, okay, that's a step," Pittman said, thinking. "She remember enough to work with a sketch artist?"

"Maybe if you give her a few days. She said it was pretty dark and he was wearing a hood of some kind, but she saw the pistol in the moonlight."

"A few days," the chief said, staring off into space.

"Or send one now and send another in a week," I said.

Pittman snapped his fingers. "Good thinking. She still in the hospital?"

"Yes. For two more days at least."

"I'll make it happen, then. Keep me posted on all new developments."

"Absolutely," I said, and left his office.

I went to my desk and found a small pile of faxes, almost all of them the results of various tests in the Conrad Talbot case. On top, the most recent, was an extensive report of the crime scene.

I looked at the photographs of the scene from multiple angles but spent more time studying a diagram that included the line of indistinct footprints between the cutoff road and the Bronco. There was an asterisk by the footprints. I looked down at the comments and saw: *Prints show wool fabric, possibly indicating a covering pulled over assailant's footwear to avoid leaving identifiable tread marks.*

I closed my eyes for a second, trying to imagine the killer pulling woolen coverings over his shoes and a hood over his head, then sneaking out of the woods, seeing the Bronco, and creeping forward.

When I opened my eyes again, I looked at the roughly northeast angle the footprints took toward the Bronco. *Why that angle? Why not come from directly behind and then slide up the side for the shot?*

I went back to the photographs and saw the reason plain as day.

"He was trying to stay in the side-view mirror's blind spot," I mumbled, feeling excited.

I put my forehead in my hands and looked down as if I were studying the crime scene map, but then I shut my eyes. Remembering that Abby said she'd seen the shadow along the left side of the car, I imagined the killer as if I were looking at him from above, watched him angling, cutting in for the close-range shot.

Something about his position at the shot bothered me, but I didn't know what.

I decided to try to see the map from the killer's point of view. He was stalking, moving quietly, very precise, very sure of his steps. He stepped by the back left window and then forward to the driver's window. He raised the gun and pointed it at the window and the back of Conrad's head.

Abby sees him at this point. She wants to scream but can't.

Does he see her move?

No, he's intent on his target.

I froze him there in my mind, a split second away from pulling the trigger. This time, I tried to spin my perspective around, to see the killer as Abby had seen him — she'd been uncertain she'd seen anything at first, distracted by Conrad's attention, and then she became sure enough to try to scream when he appeared right outside the window and raised the gun in the moonlight.

Once more, I froze the shooter in dark silhouette, facing Abby, a moment before he shot. For some reason, this triggered an image in my mind: a police sketch artist's drawing of a man positioned just like Conrad's killer.

I opened my eyes, frowning, trying but failing to place the image. I set that aside and continued to plow through the reports, starting with the toxicology results. They revealed that Conrad had been drinking the night he died, although his blood alcohol level was fairly low.

I decided it didn't really matter and reached the bottom of the stack, a ballistics report on the two large bullet fragments taken out of the ceiling of the Bronco, just above the window frame on the passenger side, behind Abby.

The fragments were identified as pieces of a 246-grain .44-caliber boattail bullet, lead core with a copper jacket.

A 246-grain boattail bullet?

Wouldn't that be heavy enough to take down a charging bear?

If it was a .44 Magnum, yes. But it couldn't have been a Magnum; if it were, the bullet pieces would have hit Abby more directly and with more force, killing her.

No, the gun that killed the lacrosse star was a straight .44-caliber pistol.

For some reason, the unusual caliber of the pistol struck me as a throwback. An older gun, certainly. We had reference books on firearms in the office. I went to one and searched through it for .44-caliber pistols.

It took a while, but I found several, including one called the Bulldog, produced by Charter Arms. That triggered a memory from my early doctoral research: a microfiche image of the front page of the *New York Daily News* in early June 1977.

The headline:

Breslin to .44 Killer: Give Up! It's Only Way Out

Sampson came back into the office. "I hate the dentist."

"Everyone does," I said, getting up.

"Yeah, but I have to go back to get a root canal."

"Let's go talk to Pittman. I think I got something."

Detectives Diehl and Kurtz were at their desks working on reports. As I passed them, I said, "I found something on the Talbot case. You're going to want to hear this."

Both senior detectives got up and followed us into the chief's office.

I knocked on the doorjamb. Pittman looked up, saw the four of us.

"Can it wait? I'm supposed to brief the media. Unless it's something new about Talbot's murder?"

"As a matter of fact, it is," I said. "But I don't think you want to go telling the press about this just yet, Chief."

Chief Pittman looked at me suspiciously. "Why don't you spit out what you've got and let me decide what I tell the press."

"I can show you all the similarities, the parallels, even the forty-four-caliber pistol," I said.

"Cross," Pittman said, drumming his fingers on his desk. "Forget the details. Give me the headline for now. I have places to be."

"The shooter, Chief. He thinks he's the Son of Sam."

CHAPTER 18

CHIEF PITTMAN LOOKED AT me like I'd lost my mind. Senior detectives Kurtz and Diehl did as well. Even Sampson was giving me a high eyebrow.

"The Son of Sam?" Pittman said. "You mean David Berkowitz? I'm pretty sure he's still in Attica."

"He's at Sullivan Correctional, actually," I said. "And I didn't say our killer *was* the Son of Sam. I said he *thinks* he's the Son of Sam."

"Gimme a break, Cross," Diehl said.

"Okay, maybe he doesn't think he's Berkowitz full-time, but he is undoubtedly following the MO of the killer who terrorized New York in 1977."

"Challenge," Detective Kurtz said. "I have close friends who worked that case. I know a lot about it, and this does not look like

Berkowitz. His first victims were not a male and a female, they were two women in a car talking."

"One killed," I said. "One wounded. The survivor was able to describe her assailant, just like Abby did for us."

Pittman shook his head. "That's not enough to say he's a copy-cat Berkowitz."

"There's more," I said. "The gun used to kill Conrad Talbot was a straight forty-four, probably a Charter Arms Bulldog, and the bullet was definitely the same kind that Berkowitz used, a two-hundred-and-forty-six-grain boattail."

"*Probably* a Charter Arms Bulldog?" Kurtz said.

"Forensics says there was gunpowder residue on the window consistent with someone shooting a relatively inaccurate short-barreled forty-four, such as a Charter Arms Bulldog, which is what Berkowitz used."

Diehl said, "I'm still not buying it. Next you'll be telling us there were satanic symbols found around the car."

"I'm sure Detective Kurtz can tell you that Berkowitz was messing with the police with those symbols," I said. "And what he said about hearing the Labrador retriever Sam commanding his son to kill and all the satanic stuff? Not true—he didn't hear anything. He made it up."

Kurtz nodded. "I'll give you that, Cross. What else you got?"

"The angle of approach. Like Berkowitz, this guy planned his approach to take advantage of the blind spot in the car's side-view mirror."

Pittman said, "Conrad's killer did that?"

I nodded. "Check the diagram of his footprints."

"Who told you Berkowitz moved so he'd be in the mirror's blind spot?" Kurtz said.

"Berkowitz," I said.

Sampson said, "Alex interviewed him for his PhD dissertation."

Kurtz said, "Yeah? Is it true he got religion in the stir?"

"That's what he claims."

The chief said, "You've got to give me more than that, Cross."

"One more thing," I said. "The Forty-Four-Caliber Killer targeted victims in lovers' lanes. Exactly what that pullout on the Potomac could be considered."

Pittman sat there a few moments chewing on the evidence to support my theory, but even I could see the flaws. There were a lot of *probably*s in my argument.

"Still thin, Cross," the chief said at last. "And I don't want to set the public off by saying we're investigating a Berkowitz wannabe in the killing of Conrad Talbot without concrete proof."

"I don't think we should tell the public anything at this point," I said. "We keep it in the backs of our minds. If I'm right, there'll be more evidence surfacing. If I'm not, nothing else will come up and I'm just an overeager rookie."

"Smells like that flip side," Diehl said, and she left.

Kurtz looked at me, said, "*Dr.* Cross," with an ironic emphasis on the *Dr.*, and followed Diehl out.

Sampson and I started to leave too.

"Cross," Chief Pittman said. "Stay, please."

When Sampson was gone and the door was shut, the chief said, "I took a huge risk, bringing you in the way I did, Cross."

"Yes, sir, I know that, and I deeply appreciate it."

"I felt, and feel, that this department—every big-city police department, for that matter—should have someone with your background. Someone who knows how criminals think."

"I agree."

"Then why is the first thing you bring me a theory with rickety support about a copycat of a guy who's been incarcerated for over a decade? If this gets out, it's going to spread like wildfire in the department, and there's already enough bad will toward you among the rank and file. You don't want to throw gas on the fire."

I blinked several times. "I didn't know anyone had bad will toward me."

"It's because you didn't come up through the ranks, and they resent that, evidently."

I didn't know what to say. "I promise you it won't happen again. Next time I come to you with a theory, it will be bombproof."

"See that it is, Detective Cross," Pittman said. "Dismissed."

CHAPTER 19

I RETURNED TO MY desk in the squad room. Detectives Corina Diehl and Edgar Kurtz glanced at me as I passed them, then went back to their work. Sampson, who sat across from me, noticed I looked shaken.

"It's past five o'clock," John said. "Want a beer?"

"More like *need* a beer," I said. I picked up my bag and coat and followed him to the elevators, which were crowded. We didn't have another chance to talk alone until we were outside, trying to hail a cab.

"What was that all about with the chief?" Sampson asked.

"He sounded like he had a bad case of buyer's remorse, and I felt like I'd been called into the principal's office," I said quietly. "Did you know there's resentment against me among the rank-and-file officers?"

He nodded. "Because you leapfrogged into the elite unit."

"I get it," I said. "But Pittman and Chief Williams approached *me*. I didn't ask for this position. It was offered."

John shrugged. "That distinction might be lost on some of the guys. But so what? And everyone gets carried away when they come up with a theory like that."

"You think I got carried away?"

"Maybe a little. I wouldn't have said anything to anyone until I had it nailed."

"Anyone except me."

"I'll tell you when you don't have it nailed, and I expect the same of you."

I sighed. "Guess I do need some checks and balances."

"We all do, brother. There's no going it alone in modern policing. The cowboy, lone-wolf, Dirty Harry detective is in the past. We're part of a system now."

I nodded. "Learning."

"Every day," he said. "Are we ever going to find a cab?"

"Seems like a message," I said. "Think I'll skip the beer, take the Metro, and go home."

"Don't take that trip to the principal's office too hard."

"I'll try not to."

But try as I might, I was still chewing on Chief Pittman's comments long after I'd gotten home and while I was cooking dinner: baked salmon, green beans, and egg noodles with garlic and oil, which pushed the boundaries of my culinary expertise. Maria got home from work after picking Damon up from day care.

He fast-waddled to me, and I scooped him up in my arms.

"I missed you, Daddy," Damon whispered into my neck.

"I missed you too, little buddy," I said, kissing the top of his head, my eyes misting. Maria took off her coat, somehow looking as fresh as she had when she'd left for work that morning.

Maria and I kissed hello, then we both kissed Damon on opposite cheeks at the same time, which got him laughing.

I asked Maria about her day. "Not bad," she said. "Baby was kicking a lot. I took care of some follow-up calls I'd been putting off. Thanks for cooking."

"Pretty straightforward meal."

"I still appreciate it," she said. "Come talk to me while I change."

I shifted Damon to my other arm, checked the timers, saw I still had twenty minutes before dinner was done, and carried him with me down the hall.

Maria was in our closet, putting on sweatpants.

"What's up with you?" she asked. "Lot of weight on those shoulders."

"Is it that obvious?"

"Yeah. I saw the hound-dog look on your face before Damon toddled over."

"I got a private spanking from Chief Pittman because I came up with a theory I was excited about, called the entire team into his office to tell them about it, and then realized how many holes there were in my argument."

"Daddy spanked?" Damon said, lifting his head off my shoulder.

"Sort of," I said.

Maria said, "Pittman will get over it. Enthusiasm never hurts."

"In the future, I think I'll be more, I don't know, disciplined about who I tell things to."

"You can be enthusiastic and disciplined. That's not hard."

As we went back out to the kitchen, I told Maria about the resentment toward me among many of the junior officers.

"I can see that," she said.

"I can too. Doesn't make it easier to deal with people watching you and wanting you to fail."

"Well, you won't fail."

"You have more belief in me than I do."

"Of course I do. I'm your wife. That's what I'm here for. You're the same way about me. Damon? Do you want some noodles?"

"Yes, please, Mommy," he said as I lowered him into his high chair. He threw both hands up and crowed, "Noodles!"

Any kind of pasta was his favorite food, and when he cheered, I realized just how right my life was.

CHAPTER

20

Newark, Delaware

IN A CARREL DEEP in the stacks on the second floor of the University of Delaware library, Gary Soneji was engrossed in *Practical Homicide Investigation: Tactics, Procedures, and Forensic Techniques* by Vernon J. Geberth.

He'd read the book during his undergraduate years but had returned to study so-called equivocal-death investigations, specifically ones where detectives believed they were dealing with staged murder scenes. He wanted to know what they took into consideration beyond fetishistic posing. He wanted to know what would make them suspect that the victim had been killed elsewhere and then moved.

He found what he was looking for. One tip-off was the location of internal blood pooling in the body being contradictory to a corpse's position at discovery. Another was fibers on the body suggesting that the victim had been wrapped in a rug or a blanket. A third was an injury on the body at odds with the manner of death.

Too many things could go wrong if you moved them, Soneji decided. You didn't leave them to be found. You didn't move them anywhere but to their graves. *This is pleasure. But it must be done so the pleasure can last longer.*

He shut the book on homicide investigations and turned his attention to an FBI manual he'd found in the stacks that focused on kidnapping investigations and included a detailed narrative about the Lindbergh-baby kidnapping case, which he read with great interest.

He'd grown up in Princeton, near where the crime had occurred, so he'd always been fascinated with that case. The idea of kidnapping—and killing—a celebrity's child held a particular thrill for him.

Death was intensely interesting to him, and it gave him immense pleasure to see people die at his hands. He felt a fierce adrenaline rush, an exhilarating explosion of power.

Murder was fun, Soneji allowed. And strangely fulfilling. *Like a glimpse into the unknown,* he thought, and felt a chill go through him.

Yet there was something about an abduction that moved Soneji equally if not more. As he devoured information on the Lindbergh case, his mind flashed back to scenes from his first take.

Joyce Adams. Very pretty. Very arrogant.

That had changed quickly, hadn't it? She'd been begging for mercy by the end.

Joyce had left the Princeton University campus to go to a local county park for an early-morning run in the woods, a fairly routine habit for the freshman co-ed. She had never emerged from those trees.

Dressed in camouflage, Soneji had ambushed her, knocked

her out with injectable animal tranquilizer he'd stolen from a vet hospital he volunteered at, and bundled her into his old VW van. He'd taken her to a small house in the Pine Barrens that he'd inherited from an uncle on his mother's side. It had a basement that suited his secret purposes perfectly, allowing him to toy and play with Joyce for several days before ending her life.

At the memory, Soneji felt warm and fuzzy inside. But also hungry for more, wanting that buzzing sense of power that had surged through him while holding Joyce against her will. He wanted it again and he wanted it soon.

The more efficient side of him, however — the side that thrived on the order and rigor of math and computer science — kept him in check. Soneji had promised himself he would finish what he'd set out to do: to study all the masters, teach himself every possible way a crime could go wrong, then resolve all the issues before he acted.

But he had to admit he'd already made two mistakes. He hadn't stayed to put a second shot in Abby, and she'd lived, and he hadn't finished off the guy on the bike, though he was evidently critically injured. On a positive note, Soneji had been reading the newspaper stories about the shooting closely and had seen no mention of a white van.

Soneji told himself he was okay. Abby and the bicyclist were alive, but he was okay. This was no time to quit. He would just have to do better next time.

He closed the FBI manual on kidnap investigations and realized that it had been more than a week since he'd taken the shot at Conrad Talbot — almost ten days, actually. It was time to practice becoming David Berkowitz once again.

CHAPTER 21

SONEJI CHECKED HIS WATCH. Three thirty p.m. He'd gotten to the library around eleven a.m.

He did some calculations in his head and decided to visit his secret little cabin in the Pine Barrens, making some important client visits on the way. He could check the place, take a few shots with the Bulldog, and be hunting for targets by sundown.

He picked up his briefcase, left the library, and headed to the parking lot and his black Saab. As he got in, his big Motorola car phone started ringing. Marty Kasajian, his boss and brother-in-law, had bought the insanely expensive device for him.

Soneji answered, figuring it was Marty, but instead he heard Meredith Kasajian Murphy's voice say coldly, "Hello, Gary. It's your wife."

"Missy?" he said, frowning. "You know this phone is only for work and emergencies."

"You didn't call last night, Gary," Missy said.

"I'm sorry. I was beat after a long day making cold calls and just crashed when I hit the motel. I know I should have called, but the pay phone there was out."

"You could have used the car phone."

"And have Marty explode about the charges? Do you know how much this thing costs a minute?"

Missy said, "Marty can afford it for my peace of mind."

"I hope you'll be the one telling him that."

There was a silence, then his wife said, "I'll do that. When are you coming home? Roni and I want to know."

Roni was their two-year-old daughter. Wanting to pound the heel of his hand against the side of his head, he replied, "As soon as I make monthly quota on new business, probably dinnertime on Friday."

"Promise?"

"Promise."

"I'm going to tell Marty I want you home Friday whether you make quota or not."

"Good luck with that," Soneji said and hung up, kind of wishing Missy and Marty were in front of him right now so he could slap his bitch wife silly and kick his dickhead brother-in-law in the nuts.

Marty Kasajian was the kind of guy who'd been born on third base and believed he'd hit a triple. He'd inherited his family's booming heating oil and propane company but acted like he was the big entrepreneur who'd built the place. He'd given Soneji a job, not in computers, but as a traveling salesman, drumming up business along the middle Atlantic Seaboard.

As jobs went, it wasn't bad. The pay was more than decent. And it allowed him chunks of time to play hooky and try out this private-school-teacher identity. He could spend his days around elite kids, studying them and fantasizing about kidnapping them.

But at the moment, he had more important things to think about. Like where to hunt his next victims.

CHAPTER 22

THE MORNING AFTER MY ill-fated meeting with Pittman, Kurtz, and Diehl, John Sampson and I were called to a homicide in Fort Circle Park in Southeast Washington, DC.

A jogger had come upon a dead male on one of the park's interior paths.

We found the body beside the path, arms circling the trunk of an oak tree, wrists tied together with wire that had cut deeply into the skin.

It had rained overnight. The skies were still threatening. We stood back while patrol officers erected canopies over the scene, then moved closer.

"No prints in the mud except the runner's," Sampson said.

"Rained hard last night," I said, moving around the tree so I could see the victim more clearly.

The left side of his face showed him to be young, in his mid-teens, and of mixed race. Hispanic and Black would be my guess.

I kept moving and saw that the right side of his face, against the tree trunk, was battered and grossly swollen. A rag had been stuffed in his mouth.

I took a few more steps and saw that his back had been struck repeatedly with something long and narrow and with such force that his bloody T-shirt had ripped, showing livid welts and torn flesh beneath.

"Jesus," I said, turning away, nauseated.

"Take a few breaths," Sampson said. "I'll check his pockets."

I walked several yards away and leaned against a tree, swallowing at the aluminum taste building at the back of my throat.

"Nothing," Sampson said a minute later. "Looks like he was cleaned out."

Emily Chin, the chief medical examiner, showed up shortly after I'd gotten my gut under control enough to return to the scene.

"You're taking field calls now, Doc?" Sampson said.

"Two deputies are on vacation, and we're understaffed, so here I am," Chin said.

I said, "Looks like the right side of his head was beaten against the tree after his back was slashed by something."

Chin took multiple photographs of the scene before the criminology team showed up. Then she moved to examine the body, Dictaphone in hand. She spoke into the recorder loud enough for us to hear.

"Victim is male, mixed race, appears to be fifteen or sixteen, with facial skin split raggedly in several places, probably from being hit against the tree trunk," Chin said. She got out a flashlight and bent over to look at his back. "Posterior torso has been lashed in multiple places."

I waited until Chin had clicked off her recorder. "Can you tell what was used?" I asked.

"Not leather," she said. "More like a long thin rod or a dowel of some kind."

Sampson said, "Like something you'd use to cane someone?"

Chin pocketed the flashlight. "I'll have to look at the tissue under a magnifying glass, but yes, it looks like a caning to me."

"He die from the head trauma?" I asked.

"We'll know more after the autopsy, but I'd say he was rendered unconscious from the head blows. When he collapsed, his weight caused the wires to slice into his wrists. Rain washed the blood down the trunk and into the leaves."

From his body temperature, she determined he'd died about five hours before the jogger found him, so around one in the morning.

At this point, a very attractive young Black woman in jeans, hiking boots, and a black windbreaker came trotting down the path toward us.

Sampson said, "Stop right there, ma'am."

She stopped, breathing hard, and held up a badge. "I'm Officer Nancy Donovan, Metro PD. I work gangs undercover, and when I heard there was a kid found in the park, I—" Donovan saw the body hanging off the tree trunk. "Can I take a look at him?"

I said, "He's pretty beat up, but have at it."

Donovan gave me a wan smile, walked past us in an arc around the crime scene, and stopped to gaze at the good side of the victim's face. She shook her head.

"I know him," she said. "Shay Mansion. Lives in Grant Park. Dropped out of Woodson last year after two trips to juvie. I've seen him multiple times in the past six months with members of Los Lobos Rojos—the Red Wolves. He was a recruit."

CHAPTER 23

SAMPSON KNEW ALL ABOUT the Red Wolves, but I was not up to speed on the nuances of gang activity in the nation's capital beyond what I'd learned in the case of Tony Miller, the boy who'd been found in the Potomac.

While John continued to take notes on the scene, Nancy Donovan, the undercover officer, and I went to a nearby coffee shop, where we took a back table and she gave me a primer on the situation.

"At the moment there are six or seven gangs in and around the edges of the District," Donovan said. "But the ones that matter these days are Los Lobos Rojos, a Latin gang, and LMC Fifty-One, who are mostly Haitian refugees."

"Rivals?"

"Bitter."

"Are LMC members capable of this kind of murder?" I asked.

"They didn't used to be, but lately their leader, Patrice Prince, has gotten bolder and more ruthless. Now I think he or his captains could do something this violent."

Prince, she said, was the son and grandson of members of the notorious Tonton Macoute, the brutal death squad feared by generations of Haitians. He was orphaned at fourteen and had come to the United States as a refugee when he was sixteen.

He soon joined La Main Cachée—the Hidden Hand—an organized-crime group in Miami. He'd been investigated and jailed briefly twice, suspected of involvement in several killings during a gang war there, but he was never convicted.

"The heat got too much, so about six years ago Prince convinced his LMC brothers to let him come north and set up a second operation."

"So the Fifty-One refers to the District of Columbia, the so-called fifty-first state."

"And the surrounding counties in Maryland and Virginia." When Prince first came north, she said, he had used proxies instead of appearing as the front man in the emerging gang. He functioned behind the scenes, building a growing network of disgruntled youth, his organization's hands reaching into narcotics, armed robbery, illegal gambling, and human trafficking.

"But about eighteen months ago," Donovan said, "the Red Wolves started feeling like their turf was being stepped on, and it got ugly from there. Los Lobos killed the two proxy front men of LMC Fifty-One about nine months ago, and Prince had no choice but to step out. Yeah, I could see Prince ordering this to make a statement."

"Any idea where we can find Mr. Prince?"

Donovan chewed at the inside of her lip before meeting my

eyes. "Look, I know who you are, Detective Cross, and I have no grudge against you. I think they were right to bring someone like you onto major cases like this."

I smiled. "Thank you, Officer Donovan. I appreciate that."

"But at the same time, I've been undercover almost fourteen months. I do know where Prince is, but if I tell you, suspicion will fall on a specific circle of people as the leak."

"Including you?"

She shrugged. "I'd be considered on the perimeter of it, but Prince is not stupid."

"I understand your situation, but this is a homicide investigation."

Donovan held up her hands. "I get it. Tell you what—Prince moves around a lot. The second I have a line on him out in a public place, which happens often enough, I'll notify you."

"What about Los Lobos?"

"I'll give you everything I know," she said.

Donovan told me that she believed the leader of the Red Wolves—behind the scenes, anyway—was Guillermo Costa, a forty-something ex-con who owned a body shop in Bowie, Maryland.

"Costa had trouble as a juvie, involvement in the precursor gang to Los Lobos, then he turned his life around for quite a while," the undercover officer said. "Became a Marine. Made recon, then got court-martialed for stealing and selling weapons. Did four years in Leavenworth. Came out, joined Los Lobos, and got arrested for grand theft auto. Did another three years hard time but learned auto-body repair, a skill he used to start his business.

"Speaking of, it's unclear where the money came from to buy the place," she went on. "I'll give you the address."

I handed her my notepad. "How does it work? He comes into the city to run the gang?"

The officer shook her head as she wrote. "Costa never leaves Bowie, from what I understand. The Red Wolves go to him. They talk in secret and leave."

"How do you know all this?"

"Prince studies him, has him watched. Word gets around."

"In French?"

"Haitian Creole. My grandmother was from Haiti. She raised me bilingual."

"You're one surprise after another."

She grinned and handed me back my notebook. "Thank you. Any help you need, you can page me at the number I wrote under Costa's address. I'll try to get back to you within the hour."

Donovan got up and turned to leave. I called after her, "Officer?"

"Detective?" she said, looking back.

"Be careful out there."

"I always watch my six."

CHAPTER 24

THREE HOURS LATER, AFTER wrapping up the crime scene, Sampson and I decided to pay Guillermo Costa a visit at his auto-body shop in Bowie, Maryland, about nine miles from where Shay Mansion had been found.

Our thinking was we'd start with Costa and see if he could tell us anything about Mansion, Los Lobos Rojos, LMC 51, or Patrice Prince before we did the heavy deed of informing yet another parent that their son had died. First, however, Sampson found a pay phone and called the Woodson High office, trying to track down Shay Mansion's parents.

I parked but kept the car running, waiting for him. I had WTOP, all-news AM radio, playing softly in the background, an old habit.

"Yes, I know Shay is no longer a student," John said, then listened. "Expelled, right. But a last address for him would be very helpful."

He looked at me in despair and then brightened. "Great. Okay."

Sampson scribbled something, nodded. "You've been a great help."

He hung up and slid into the car, and we headed out. "Rosalina Mansion. Shay's mom. We've got an address and a home number, but the Woodson secretary says the mom's a nurse's aide. Husband died a few years back. She works crazy hours, two jobs, never home. Probably part of the reason the kid got involved with Lobos Rojos."

On the radio, I heard: "Prince George's County Sheriff's investigators are said to be converging on a homicide scene in Beltsville this morning. WTOP's Bill Johnson is there. Bill, what can you tell us?"

Before the reporter could reply, Dispatch called on our police radio, so I turned the broadcast off.

"Roger, Dispatch, this is Sampson."

"Call Chief Pittman."

"Roger that." Sampson sighed, shrugged, and we found another pay phone and pulled over again. This time we both got out of the car and huddled over the pay phone's receiver so we could talk to him together. Pittman answered on the second ring.

"I heard it's damn gruesome, this kid in the park," the chief said.

"It's not pretty, sir," said Sampson.

I said, "Downright brutal if you ask me, Chief."

"Motive?"

Sampson said, "We're thinking it might be gang-related. According to intel, Mansion was a recruit to Los Lobos Rojos, so this could be a statement killing by rival gang LMC Fifty-One and its leader, Patrice Prince."

"I saw a report on Prince. Any link to the other kid, the one in the Potomac?"

"Tony Miller," I said. "Possibly, but I haven't looked into it yet."

Sampson said, "Sorry, sir, but we haven't had much time to devote to the Miller case because of our focus on—"

"Conrad Talbot," Pittman said. "And that's right where I wanted your attention and still do. That kid's death is priority one. It takes precedence. Even over this case."

"Because Talbot's white, sir?" I couldn't help asking.

"No, and don't play the damn race card with me, Cross. Talbot gets attention because he was a first-team, all-state, Division One–bound athlete who was also smart enough to get into several Ivy League schools."

"Exactly my—"

"Cross," Pittman said, cutting me off, "you're not letting me speak. I want to be clear, okay?"

Sampson slapped me on the upper arm.

"Okay, Chief."

"Black, Latino, Asian, white, whatever—a kid with those credentials who was killed like that? I'm sorry, but we are giving his murder investigation priority over gangbanger kids who got caught up in a turf war. If that sticks in your craw, swallow hard, because my stand on that is not changing. Clear?"

"Clear, Chief," Sampson said.

I said, "But also, one last thing, Chief—I don't know much about Shay Mansion at this point, but I know Tony Miller was a hell of a student. My grandmother knew him and thought he was brilliant, capable of getting into a great school."

There was a pause, after which Pittman said in a calmer tone, "I'm not telling you to ignore Miller's death, Cross. Or this kid's. I expect you to work them too. But you've got to learn that as a big-city homicide detective, you've got six to eight burners on your stove, and some cases are front burner and others are back burner."

He hung up.

I said, "I hate when he does that."

"I do too, especially after he's said something that makes total sense."

I frowned, and we got back in the car again. "About prioritizing the Talbot case?"

"About there being a lot of cases you've got to keep track of all at once. It takes time to learn how to do that and not lose momentum on any of them."

"I can see that," I said. "Still learning."

"Always," Sampson said.

CHAPTER

25

COSTA'S BONA FIDE AUTO-BODY and Engine Repair took up several lots and was spotlessly maintained, in contrast to a lot of similar places I'd been. No oil stains. No auto parts scattered about. The place was well cared for.

Indeed, when we pulled up, a ripped, heavily tatted, shaved-head dude in ironed black jeans, a black T-shirt, and polished black tactical boots was spraying down the sidewalk and pavement out front with a pressure hose. I recognized Costa from his booking photo. He turned off the spigot when we climbed out.

Sampson said, "Guillermo Costa?"

Costa took one look at us, smiled sourly, shook his head, and said in a thick accent, "I don't know what you're doing here, man, but Costa is clean. Costa's whole life has been clean since he did his time."

"Nice clean place," I said agreeably, holding out my badge and ID. John did the same.

Costa was in his early forties and built like a welterweight. When he dropped the hose and came toward us, his movements were fluid and balanced, like a cat's.

Sampson and I each had several inches and thirty pounds on him, but Costa was jacked, and his file said he had Special Forces training. Both of us were on high alert as he came closer. He stopped to peer at our credentials from three feet away.

"Metro Homicide," he said, taking a step back, palms up. "Detectives Cross and Sampson. What's this about?"

Sampson said, "The body of a sixteen-year-old male was found in a park not far from here. He'd been tied to a tree with wire and lashed. We have it on good authority that the kid was connected to Los Lobos Rojos."

Costa went unreadable, shook his head, and took another step back. "Man, Costa told you, he is clean. Long time clean." He waved his hand at the auto shop. "Do you think Costa would take any chance of losing this? After working so hard to build his business and get his life back? No, man, Guillermo the Marine and Guillermo the gangbanger, he left both behind the day he started his last stretch. When he got out, he was Costa, and the Red Wolves knew this new person wasn't ever coming back to the street. Costa was a different person. He has no beef with them, and they have no beef with Costa."

I said, "Quit talking about yourself in the third person. It's really annoying."

Costa looked like he wanted to deck me. "I am clean. We are talking three different people is all."

Sampson said, "Right, and yet high-ranking members of the gang are known to frequent your business."

"As customers, sure. We fix cars here. We are good at it. Some of those people know me from the old days, but we do not see each other as close friends anymore. They have to pay me for what I am skilled at. End of story."

I said, "So you've never heard of Shay Mansion?"

Ripped welterweight or not, changed man or not, Costa looked like he'd gotten a solid punch to the solar plexus. His stony expression cracked, and he gazed at us in bewilderment.

"Shay?" he said softly.

Sampson said, "You knew him, Mr. Costa?"

"You're sure it's Shay Mansion?"

I said, "We have a preliminary ID. We're leaving here to contact his mother."

"Rosalina," he said, and all his defensive bluster seeped away. "My cousin. Oh, Jesus. She don't know?"

"Not yet," I said.

"Jesus," he said, wiping away tears with his forearm. "It's gonna…"

"What?" Sampson said.

"Rip her up. She lost her husband back five years ago. Shay's her only kid."

"You two close?"

He shrugged. "Growing up, we were. Our mothers were sisters, and Rosalina and I are almost the same age. We still talk now and then. I help her when I can."

I said, "She say anything about Shay joining Los Lobos?"

He tightened ever so slightly. "Nah, nah, that I would remember. But you know what? If he was Los Lobos, you don't want to be talking to me or Rosalina. You want to be talking to that son of a bitch Patrice Prince."

"From LMC Fifty-One."

"Damn straight LMC Fifty-One. Bloodthirsty Haitian. Don't give a damn about life."

Sampson said, "Wait a second. I thought you said Costa's not a part of a gang anymore."

Costa looked like he wanted to punch John now, which would not be a good idea. Built like a brick wall, my friend and partner was six nine, weighed about two fifty, and was capable of sudden and devastating violence when required.

"I am not a part of gang life, but I have ears," Costa replied evenly.

I said, "What have you heard?"

"You'll let me go with you to tell my cousin her son is dead?"

I glanced at Sampson, who said, "It's not a bad idea."

"Okay," I said. "What do you know about Patrice Prince?"

"A lot," he said. "Come in my office and I'll tell you."

CHAPTER 26

I TRUDGED HOME THAT evening, feeling emotionally drained but happy that we'd made such strong progress in the fourteen hours since we'd caught the Shay Mansion homicide investigation.

Sampson and I were not entirely sure that Guillermo Costa was walking the straight and narrow. *Still*, I thought, *the guy sure knows a lot about—*

All thoughts of the ex-con, the murdered boy, and his shattered mother fled as I reached the front door and smelled a familiar aroma. Before going in, I closed my eyes to savor the glorious scents pouring out. As I opened the door, the river of smells became a wave and then a flood that carried me straight into the kitchen, where Maria was stirring a pot on the stove.

"Daddy!" Damon called from his high chair. His face held evidence of every item he'd eaten, from applesauce to ground meat to squash.

"Damon!" I cried. I managed to kiss him without getting the remnants of his meal on my chin and went over to Maria. I looked into the simmering pot, put my hand over my heart, and moaned. "Your mother's secret spaghetti sauce. Welcome back, old friend. Welcome back."

"Hey, what about me?" Maria said, feigning hurt.

"I am always about you."

"Is that right?" She set down her spoon and embraced me, her belly bumping mine.

"Always," I said. "I am here to protect my queen and give her what she needs."

Maria squeezed me. "And I'm here for you in every way I can think of, Alex."

"Mommy?" Damon said.

"Hold on, kiddo," she said, peering up at me. "Long day for you?"

"Tough day," I said.

"Tell me what you can while we eat."

"Mommy? I finish!"

"Okay, baby. Peaches now," she told Damon, breaking our embrace. In short order, Maria had diced peaches in Damon's bowl, and our pasta was steaming on plates on the table. My boy loved peaches and wolfed them down, ignoring us.

I took a bite of the spaghetti with Maria's mom's incredible secret sauce and groaned with pleasure. "What *is* it? What is it that makes it so good?"

"Can't tell you."

"I'm your husband. Your soulmate. You won't share the secret with me?"

Maria set down her fork and gazed at me with a dead-serious expression. "If I gave you the recipe, you could leave me."

"What? I would never leave you."

"But if you knew the secrets of the sauce, you could."

"Are you telling me you think that's all that's keeping us together?"

"Not even close. The sauce is just part of the…"

"What?"

I could tell she was trying not to laugh, but then she did and flashed her eyes in that way that always melted me. "The sauce is part of the spell I weave over you."

"You are mesmerizing," I said. "And you do weave a spell over me."

"Good," she said. "So forget about how the sauce is made and how the spell is cast and just enjoy."

CHAPTER 27

I LOVED EVERY BITE of that spaghetti and took several trips back to the stove for extra spoonfuls of the sauce while describing my day. I left out the goriest details of the Mansion crime scene but explained that we'd gotten deep insight into a Haitian gang from a guy who was rumored to be the leader of an opposing gang, although he claimed he wasn't.

"LMC Fifty-One and Los Lobos Rojos?" Maria said. She lifted Damon out of his high chair and cleaned his face with a washcloth.

"You know them?"

"They get shot and stabbed a lot. End up in the ER and then the operating room. It's my job to find them aftercare if they're not heading to jail."

"What do you know about Guillermo Costa?"

She shrugged and put down Damon; he giggled and ran over to his toys in the living room. "Honestly, I never heard of him. Why?"

"Long story," I said. "What about Patrice Prince?"

Despite her small stature, my wife was rarely intimidated by anyone. I'd seen her walk up to dangerous men who outweighed her by a hundred pounds and quickly put them under her spell. But when I mentioned Prince's name, Maria lost color and sat down in her chair. "That is one scary person, Alex."

"You know him?"

A sour expression crossed her face. "I met Prince once. Last year."

Maria said one of Prince's young cousins was beaten and left for dead in an alley in Southeast. The gang leader had come to the hospital.

"He was very polished," she said. "Nicely dressed. Expensive clothes, but not flashy. His English was very good. He was polite and soft-spoken, but…"

"What?"

She looked at me, the memory of a repellent experience etched on her face. "Alex, you know I've encountered more than my fair share of bad people at work."

I nodded.

"Prince?" she continued with the barest of shivers. "He had the deadest eyes I have ever seen. No empathy. No compassion. No recognition. No soul. I mean, I felt like I was a few feet away from someone who wasn't entirely human. He seemed reptilian to me, and I doubt he saw me as an equal."

"He probably didn't. Sounds like antisocial personality disorder."

"I could see that," Maria said, glancing over at Damon, who was playing with his blocks. "And now I don't want to talk about that guy anymore other than to say I hope you find him doing something bad enough that you can put him in a cage for a long time."

I got up to clear the plates. "If he's behind the murder, that's my plan."

"Be very, very careful around him, Alex," she said. "I'm telling you, I don't think I've ever met anyone who radiated such a sense of threat."

"I hear you loud and clear," I said, and went to the sink with the plates.

On an impulse born of old habit, I reached over and turned on the little portable radio we had on the counter. WTOP all-news radio came on. The announcer finished the local forecast and began a recap of the day's events.

"The Prince George's County Sheriff investigators are still gathering evidence in the Beltsville double homicide of two young medical technicians. Twenty-three-year-old Selena DeMille and twenty-two-year-old Alice Ways were found this morning in Ms. DeMille's vehicle.

"Sources say that the two women appeared to have been approached while they were parked on a secluded stretch of road and were shot multiple times at close range. Investigators concede they have very few leads and are asking the public to come forward with any information regarding the—"

Maria turned the radio off and fixed me with her irresistible smile. "Less attention on crime, more attention on the spell caster and our boy."

But I couldn't concentrate after hearing that another pair of victims had been shot while sitting in a parked car. It had to be related to the Talbot case. I felt pulled in multiple directions, but I quickly decided on the right one.

I put my hands on my wife's shoulders. "Maria, I love you. I adore you and Damon. But you'll have to hold that thought. I promise all attention will be on the spell caster and our boy tomorrow night."

I kissed her and walked to the front door.

"Where are you going?" she asked in frustration.

"Beltsville," I said, and left.

CHAPTER 28

AT TEN O'CLOCK THE following morning, I was under fire from multiple sides.

Maria had given me the cold shoulder at breakfast and left early to take Damon to day care. When I arrived at the office, Sampson was out getting his root canal, and I had a note on my desk from Chief Pittman ordering me to go see him as soon as I got in.

I knocked on the chief's doorjamb a few moments later. Pittman looked up from some paperwork, his face expressionless.

"Come in, Cross," he said. "Shut the door behind you."

I did, getting the distinct feeling I was headed to the principal's office again.

"I'm thinking I made a mistake in hiring you, bringing you on this way," Pittman said.

"Chief?" I said, feeling a surge of fear that he was about to fire me.

Face flushed, the chief of detectives said, "You do understand the concept of jurisdiction, don't you? Or don't they teach that at the police academy or in psychology PhD programs?"

"I understand the concept, sir."

He glared, then slammed his hand on the documents on his desk, sending several flying. "Then why in God's name did you try to take over someone else's crime scene last night?"

"I—I didn't try to take it over," I said, stammering. "I was just—"

"You were just telling detectives in another jurisdiction what to do and how they should do it! I got a goddamned call about you at six thirty this morning from the Prince George's County sheriff himself! He's seriously pissed, and I don't blame him."

I did not know what to say. I figured Chief Pittman didn't really want to hear my explanation, and anything I said to defend myself would likely make him even angrier.

I puffed out my cheeks, blew the air out, and said, "I understand your concern, Chief. I just get carried away trying to make things happen in cases I care about deeply. Like the Talbot case."

When Pittman spoke again, his voice was several decibels lower. "The Talbot case is only your second case, Cross. You've been on the team less than a month. And now it's not just the younger officers in the department who are upset with you. I've got senior detectives and top brass wondering whether I hired a loose cannon."

"You didn't. I promise you, Chief. I...I was just thinking that—"

"I don't care what you were thinking, Cross. You're still on probation. One more stunt like last night and you're out. Got that? Dismissed."

I went back to my desk feeling like I'd blown everything I'd ever dreamed of, sensing that all eyes in the squad room were on me, and wishing I'd never gone out the door last night, that I'd stayed home under the spell of Maria and Damon.

When I sat down, I found an envelope from Ellen Bovers at the FBI containing a videocassette with the footage I'd requested from the Chain Bridge camera on the DC side of Canal Street. I could have gone into the conference room and watched it on the video player there, but instead, I stewed, unable to stop thinking about my talk with Chief Pittman. It made me ill.

From the time I decided to get serious about academics in high school, I had prided myself on excellence in the classroom, in the clinic, and in my research. I had made a habit of not only succeeding in those worlds but flourishing in them.

I am not flourishing either here or at home these days, I thought. *I am flailing.*

Rather than giving in to a growing sense of confusion, doubt, and fear that I was not enough, that I was not a detective who understood the criminal mind better than most, I called an all-stop to the rush of my thoughts.

Martha Warner, my adviser and clinical professor at Johns Hopkins, once told me that when confused, fearful, or upset, one should stop and recognize that the emotional crosscurrents are often created by not facing up to one's own role in whatever the crisis at hand is.

Reflect on yourself, not others, Martha always said. *See clearly what error you might have made, what hurt you might have caused, and take responsibility for it. Your confusion and fear will fade away.*

So I did that for quite a while. I saw how I'd left Maria when she needed me, left Damon when he needed me. I went to the police lines at the Beltsville shooting and asked the detectives who'd been there all day to let me in to look, and when they refused, I told them about the Talbot shooting and how I thought there might be a David Berkowitz copycat on the loose.

Matthew Brady, the lead detective on the case, looked at me like I had two heads and ordered me to leave the area.

"Fine," I'd said. "Don't believe me, Detective. But please call me when your ballistics report comes in."

Sitting there in the conference room, I remembered Brady, a lumbering guy in his fifties with a cynical, seen-it-all attitude, walking away from me with the middle finger of his right hand held high.

CHAPTER

29

WHEN JOHN SAMPSON RETURNED to the office with a thick tongue and a slightly swollen left jaw, I was in the conference room watching grainy video footage of the intersection of the Chain Bridge and Canal Street taken on the night of Talbot's murder.

I was trying not think about my—to put it frankly—arrogance of the night before. I was going back to basics and humbly doing the raw legwork. I felt that was my best chance to break the Talbot case and get back in Pittman's good graces.

"Hey, shunshine, why the long face?" John slurred as he came into the conference room. "I'm the one with a mouthful of Novocain."

"I'm not going there right now." I waved off his comment. "My friend at the FBI came through with CCTV footage of the bridge intersection and Canal where it meets the Clara Barton on the night Talbot was killed."

"Anything?"

"The camera must be mounted over the top of the traffic light facing the bridge because the Bronco passes under it, gunning through a yellow light, at ten twelve in the evening," I said, playing the sequence.

We watched as a Ford Explorer and a Volkswagen Scirocco took a left onto the bridge when the light on Canal changed. The third vehicle in line, a dingy white Ford Econoline van with tinted windows, continued on in the northbound lane, followed shortly after by a Dodge pickup and a Toyota Corolla. Then three cars came across the bridge from Virginia. Two went north into Maryland; one headed south toward Georgetown.

I stopped the tape and sighed. "I don't know what I'm looking for."

"Commonalities," Sampson said. "The ME is putting time of death around ten thirty p.m. Let it play for a while."

I sat back and watched the intersection footage for almost twenty minutes before spotting a dingy white van with its high beams on heading south toward Canal Street.

I gave a little whoop, stopped the player, rewound the tape several seconds, and froze it on the image of the van just as it entered the intersection. "Looks like the same van to me."

"It does to me too," Sampson said, moving closer to the screen. "Tinted side windows. No passenger. Driver's got the visor down, blocking his face. And the bulbs over the license plates are out. But could be old Pennsylvania plates, the blue on yellow ones with the keystone in the middle?"

I moved closer too. "I think so. And look at the front left headlight. Is the cover busted?"

"Something's off about it," he agreed. "We'll get someone to really blow up the image."

"If this is the van that hit Carl Dennis, we've placed him within—"

My pager went off. A Maryland number.

"Rewind and check if the van's headlights were intact on its first trip through the intersection while I make this call," I said. I went back to my desk, picked up my phone, and dialed the number from the pager.

"Brady, Montgomery County Sheriff's Office," said the same detective who'd given me the finger the night before.

When Sampson came out of the conference room a few minutes later, he saw the difference in my posture and attitude.

"Headlight's intact going north," Sampson informed me. "Who paged you?"

"I'll tell you in two seconds, John," I said. "Someone else needs to know first."

I went straight to Chief Pittman's office and knocked on his closed door. He barked something, so I opened it.

He took one look at me, rolled his eyes, and grumbled, "What now?"

"We may have identified the vehicle that hit the Senate aide, and it might belong to Talbot's killer."

"What do you mean, 'may have'?"

I held up my hands. "More important, I just got off the phone with Matthew Brady, the detective in charge of yesterday's Beltsville shootings. Preliminary ballistics say the two women were shot at short range by a forty-four-caliber snub-nosed pistol shooting two-hundred-and-forty-six-grain boattail bullets. Just like the one that hit Conrad Talbot."

CHAPTER

30

GARY SONEJI FOUGHT THE urge to exit Interstate 495, cruise into Beltsville, and roll past the scene to see what the cops were doing.

That would be a rookie move, he decided, shaking his head as he passed the exit. He'd been near perfect the other night and wanted to be as meticulous in every aspect of his follow-through.

With that motivation taking firm hold, Soneji got onto I-95 heading north toward Baltimore and Wilmington, Delaware. He set the cruise control in the Saab to sixty-seven, just two miles above the speed limit. He had no desire to attract the attention of a state trooper, especially with the items he had stowed in the trunk.

As Soneji drove, he listened to a jazz station out of the University of Maryland. With Herbie Hancock providing background music, he relived last night, saw every moment of his flawless stalk, every step an exquisite eternity of anticipation.

He'd had the angle coming at the green Chevy Malibu, was positive he would not be noticed as he eased his latex-gloved hand into the pocket of his dark hoodie and slipped the Bulldog from a plastic bag.

The young women had been talking. He'd heard their murmurs and laughter.

He saw the silhouettes of their heads inclined toward each other as he moved into point-blank range. For an interesting moment as he raised the pistol, Soneji thought they might kiss.

If that was their intention, they never got there. He fired through the right rear window, hitting the driver high in the right cheek, just below her eye.

The passenger screamed in horror; her hands gripped her head as she twisted away from her dead friend, looking in terror for the shooter. She never got to see him.

Soneji stepped sideways and shot. The bullet went through her right hand and into her temple.

They were both clearly stone dead. But remembering his blunder with Abby, he put one more round into each woman. Then he leaned into the car and tore off a flap of scalp from the gaping wound on the side of the passenger's head.

After that, he'd run back to the Saab and taken the same route he was driving now, north on I-95 past Baltimore and Aberdeen, heading toward the Delaware line. He reveled in his flawless execution until a sobering thought came to him.

He had mastered David Berkowitz. It was time to move on.

But he had things to take care of before he could decide whom to study next. A few tasks he'd left undone the night of the first shooting.

He'd been emotionally and physically exhausted then and had decided to take care of those jobs later. It didn't matter. There'd been no real rush.

Soneji left the interstate just shy of the Delaware border and headed north on Maryland 272. He passed through Bay View and soon after crossed the Pennsylvania line. The state highway cut through a checkerboard of farms and small woodlots in full fall foliage, all of it so familiar to him.

He turned off south of Oxford, Pennsylvania, and wove his way on county roads toward the Chrome Barrens, a large nature preserve with forests and prairie-like grasslands that were managed as American Indians had managed them centuries ago—with fire.

Indeed, as Soneji got close to the Chrome Barrens, he could smell and see smoke. He crested a rise. There were fire trucks and police cars parked up on the road ahead, ready to act should the flames jump beyond their intended areas.

He debated leaving and returning another time but decided to push on. He took a left on a dirt road well short of the police and fire vehicles, headed north, then pulled over and parked.

Smoke wafted through the trees. Fingers of it crept out onto the farm fields across the road from the preserve.

Soneji had not planned for a controlled burn. Still, it might be a good thing. He was sure he could slide in and out unseen, but the smoke couldn't hurt—it would give him one more layer of concealment.

He went to the Saab's trunk, took out knee-high rubber boots and latex gloves, put them on, then pulled out a hiking pack and shouldered it. The pack was an easy load, and he set off into the woods, moving diagonal to the burns. On the far side of a knoll deep in the woods, he dropped into a natural ditch of sorts that ran east.

Glad that the gully concealed him almost to his shoulders and that the damp leaves deadened all sound beneath his feet, Soneji moved quickly to the edge of a clearing. Much of the opening was knotted with thorny brambles, but weeks before, he had used garden shears to trim a path into the yard of a ramshackle uninhabited farmhouse. Beyond the house was a long, low shed, one side open to a rutted driveway leading toward thick pines.

As Soneji crept along the cleared path, he paused often to listen but heard only the chattering of squirrels and crows cawing off in the pines somewhere. Soon he was there at the edge of the yard again.

He crouched and studied the area, trying to see if something was different from his last visit, something that would tell him he was being watched.

CHAPTER

31

WEEDS FOR GRASS. SEVERAL crooked apple trees in desperate need of pruning. The farmhouse stood to the right of the trees, its once white walls now begrimed with time, paint peeling off the clapboard siding.

The windows appeared intact, but the roof sagged and shingles were missing. A gutter dangled, creaking in the breeze.

A local farmer leased and tilled the fields beyond the pines, but no one had lived in the house since elderly LeeAnne Lawton had died there five years back. Eamon Diggs, her grandson, inherited the land but had shown no interest in selling it, living there, or renting it.

Soneji knew all that for certain. A few years back, he'd read an article in the *Philadelphia Inquirer* about Diggs, who'd been released from prison after doing ten years for the rape and attempted rape of several young women. The story had noted Diggs's inheritance and current employment in a granite quarry along with several other ex-cons. Soneji had been intrigued by the serial rapist and was drawn to find the farm.

On that first trip, he'd discovered little to explain Diggs's hatred of women, but he did find things that intrigued him even more, things that set his imagination free with possibility, things that caused him to return to the abandoned farm with increasing frequency.

Finally satisfied that he was alone and that nothing had changed since his last visit, Soneji moved quickly, staying in the weeds, not wanting to be anywhere near mud as he traversed the yard heading for the long, low, three-sided shed connected to an old workshop with cinder-block walls. He ignored the workshop and halted where the weeds gave way to the shed's dirt floor.

The shed was divided into six bays. Four were filled with rusting farm equipment. One was largely empty. A filthy beat-up white panel van was backed into the nearest bay, an old tarp over the front end. Soneji studied the dirt around it, saw no prints in the lightly raked soil.

Emboldened, he put on latex gloves and pulled back the tarp, revealing the broken headlight and turn signal. Soneji put down his pack and took out a new headlight, a new bulb for the turn signal, and new covers for both.

He put on reading glasses to make sure he was seeing everything clearly and in the minutest detail. Kneeling, he studied the bumper and saw a little blood spattered there; a ragged strip of stretchy black fabric was stuck in the cavity of the broken headlight.

Soneji removed the fabric, set it aside, and installed the new bulbs. Before he put the replacement covers on, he worked the fabric into a gap in the upper right corner of the grille.

Satisfied, he went to the rear of the van and looked at the smears in the dirt where the bicyclist's message had been written across the double doors. Then he reached up to a shelf behind the vehicle, moved a coffee can filled with wood screws, and found the key.

The rear of the van's interior was a mess, just as he'd found it the first time, strewn with empty beer cans, old nudie magazines, newspapers, trash, papers, leaves, and everything else that belonged in a dump.

From his pack, Soneji fished out a baggie holding the piece of hair and scalp he'd torn off the dead woman after the second shooting. Another baggie held the Bulldog pistol. A third held the latex gloves he'd worn last night, fingertips covered in dried blood.

He opened the driver's-side door, got out the pistol, set it aside, and turned the plastic bag upside down. He shook it out over the console between the two bucket seats and on the dash.

Then he opened the cylinder and extracted two of the four spent rounds. Soneji crouched down and carefully pushed the bullet casings into a frayed and separated seam in what was left of the van's floor fabric.

Soneji closed the driver's door and locked it, then returned to the rear of the van and opened the baggie containing the latex gloves. He'd worn two layers of gloves on his gun hand that night, and now he carefully separated the inner glove from the one with gunshot residue and blood from the dead passenger. He lobbed the contaminated glove into the mess, then opened the baggie with the bloody hair, scalp, and flesh in it. He flicked the treasure into the trash heap in the van's rear, closed the van's door, and locked it.

He returned the key to the shelf and set the coffee can on top of the key, put the pieces of the headlight and turn signal into his pack, then shut the door. He picked up the rake and gently stirred the dirt behind him as he backed out.

He threw the tarp over the front end and raked everywhere he'd been on the shed floor. When his boots reached weeds, where he would no longer leave tracks, he leaned over and placed the rake against the wall.

The air still stank of woodsmoke. It made Soneji's eyes sting as he set off on the path through the bramble, toward the Saab and a dreaded, dutiful long weekend with Missy and Roni.

PART THREE
A More Intimate Way to Kill

CHAPTER 32

THE THURSDAY AFTER THE Beltsville shooting, Sampson and I went to the rehab facility in Bowie, Maryland, where Senate aide Carl Dennis was being treated for his many injuries. Before we went to his room, his wife, Kathleen, warned us that he was heavily medicated and remembered very little of the night he was run over.

But we had to try. It was hard to look at all the casts, traction cables, tubes, and IV lines that held Dennis together. His head was heavily bandaged. His face was swollen and bruised.

"Carl, hon," his wife said. "These police detectives want to talk to you about the night you were hit."

He said, his words sounding slurred, "Don't 'member."

"Nothing?" Sampson said.

He thought several beats before he said, "A shot?"

"You heard a shot?"

"Think."

"What else?"

He closed his eyes a few moments, then opened them. "Lights. Fast. Low lights."

I thought about what we knew. "Fast, low headlights?"

"Guess." He shrugged.

I said, "Could it have been vehicle headlights coming at you?"

The Senate aide nodded.

John opened a folder and retrieved a still shot of the white Ford Econoline van. He showed it to Dennis. "Is this the van that ran you over?"

He studied the picture for a long time before shaking his head. "Don't know."

"But it could be," Sampson said.

"Don't know," the injured man said, tears coming to his eyes as he looked to his wife in desperation. "Don't know anything, Kat."

He began weeping.

His wife moved to his side, rubbing his arm and soothing him. "It's okay. You heard what the doctors keep saying. This is going to take time, hon."

He sighed again and shut his eyes.

Kathleen said, "He had a difficult night, Detectives. Can I call you when he begins to remember more of what happened?"

"Of course," we said, and we left, feeling frustrated that we could not say for sure that the driver of the white van was responsible for the murder of Conrad Talbot and the attempted murder of Carl Dennis.

The next morning, word of my Berkowitz theory leaked.

The headline across the top of the front page of the *Baltimore Sun* read:

Is Killer Mimicking Son of Sam?

The police department phones began buzzing and jangling with calls from local and national news organizations keying in on the Berkowitz angle. The media set up camp outside Metro headquarters and squawked about it for hours, even dissecting the fact that the Son of Sam had first killed two women, then a man and a woman, the reverse of the current situation.

The *Sun*'s original piece—and almost every story afterward—named me as the theorist, noting my doctorate from Johns Hopkins and the parts of my dissertation that included Berkowitz. I declined to make any comment and deferred to Chief Pittman, who actually proved remarkably adept in the spotlight, running two crisp, efficient press conferences in which he confirmed that Metro and Prince George's County detectives were looking into a Son of Sam copycat.

"It would be a dereliction of duty if we were not actively looking into Dr. Cross's theory," Pittman said on TV as Sampson and I watched from the squad room on Friday.

Detectives Kurtz and Diehl were there in the squad room as well, both with their arms crossed. Pittman went on, "We're telling people in the greater DC area to beware. He's now killed three people and gravely wounded a fourth. We want to stop him before there is a fifth."

Kurtz reached over and clicked off the TV. Diehl shook her head.

"He's left you dangling, and you don't even see it, *Dr. Cross*," Diehl said, putting heavy sarcasm on the title.

"How so?" I said, ignoring the edge.

Kurtz snorted at my naïveté. "Pittman's smart. He's thought ahead. He's pinning this all on you, so if things go more sideways than they already have—if you don't catch someone acting like Berkowitz or if the real killer's off in a completely other direction and someone dies because of it—well, Pittman can say it was all your idea. Maybe you don't survive your three-month probationary period."

"Yeah," Diehl said as she walked away. "Wake up, Doc. You're in the big leagues now."

CHAPTER 33

SAMPSON SAT DOWN. I caught him looking at me as I took my chair.

"Tell me I'm wrong about this," I said, arms crossed.

"You're not wrong," John said. "Or at least, I don't think you're that far off. Let's just get back to work and prove it."

I nodded, feeling more pressure than I'd ever experienced in my career. And my home life was strained too. Maria and I had made up after our fight, our first real one in a long time, but damage had been done. I'd still sensed friction between us that morning when she set off for work.

Rather than think about that, I forced myself into action by taking a hard look at where we were in the four different cases battling for our attention.

John and I remained largely stalled in our probes into the deaths of Tony Miller and Shay Mansion, but I went back through my notes on our second interview with Mansion's mother, Rosalina Mansion.

Her cousin Guillermo Costa had accompanied us when we'd informed Rosalina of her son's death. She'd collapsed into her cousin's arms, inconsolable. In our second interview with Rosalina, she'd been alone, but she claimed to have had no idea that her son had joined Lobos Rojos and vigorously disputed the suggestion that her cousin was the gang's leader. She said that Costa had gone straight after prison.

"You cannot blame this on Guillermo at all," she insisted. "If Shay was involved, it's on him. Once he quit school, I lost control over him. With his father gone, he was out at all hours, sometimes sleeping at home, sometimes not. And he never asked for money."

She hung her head. "I think I lost him almost a year ago, to be honest."

I'd written that down, and now I stared at that sentence in my notebook, feeling the poor woman's sadness all over again. Then I set the file aside and turned once again to the Bulldog murders, as I'd taken to calling them, after the unusual gun that had been used.

Over the past few days, Sampson and I had formed a decent alliance with Detective Matt Brady, who was damn good at his job.

In the first forty-eight hours, Brady and his partners had focused on the victims, both of whom were medical techs who worked at a hospital not far from the murder scene and who had been friends since their early teens. We checked everything they found out about the two women against our evidence in the Talbot murder case.

At first, John and I saw no definitive crossover, no commonality save the caliber of the weapon and the angle the killer had shot from. Then, yesterday afternoon, the full ballistics report came back from the Maryland crime lab, confirming that the bullets in both attacks had been fired from the same gun.

"This is interesting, Alex," Sampson said now.

I looked up from the ballistics report. "What's that?"

"The medical examiner's autopsy report," he said. "It notes that a sizable piece of scalp and hair from Alice Ways, one of the victims, is missing."

"Saw that last night," I said. "And Brady confirms the piece was not found in the car."

"You think the shooter took it?"

"That's what it looks like."

"Why would he do that?"

"Could be a trophy."

"Why didn't he do it with Conrad and Abby?"

I shrugged. "Maybe he didn't think of it. Maybe this time he thought having that piece of scalp and hair would remind him of the event more vividly."

"That's disturbing. I've heard of killers taking little mementos like bracelets or necklaces, but not a hunk of scalp."

"I'm not saying it's normal behavior, John. Quite the opposite. We're dealing with an abnormal mind at play, which is how I think he sees this. As a game."

"Like he's saying, *Catch me if you can?*" Sampson said.

"Partially. It's also a sign of increasing boldness."

"You're thinking he'll do it again soon?"

I nodded. "He'll escalate. Broaden the number of victims taken at once or kill again sooner than he did between the first and second murders."

"So in the next five days?"

"That's what has me on edge."

Sampson's desk phone rang. He answered. I returned to the Bulldog murder book.

"Thank you, Officer," John said a moment later, and hung up. "We're out of here, Alex."

"What's up?"

"That was Donovan, the undercover working LMC Fifty-One. Patrice Prince is on the move, and she thinks she knows where he's going."

CHAPTER 34

Chesapeake Beach, Maryland

SAMPSON PULLED OUR SQUAD car into a parking stall a block off the shore. Despite it being October, the resort town was surprisingly busy.

I commented on it as Sampson climbed out.

"It's the warmth," he said. "We haven't had a really cool day yet. Might as well be August."

That was true. Temperatures along the mid-Atlantic had been in the seventies or higher since August.

I got out, regretting the jacket almost immediately, feeling sweat beading on my brow and the nape of my neck. "I hope Donovan's right. I'm going to have to dry-clean this coat, I'm sweating so much."

"Good chance she is right," John said. "Jibes with what Costa told us."

"It does. Worst case, we have spicy crab for lunch."

"Hope my gut can handle it."

We walked past a British pub, crossed a street, and made our way to a restaurant in the middle of the next block.

This was TANTE COCO'S HAITIAN CRAB SHACK, according to the sign, and it featured eight picnic tables inside, five of which were occupied, two by older tourists, two by younger couples, and one by three surfer dudes in their late teens. The reputed gang leader of LMC 51 was nowhere in sight, although both Costa and Donovan had told us that Patrice Prince was often here. Prince loved the crab and spice in Tante Coco's secret boil recipe.

The spice in the air tickled my nostrils and made my mouth water.

The other patrons hardly looked at us. They were eagerly breaking shells with wooden mallets and picking out the crab until they had suitable piles to gorge on.

The waitress, a big gal in her thirties, came out with several large sheets of brown wrapping paper that she taped to the top of one of the empty picnic tables. Then she nodded to us, set out two mallets, shell crackers, metal picks, plastic bibs, and a pile of napkins and motioned to us to sit.

"Your drink order?" she said in a light Haitian accent. "We have cold Pepsi products, homemade lemonade, Coors beer, and boxed white wine that isn't half bad."

"Lemonade," I said.

"Same," Sampson said.

The waitress turned to leave. I said, "Can we see a menu?"

She shook her head. "Boil's the only thing we serve."

John said, "Boil for two, then."

"Way ahead of you, *mon ami*," she said and went through a set of double doors.

About five minutes later, she returned with the drinks. She

also brought warm corn bread in a basket and a heaping bowl of fresh coleslaw, both of which were some of the best I'd ever had. The boil that followed was equally impressive.

I'd been eating boiled crab since I was a kid, and I wasn't bad at making them myself. But the spices used at Tante Coco's gave the shellfish a smoky beginning and a fiery ending with just the right amount of balance between sweet and heat.

We were halfway through the mound of crabs set before us when a lean, powerfully built Black guy in his mid-twenties wearing Versace sunglasses, a black T-shirt, and dark slacks and sneakers came in. He scanned the place.

I did my best businessman-having-lunch-with-a-client act, laughing with Sampson as I picked at a crab leg. Versace left.

"Scout, probably," I said quietly.

"My bet too," Sampson said.

Three minutes later, Versace returned, this time followed by another big dude wearing a similar outfit. The waitress came out, taped wrapping paper onto the empty table next to us, and nodded at them.

The second guy went to the door and waved. A third man, the tallest of the three, entered. He wore pressed black slacks, black loafers, a black long-sleeved shirt, and Vuarnet cat-eye sunglasses with a mirror finish.

It was like Maria had said. When Patrice Prince came through the door and made his way to the table next to us, I felt a sense of menace, though I could not pinpoint exactly what about him was causing it.

Prince ignored us, sat between his two men, and began speaking in Haitian Creole. I put down my crab mallet, took off my bib, reached in my jacket, and retrieved my ID and badge.

I went over to their table, right hand inside my jacket, on the butt of my weapon. Versace and his friend saw me and started to reach around their backs, low at the waist.

"That would be a bad idea," I said in a soft voice, showing them my badge, which I held cupped in my hand to the side of my hip.

"A very bad idea," Sampson said, equally low-key. He was standing beside me now, one hand on his service weapon, the other holding his badge in a way that only Prince and his guys could see. "Hands on the table, everyone. Mr. Prince, we just want to talk."

"About?" he said, not looking at us.

"Why don't you lose the shades and join us," I said. "We'll take just ten minutes of your time. And the box wine is on us."

CHAPTER 35

"I'LL PASS ON THE box wine." Prince sniffed, then nodded to his men, got up, and moved over to sit at our table. He took off his sunglasses, revealing hazel agate-like eyes that cut back and forth over us, and calmly folded his hands on the table. "What is it you want from me?"

"Information about Shay Mansion," Sampson said.

Prince raised and lowered his shoulders slowly, his attention never leaving us, his calm demeanor and sharp gaze unchanged. "I do not know this name."

"Sixteen-year-old kid," I said. "Recruit to Los Lobos Rojos. Found wired to a tree in a park in Southeast DC. He'd been caned to death."

The reputed gang leader winced, closed his eyes a second,

then opened them and gazed at us unmoved once more. "How terrible. Who would do such a thing?"

Sampson said, "I don't know. The son and grandson of Tonton Macoute members?"

Prince made a clicking noise and said in that same even, disarming tone, "I am hardly a secret policeman, Detective. But—how do you say it? The jury is out on you two."

"We're homicide detectives with Metro police," I said.

"So you say. But who knows where your true allegiances lie."

"They lie with the dead," Sampson said, getting irritated.

"As they should," Prince said. "But that has nothing to do with me."

I said, "Or LMC Fifty-One?"

He did not react, just trained those odd hazel eyes on me, his expression serene, and yet somehow he broadcast a sense of deep, inner darkness that made me feel he was capable of unfathomable violence. Menace seemed to seep out of the man's pores. I tried not to shiver.

"I run an import/export company," Prince said finally. "We bring in Haitian cocoa and cane sugar, which we distribute to chocolate makers across North America. We try to send back whatever money we can to the markets in Haiti, and we make donations to many NGOs operating there."

"So you're really just a misunderstood humanitarian philanthropist," Sampson said.

Prince smiled, revealing a gold canine on the lower left. "Now you're beginning to understand my situation."

I asked him where he'd been on the night of the murder.

He thought. "In bed. At home."

"Can anybody confirm that?"

"The two women sleeping with me and my friends here, who were in the outer room," Prince said. His men, who had been watching intently, nodded.

"We'd like names and phone numbers, please," Sampson said.

Prince sighed. "Is that necessary?"

"It's a murder investigation, so yes."

"I say it again: I did not kill anyone, much less a boy only sixteen."

I said, "How about Tony Miller? Kid who got stabbed and thrown in the Potomac?"

"Can't say I know that name either," Prince said, sounding weary. "And now I see my favorite corn bread and coleslaw coming. I wish to eat in peace. Any other questions, you must talk to my lawyer."

He got up. "By the way, how did you know to find me here?"

We had prepared for that. John said, "Street soldiers with Lobos Rojos told us."

Looking into those strange, agate-like eyes, I said, "Didn't you know? They keep close tabs on you. They follow you, know all sorts of things about you."

For a second, before Prince put his sunglasses back on, I saw rage flicker through his mask of a face.

CHAPTER 36

WITH A SATISFIED GROAN, Soneji rolled off his wife around ten p.m.

He'd seen her scowl as they'd started to make love, but he didn't care. He'd just turned her facedown so he didn't have to see her dissatisfaction.

Missy got up without looking at him and went to the bathroom. He closed his eyes, expecting their evening together to be done.

He'd needed the release. He'd read the story about the DC cop who theorized that he was copying Berkowitz. PhD in psychology. Profiler.

It doesn't matter, Soneji told himself. He'd mastered Son of Sam, and he was restless, ready to move on.

Now I just have to make it until Monday to—

"You are not going to sleep on me, Gary Murphy," Missy said.

He opened his eyes, saw her standing at the foot of their bed, nude, arms crossed, rage flaring in her eyes.

"What now?" he asked. *Blond cow,* he thought.

"You come home, spend half an hour at best with Roni, then disappear into your office to do God only knows what. You didn't even kiss your daughter good night, you shit. And then you just get in bed and jump my bones."

Soneji gazed at Missy dispassionately, had a fleeting fantasy of killing her naked.

Everything she'd said was spot-on. He'd come home to their perfect suburban house, a two-story white brick gingerbread Colonial on Central Avenue in Wilmington, and played with his toddler daughter, but there wasn't really a connection between them. At least, he hadn't felt one. Ever.

And he'd had to go into his home office to phone the Charles School and see about more opportunities to substitute-teach in the coming week.

Headmistress Jenny Wolcott had gotten on the line herself and informed him that there were no subs needed at the Charles School, but she'd heard there might be a longer-term substitute position opening up at Washington Day School. A teacher there was going on maternity leave.

His response to Wolcott was noncommittal, but afterward he'd immediately researched the school. It was an elite private school, an academy that catered to the children of the powerful, the celebrated, and the wealthy.

The Washington Day School, he'd thought excitedly. *It's perfect. I mean, we're talking Lindbergh-baby territory. Who knows who walks those hallowed halls?*

He knew his real résumé would not be enough to score the gig. He'd need academic credentials and references. But luckily, he'd already created a fictitious background for Gary Soneji. He had forged documents claiming he'd received undergraduate and graduate degrees from the University of Pennsylvania as well as letters of recommendation from three professors and the superintendent of a school system in Delaware. He'd quickly written a cover letter and faxed copies of everything over to the school. Then he'd left his office, wanting a drink and sex.

"Say something!" Missy shouted now, breaking into his thoughts. "This is not a real marriage any more than our wedding was real."

"Okay, here we go!" Soneji shouted. "Our wedding *was* real. We have a marriage certificate, Missy."

"It was shotgun," she said, and she burst into tears. "No one but us and some drunk stranger for a best man. Everyone told me not to go through with it. And now you won't even look at me while we make love."

"Who wants to have sex with someone who's always angry at them?" he spat back.

"I have reason to be angry! You're gone all the time. And when you're here, you're Mr. Secrets."

"I have a job with your family's company that requires me to be on the road five days a week. Ask your brother. But you know what? You're right. I'm sorry that I have to be gone five out of every seven days. But that's the job, and you knew it when I took it. You encouraged me to take it, remember? I wanted to teach."

She said nothing.

"Remember?" he said again.

She shrugged and started to cry.

"Ah, Jesus," he said, wanting to kill her again. "Now what's the matter?"

"Since my dad passed last year," she said, sniveling, "I've just been wanting to make it real, you know?"

"Make what real?"

"Our marriage, Gary," she said. "I want a real wedding with all my friends and family and a beautiful reception. The way it should have been at the start."

They'd met her senior year at the University of Delaware. He'd swept her off her feet and into bed within three dates. Three and a half years ago, after finding out she was pregnant, they'd eloped to Atlantic City.

"I don't know," he said.

"C'mon, Gary," she said. "I know you hate crowds and all. But this will put us right, give us a new beginning."

"You think having a big wedding is going to change things in our marriage?"

"It could be a start," she said, wiping at her tears. "A restart?"

Soneji didn't mind crowds as long as he was anonymous. But he did hate being the object of other people's attention. Scrutiny made his skin crawl.

The members of Soneji's own family were all long dead. But Missy had a huge extended family. Their tribal get-togethers always made him feel claustrophobic and cornered.

The idea of a wedding involving the entire Kasajian clan was sheer misery as far as Soneji was concerned, and he groped for a way out.

"But we don't have the money for a big wedding. You know what I make."

"My mother has money, and I'm going to inherit lots of it when she dies anyway. She could give me an advance on that."

"You've talked with your mom about this?"

"A little."

"And?"

"She's for it," Missy said, coming over and getting back into bed. "As long as you are, Gary." She rolled into his arms. "Okay?"

He kissed her. "Tell you what—I'll sleep on it."

Missy stiffened as if to fight. He gazed at her neck, imagining what he could do to it if provoked further.

She sighed, shut her eyes, and rolled away from him, leaving Soneji with a different perspective on dear Missy's neck. And in that moment, the student of homicide and kidnapping geniuses knew whom and what to study next.

CHAPTER 37

THOUGH HE MADE MORE of an effort to play with and care for his daughter and stayed attentive to Missy's conversation, Soneji managed to avoid giving his wife a concrete answer all weekend.

He kissed Roni and Missy goodbye on Monday morning and told his wife he'd call in the evening.

"What about the wedding?" she asked just before he left.

"I don't know," he said evasively. "I don't know if this is the right time, and I'm conflicted. Got to work some things out."

"Like the fact no one from your family would be there?"

"You got it in one, smarty-pants," he said, which made Roni giggle. He kissed Missy again and left.

He spent his day doing just enough sales work to satisfy his brother-in-law, then pulled the Saab onto I-95 and headed south toward Maryland. He thought about the power of simplicity and then about the power in his own hands and the ways that power could be enhanced with a rope, a sash, a noose, a wire garrote.

He saw himself throttling Missy in multiple ways and then imagined other women, nameless women, all of them fighting for air, their struggles as real to him as if he'd had a big fish on a line. It didn't really matter to him who they were. They were all fish, swimming below the surface until he lured and caught them.

The idea of actually strangling someone, up close and personal, began to overtake Soneji's mind. A part of him wanted to start casting about for a victim right then.

But he had not done his homework yet, and he had more important things to do. He began to breathe deep and slow, telling himself to calm down, to be patient.

Fifteen minutes later, he took the exit for Route 272 toward Bay View and the Pennsylvania line. He quickly drove north, passing the turnoff to the old Diggs farm, continued on through Oxford, and took Pennsylvania Route 472 toward Kirkwood and Quarryville.

Five miles beyond Kirkwood, he passed a sign for Keegan's Granite, drove on a mile, then pulled off onto the shoulder. He waited until the road was clear, then took out his binoculars and a pack and entered the woods.

He heard a series of thuds, muffled explosions, then crashing. The temperature was dropping as he slipped forward, hearing cutting machines ahead. Within minutes he was in the shadows near a chain-link fence that surrounded the granite quarry where Eamon Diggs worked.

Soneji had done some research and discovered there was more

than one sex offender working in the quarry; he wanted to see if he could spot the other man, Harold Beech.

He lifted the binoculars to his eyes and saw men moving through dusty air toward the big slabs of granite that had just been dynamited off the wall. Other workers maneuvered stone saws into position to cut the slabs into more manageable pieces.

A few minutes later, a horn sounded, announcing the end of the workday.

Soneji scanned the men walking out of the quarry and exiting the cabs of the big machines. He spotted Diggs—big dude, long beard, ponytail sticking out from under his hard hat. He was climbing down off a backhoe that had been clearing scrap rock from the quarry.

Diggs did not join the other machine operators climbing the hill to clock out at the end of their shift. He stood waiting until he was joined by another man, a squat little guy in a coverall, respirator, goggles, and yellow safety helmet, all of it covered in pale dust from cutting stone.

The man tore off the respirator and goggles, grinned, and laughed at something Diggs said. Together, they started up the hill.

It wasn't until both men were close to Soneji and he saw them in full profile that he recognized the squat little guy as Beech. He smiled.

He suddenly had a desperate need to know what they were talking about and just how buddy-buddy the two sex offenders were. Soneji trotted back through the woods, dodging low-hanging branches, and skidded down the bank to the Saab.

Within minutes he was on the shoulder of the road across from the entrance to Keegan's Granite. He watched a line of vehicles leave the quarry until he spotted Diggs's old black Chevy K-10 four-by-four, followed by a very loud, very rusted Subaru sedan with cardboard duct-taped across the back window and a perforated muffler hanging by a wire.

The front passenger-side window was down. Beech was at the wheel, trying to light a cigarette as he followed Diggs toward Kirkwood.

Keeping a car or two between them, Soneji followed; he pulled over when they turned off and headed toward Diggs's place, a dilapidated double-wide trailer. He waited five minutes and then drove there, saw the duo on the stoop drinking bottles of Budweiser.

To the far left of the trailer, closer to the road, a dead whitetail doe hung upside down off a rope rigged to a pulley and crossbar bolted into the trunks of two pines. An archery target sat a few feet away.

He drove past. The two sex offenders were laughing at some shared joke and barely noticed him. That was how he wanted it. Soneji noted faded clothes on a line close to the trailer and decided a return trip was needed in the near future.

They did time for their crimes, but they haven't changed, he thought. Sexual violence was as much a part of Diggs and Beech as the insatiable need to watch the light go out in someone's eyes was for Soneji. He couldn't change that if he wanted to, and neither could they.

Heading south toward the interstate a few minutes later, Soneji felt confident that given the chance, Diggs would rape again, and given the same chance, Beech would go at some young girl with a broomstick or whatever.

They would not be able to help themselves. He was certain of it.

Soneji laughed. The situation could not have been better.

He decided to stop on the way home at a marine-supply store near Baltimore. There was a tool he needed to get that would be critical if he was to learn the lessons of the greatest asphyxiator of them all.

CHAPTER

38

I GOT HOME AROUND seven that night to find Damon playing with his fire truck and blocks.

When my little boy saw me, he dropped his toys and waddled fast toward me, arms up, crying, "Daddy!"

I scooped him up and whirled him around, which made him crack up, then carried him like a football into the kitchen, where Maria was cooking chicken marsala in a deep-sided skillet. She tapped the spoon on the side of the skillet, covered it, and turned to me with her heart-melting smile.

"The love of my life returns and look who he's carrying!"

I grinned and hugged her with one arm. "What a difference a few days make."

She snuggled up to my chest with Damon, who laughed, then

said he wanted to get down. I set him on the floor and he went back to his blocks.

"I just decided to let it go," Maria said, rubbing her belly. "Besides, you were right to head up to Beltsville that night. If you hadn't, we wouldn't know a serial killer was at work."

"Maybe, but I didn't handle it well. Given you were weaving a spell and all."

She tilted her head back and gazed at me with sparkling eyes. "I was?"

"As I recall," I said, and kissed her.

"Okay, now I kind of remember," she said. She winked at me and slipped from my arms. "Wash up, dinner's almost ready."

When I came back from the bathroom, she had plates of steaming chicken marsala and fresh fettuccine on the table, along with a cold glass of beer for me. She cut up Damon's food and I lifted him into his high chair, and he immediately started shoveling dinner into his mouth.

"Tell me about your day," Maria said, sitting down and smiling at me.

After I'd taken several bites and moaned about how good everything was, I said, "Went out to Chesapeake Beach with Sampson, ate crab, and met Patrice Prince."

Her smile disappeared. "How did that go?"

"Crab was great. Prince was as dark and unsettling as you described him."

"I told you. Like there's no soul there," Maria said. "Get anything from him?"

"He denied everything. Involvement in the murders. LMC Fifty-One's existence. He claims to be an import/export guy who's a humanitarian at heart."

She snorted. "Let me tell you another fairy tale."

"I hear you. But he's definitely aware of Los Lobos Rojos. It upset him when we said they were watching him."

We ate quietly for several minutes.

"*Are* they watching him?" Maria asked.

"Good chance, anyway," I said and drank some beer.

"Did you tell Pittman all this?"

"When we got back to the squad room. He gave us a copy of the most recent report from an officer working undercover inside LMC Fifty-One. She included an analysis of the number two and number three men in the gang and how they might be turned against Prince."

"Philippe LeClerc and Valentine Rodolpho?"

That surprised me. "You know them too?"

"LeClerc was shot in the leg last year in a drive-by and spent some time with us. Rodolpho is the one I told you about, Prince's cousin, the guy Prince came to see after he was beaten and left for dead in Southeast. I helped get him into a rehab unit."

That made sense, especially in light of Officer Nancy Donovan's report that Rodolpho was the weakest of the gang's leaders. Evidently, he had never fully recovered from the beating, and he still walked with a pronounced limp. "The undercover officer said Rodolpho isn't the smartest tool in the shed, but he's wary, always on the alert for possible threats."

Maria agreed. "Rodolpho doesn't trust anyone except Prince. I worked with him off and on during his long rehab, and he sure didn't trust me. And he checked with Prince before he said anything to me."

"He have other relatives come in to see him?"

"No mom. No dad. No girlfriend that I remember. He had

other visitors besides Prince, male and female, but I couldn't tell you what their relationships were."

"What about LeClerc?"

"Nontalker. Another suspicious, guarded guy."

"Okay, of the two, who do you think might be involved in the murders of the two boys?"

Maria considered that for several moments as she chewed the last of her chicken. "Rodolpho. He and Prince are blood-related and Haitian-born. LeClerc was born in Miami, and I never saw Prince come to the hospital to see him. I don't know how LeClerc and Prince connected."

"Probably through LMC in South Florida."

She nodded and put down her fork. "Makes sense."

"You think we can turn Rodolpho or LeClerc against Prince?"

Maria scrunched up her face. "That's going to be a tough one. I imagine it'll take some heavy leverage to make that happen."

"Two murder-one charges might do it," I said. "But we're a long way from that point, and I don't want to talk about gangsters killing kids anymore."

"Fine with me," she said, smiling. "What do you want to talk about?"

"I don't know. Spell-weaving?"

My wife threw her head back and laughed. "I was thinking the same thing!"

CHAPTER

39

AROUND NINE IN THE morning two days later, Sampson and I were parked in a dark blue utility van down the street from Valentine Rodolpho's row house in Capitol Heights. Sampson lowered his binoculars. "Our boy Valentino's sleeping in again. We didn't need to be here so early."

"Valentine," I said, suppressing a yawn.

"Not to me, he isn't," Sampson said. He reached for his Styrofoam coffee cup while I shifted uncomfortably, trying to get my right leg to stop cramping.

We'd had our eye on the number three in Prince's gang for days and he'd made no suspicious moves whatsoever. He limped out once a day around ten, caught a taxi to La Coccinelle Café and Bakery, bought two cafés créoles and a large bag of beignets, then went home in another taxi. The rest of the time he stayed in his house.

"Wish to hell we could get a wiretap on his place," Sampson said.

"Pittman said zero chance of that for the time being."

"I can dream, can't I?"

"Donovan did say in her report that Rodolpho can be reclusive."

"Looks like that leg gives him a lot of pain."

"Baseball bat will do that to you."

"That's what he was beaten with?"

"Maria said that leg was broken in six — there he is."

Clutching a black cane with a carved ivory handle, Valentine Rodolpho, a long, lean man, limped out onto his front porch and squinted at the late-fall sunlight. He rested his cane against the wall, zipped up his hoodie, slipped sunglasses on, and put a New York Yankees ball cap on his head.

"Follow or go downtown?" I asked when I saw a Yellow Cab slow to a stop in front of Rodolpho's house.

"Follow."

Prince's cousin picked up his cane, limped down to the taxi, and got in. Sampson trailed it loosely across the District line. We knew where he was going, and John took a shortcut, so we were in the parking lot of the strip mall in Suitland–Silver Hill where La Coccinelle Café and Bakery was located before Rodolpho arrived.

The past two days, he'd gone in and out quickly. This morning, however, he stayed in the small café for nearly forty minutes.

"He spot us and ditch us?" I asked finally.

John's eyes were closed. "I hope not, but one of us better go inside and check."

"I'll do it," I said. I was reaching for the door handle when Rodolpho exited. He laughed and pivoted on the sidewalk to say something to a woman behind him.

I got my binoculars on them and was shocked to see the woman following the gangster was undercover officer Nancy Donovan. She was laughing too.

Rodolpho held out his arms and she cocked her head as if considering before sliding over to him and surrendering to his kiss.

CHAPTER 40

"**THAT'S NOT BY THE** book," Sampson said.

"Bad news, you think?" I said when Valentine Rodolpho and Nancy Donovan broke their embrace.

They held each other's hands a moment. She smiled and slipped away into a playful skip down the sidewalk, then looked back at him and laughed again.

"Could be real bad news," John groaned as Donovan disappeared around a corner. "I hope to God Pittman doesn't know she's crossed that kind of line."

"We telling him?"

Sampson thought about that. "I don't know yet."

"Who's this?" I said as a black Lincoln Town Car rolled to a stop by Rodolpho. He seemed buoyed by his kiss with Donovan and climbed in easily.

"Rodolpho's rising up in the world," Sampson said. "A hired car instead of a Yellow Cab? Let's see if he goes home."

He did not go home.

Rodolpho's car took him straight east on Maryland Route 214. Thirty minutes later, the Lincoln turned north on a road just west of Davidsonville.

It was rural country, and the road was little traveled. We were nervous about being spotted and stayed well back for several miles. We lost them as the road passed through woods.

"Turn around," I said when we emerged into farm fields and could see up the road. "They must have taken one of those gravel drives back there."

John got the van turned around. We were no more than a quarter of a mile into the trees when we saw the Lincoln exit a drive on the left that had a large black mailbox out front. The car headed toward the highway.

"Drive in?" I said.

"Walk in," Sampson said, driving past the dirt lane that vanished into the forest. "See what old Rodolpho's got going on."

"'P and E Imports and Exports,'" I said, reading the words on the mailbox. "Could be Prince's place."

"Could be," he said, pulling over on the shoulder a quarter of a mile past the drive.

We got out, crossed the road, and started through the trees. Three hundred yards in, we spotted an opening in the woods several acres in size steeply downhill from us.

We reached a forested outcropping that overlooked a patch of scrub grass surrounding a high chain-link fence topped with razor wire. Behind the fence, we could make out construction equipment, stacks of construction supplies, and a large steel-gray building.

"What's with the razor wire?" Sampson said. "I mean, that's a lot of expensive equipment in there, but it seems like he's going overboard."

Looking through my binoculars, I picked up movement inside the fence to our left. "And why are the two big guys near the gate carrying rifles?"

"Gotta be to protect all the humanitarian and philanthropic pursuits going on in there."

"A Nobel Peace Prize is in the offing for Prince."

"Without a doubt."

CHAPTER

41

WEDNESDAY EVENING, GARY SONEJI kept watch on Eamon Diggs's double-wide until midnight, when a drunk Harold Beech left in his beater Subaru. Soneji waited until the lights in the double-wide had been off for half an hour before making his move.

Wearing latex gloves, he came in from the east, creeping through the pines toward the game pole where Diggs had had his deer hanging. The carcass was no longer there, but it didn't matter. The block and tackle remained, along with the rope that passed through the pulley overhead and was tied off around one of the tree trunks. Soneji went to the rope, untied a length equal to his spread arms, and cut it off.

He ground dirt into the freshly cut end, retied the remaining rope around the tree trunk, went to the clothesline and tore off a small piece of a faded flannel shirt hanging there, then hurried back to the Saab. He drove to the pull-off near Diggs's late grandmother's farm, cut through the woods wearing a headlamp, and retrieved the battered white panel van from the shed.

He navigated the van down back roads at or below the speed limit all the way to the Pine Barrens and arrived at his own cabin shortly before four a.m. He slept for six hours, then got up and went for a run. He always made sure to keep himself in good shape.

It was a crisp, chill morning in the Pine Barrens, the first real break in the weather. He could almost see his breath near the end of his route, which took him on an old two-track trail through public land that abutted the rear of his fifteen-acre property, farthest from the cabin and the road.

Soneji crossed his property line and cut left into the woods where he'd left two rocks arranged in a V shape just off the trail. His heart began to beat faster when he approached an uprooted and fallen birch tree.

He went to the massive root system, which had torn away a good foot of soil, and stood there looking at the exposed earth, knowing who lay deep in the dirt and reliving the memories of his best moments with Joyce Adams. He grew stronger and even more sure of himself.

That kidnapping had gone off without a hitch. And Joyce's terror had been more than real. For Soneji, it had been soul-affirming, everything he'd ever desired.

Thoughts of the pleasure he'd enjoyed with his captive at the cabin swirled in Soneji's mind, made him want to have another experience just like the one he had with Joyce. Maybe even better.

He looked at the grave and silently promised her she would not be alone much longer. As soon as his studies were complete, he planned to bring many others to this little cabin to feed his hungers, and when he was done with them, they would join Joyce here in the Pine Barrens for eternity.

Walking back through the trees to the trail and out to the yard, Soneji recognized that he was not ready yet for that phase of his secret life. He still had much to learn if he hoped to avoid detection later.

On the porch, he retrieved two gallon-size Ziploc bags. One contained the length of bloody, dirty nylon rope he'd taken from Diggs's place. The other held a clean white marine rope of the same length. He took out that rope and went to an old fence post along the drive.

Soneji imagined the top of the fence post as a neck. He wrapped both ends of the rope around his fists and began experimenting with how best to quickly flip the slack line over an imaginary head, clear the chin, and cinch the rope tight around the windpipe.

He had to feel his way to the best technique because the master had not given details about that, had said only that he'd used his hands or a rope or an electrical cord.

But the Boston Strangler had taught him many things. After killing thirteen women in the 1960s, Albert DeSalvo had confessed. He'd been remarkably open and comprehensive with police and with his defense attorney, F. Lee Bailey, who later wrote a book about the case.

DeSalvo had said that the key to strangling was getting close to your victim before you attacked. To do that, you had to set your victim at ease by appearing unthreatening. The Boston Strangler had often gained entry to women's apartments by posing as a repairman sent by their landlord.

Soneji's main takeaway from DeSalvo was that you had to fit

into your environment so plausibly that the victims would let their guard down and offer you an opportunity to attack. He thought about that as he practiced his garroting technique and decided the repairman angle could work for him too.

He thought about other places that his presence might be naturally accepted by a solitary victim and remembered a conversation he'd overheard between his mother and an aunt, then a real estate agent. She'd told his mother she hated doing open houses because she felt vulnerable being alone in them.

He considered that as he flipped the rope over the fence post and leaned back against it, imagining a struggle.

That could work nicely, Soneji thought. *Especially on a Saturday afternoon.*

CHAPTER 42

AT FOUR P.M. ON Saturday, Soneji parked the white Ford Econoline van on a tree-lined suburban street in Groveton, Virginia, down the road from a home with an OPEN HOUSE sign out front.

His mood swung between excitement at having been asked to come in for a preliminary interview at the Washington Day School and bubbling rage at Missy, who'd harped on about the goddamned wedding from the moment he'd walked in the door yesterday.

Missy had been so relentless, he felt homicidal toward her, and that would not do. Missy was a key part of his cover. Besides, they always suspected the husband first.

So he'd driven away before dawn that morning, leaving his wife a note saying that he needed to be by himself, that he'd be back when he was back, and they could discuss the whole wedding thing then.

Soneji was wearing the brown wig under a ball cap with a tool-company logo on it. He'd found a clean green workman's coverall with an embroidered chest patch that said DENNY'S PLUMBING on it in a Goodwill store. He'd scraped and dented the toolbox that now sat on the passenger seat so it looked like it belonged to the journeyman plumber he was impersonating.

For the next forty-five minutes, Soneji watched the house through a pair of pocket binoculars. A slow trickle of potential buyers went to the porch, put on blue booties to protect the newly refinished floors, entered, and exited not long after. At a quarter to five, there were three visitors left in the house.

A single male in his forties left at ten to five, and Soneji made his move. He put on latex gloves, grabbed the toolbox, and left the van. It was windy, raw. He marched up the short drive in the remains of the daylight.

The final two viewers, a young couple, exited the house, pulled off their blue booties, and walked down the porch steps, heads lowered against the wind. Absorbed in a discussion about the kitchen, they barely looked up as they passed Soneji, who was standing where the walkway met the short drive.

"Oh, I think she's closing up," the woman called to him.

Soneji waved his gloved hand but did not turn to them. "Thanks, I'm not a buyer."

He climbed up to the porch and put on a pair of the blue booties as the sign there requested. A help, as far as he was concerned. Then he went into a brightly lit, thoroughly renovated, and beautifully staged home.

Slate entry. Spacious great room. Hardwood floors. Nice, neutral paint job. The furniture looked custom-made.

He reached behind him to a panel by the door, flipped off the outdoor lights.

"I'm sorry, the open house is over," a woman called out in a pretty Southern accent.

A bosomy platinum blonde in her early fifties came out of a hallway on the far side of the room and walked toward him. She wore a cream-colored pantsuit, matching high heels, a pink blouse, an imitation-pearl necklace, and a name tag.

"Not looking to buy, ma'am," Soneji said, adjusting his accent to match hers. "I'm Denny Holder, just supposed to check the gas fittings on the boiler."

He could see her suspicion and knew there was fear there as well.

"What could be wrong with the boiler?" she said, close enough for him to read the name tag—BRENDA MILES—on her blazer. "Everything in this house is brand-new."

"I'm sure it is, Ms. Brenda," he said amiably. "But the gas company's done over-pressurized the lines in this part of the county. We've been getting forty calls an hour about people smelling gas, including one from the lady across the street. It's easy to check, easy to fix, and I'd hate to see a house as pretty as this one explode or something."

The real estate agent paled, looked at her watch. "Go ahead. Door to the basement's over there in the corner. But could you be quick? I've got a dinner date."

"Done in ten or less," he promised, smiling at her.

He opened the basement door, pleased at how quietly it traveled on its hinges. He turned on a light, closed the door behind him, and set his toolbox on the riser.

Soneji got out the baggie containing the rope he'd stolen from outside Diggs's trailer. He removed the rope and wrapped one end three times around his gloved left hand, holding the other end loosely with his right.

He used that same hand to crack open the door enough for him to peer into the great room. The real estate agent was nowhere to be seen.

He heard water running and then a cabinet shutting, and he figured she was in the kitchen, down the short hallway that began near the big mirror on the wall.

Quickly, quietly, Soneji crossed the great room to the hall entry and stood next to a sideboard artfully decorated with glossy coffee-table books.

"Ms. Brenda?" he called. "I need you to see something and sign something."

"Two seconds," she called in a weary voice.

CHAPTER 43

SONEJI WAITED UNTIL HE heard the *click-click* of the real estate agent's heels coming his way before lobbing one of the books at the door to the basement. It made a solid thud when it hit.

"What was that, Denny?" Brenda Miles said.

He said nothing, waited, heard her come closer. As he'd hoped she would, she stepped out of the hall and looked around for the source of the thud.

Soneji took a half a step forward and flipped the rope over her platinum-blond do, her pert nose, and her chin. When he felt the loop hit her chest and stop, he wrenched back, almost taking her off her feet.

Stunned by the assault, the woman did not fight back at first, but then she began to struggle and kick at him with her spiked heels.

RETURN OF THE SPIDER

"Whoa there, Ms. Brenda," Soneji said as he hauled her around, breaking her necklace. He got her up on her toes, both of them facing the big mirror.

Albert DeSalvo had hated seeing himself in mirrors while he attacked his victims. In one case, the Boston Strangler confessed that he became so disgusted with the reflected image of himself choking a Danish girl, he released her and begged her not to tell the police.

But Soneji had no qualms about mirrors. He leered at the reflection of Brenda Miles and himself as he twisted the rope. The fake pearls slipped off her necklace one by one as the fight seeped out of her.

Her fingers let go of the rope. Her arms dropped to her sides. Her eyes glazed over, wide open like her mouth, and she sagged down.

Only then did Soneji realize he was panting and inflamed with something like lust from her smell, from the adrenaline of it all.

And he'd been able to watch his own fascination in the mirror as the light went out of her eyes. He didn't understand why DeSalvo disliked mirrors, but he completely understood the man's obsession with strangling. He lowered Brenda Miles gently to the floor. She'd been so close to him!

He slipped the rope from her neck and admired the abraded wound it had left. Strangulation, he decided, was a very beautiful thing before, during, and after.

Soneji put the rope back in the Ziploc, which he stashed inside the coverall. He went into the kitchen and saw a crock filled with cooking utensils. He chose a wooden spoon and returned to the dead woman. He undid her pants and pulled them down around her knees with some difficulty, then rolled her over so she was facedown on the floor.

"Sorry about this, Ms. Brenda," he said. He pushed her panties aside and jammed the spoon handle where it should not have been.

Then he retrieved the toolbox, flipped off the lights, walked onto the darkened porch in the dusk, and shut the door behind him. He heard kids playing in adjoining yards and saw headlights coming in both directions. He turned his collar up, tugged down the brim of his cap, and marched to the sidewalk. He held the toolbox on his right shoulder and lifted his left arm to further shield his face as he hurried across the street between two sets of approaching headlights. He reached the white van. The car to his right passed by a second before the car to his left.

Soneji opened the van door and climbed in. The drivers might have gotten a solid look at him, but they could not possibly identify him.

CHAPTER 44

EARLY ON SATURDAY, SAMPSON and I had filed reports on our surveillance of Valentine Rodolpho. Monday was supposed to be our day off, but Chief Pittman's personal assistant called us both into work early.

When we got to his office, we found Detectives Edgar Kurtz and Corina Diehl already there, both looking hungover and pissed to be here on what was supposed to be their day off too. Also there were Lieutenant Stacey Lindahl, commander of the narcotics unit, and undercover officer Nancy Donovan, who glared at us like we were traitors.

"Lieutenant Lindahl and I have read your reports on Rodolpho," Pittman said to me and John. "You indicate, Detective Sampson, Detective Cross, that you observed Officer Donovan hug and kiss Valentine Rodolpho."

We nodded, but I felt bad about the decision to report the undercover officer. I felt worse after Donovan blasted us.

"Try 'You observed her hugged and kissed *by* Rodolpho,'" she said angrily. "Try 'She made only the slightest of hugs and no reciprocity to his kiss.'"

Sampson held up his hands. "We didn't expect you to be there, and suddenly you were in his arms and then skipping away. What did you want us to do, not report it?"

She shouted, "You could have told me you were putting Rodolpho under surveillance!"

"Calm down, Officer," Lieutenant Lindahl said. "Don't make this worse."

I held up my hands too. "You are a difficult person to get in touch with, Officer Donovan, but you're right, we should have told you."

"If you're following him without my knowledge, you are compromising my safety and my ability to work! Why were you following him, anyway?"

"Because you mentioned in one of your recent reports that Rodolpho is the weakest link."

She calmed down. "I think he is. I also think there's no way he's going to expose his weaknesses to you or almost anyone else. Even with his leg, he's too proud for that."

Detective Diehl said, "But you think he'll expose his weaknesses to you?"

"I'll have to walk a thin line, but yes, I believe there's a good chance that I can get him to confide in me. He's at that playful, flirting stage at the moment."

Chief Pittman frowned. "I don't want it going farther than that stage on your part."

Lieutenant Lindahl nodded. "If it does, you might as well

come in from the cold, Nancy, because the entire case will be compromised."

Donovan sobered and nodded. "Yes, ma'am. Of course."

I said, "What do you know about that minor fortress out in Davidsonville?"

"What?" Pittman said, puzzled. "What fortress?"

Donovan, Diehl, and Kurtz all looked clueless as well.

Sampson raised an eyebrow. "Did you read our report to the end or stop where Officer Donovan made her appearance?"

"I stopped," Pittman admitted. "Fill us in."

We described following Rodolpho to the driveway of P and E Imports and Exports outside Davidsonville and then the facility itself. Pittman, Lindahl, Kurtz, and Diehl seemed unimpressed until we told them about the fence, the razor wire, the big steel structure, and the guards with AR-15s.

Donovan said, "I heard something about that place."

Lieutenant Lindahl said, "What have you heard?"

"Just that they call it the warehouse and they have meetings there."

Kurtz said, "Who owns the company?"

Sampson said, "Incorporated in Delaware by Patrice Prince, who is listed as president. He used a rent-a-lawyer in Wilmington as counsel. Purpose of the company is import/export between the U.S. and Haiti."

"Which is what he told us at the crab shack," I added.

Diehl said, "What's so important in his import/export business that it requires an East Jesus location, a security fence, dogs, and armed men?"

Sampson said, "We asked roughly the same question in our report."

Kurtz scowled. "But what has this got to do with the deaths of those two kids? Isn't that the case you're supposed to be working on?"

I said, "We believe Tony Miller and Shay Mansion might have crossed someone in LMC Fifty-One and been killed for it. The warehouse seemed like an important find."

Officer Donovan said, "And two killings are not beyond either Prince or Rodolpho."

Pittman crossed his arms and sat back. "Well, hearsay and beliefs don't get us search warrants on a place like this warehouse. We're going to need more. Dismissed."

He turned away from us, so we got up and left the room.

Kurtz looked at Diehl, murmured, "He does that kind of thing a lot."

"He's worse on the phone," Sampson said.

"Got a personality disorder if you ask me," Lieutenant Lindahl said.

"Low social skills, anyway," I said.

CHAPTER 45

WE FOLLOWED OFFICER DONOVAN to the squad room, where we apologized again.

"Be safe," Sampson said. "And keep an eye on that line you're walking."

"I'll do that," Donovan said. She smiled at us wanly and left.

"Fine-looking woman," Sampson said when she was gone.

"Brave too," I said. "Nerves of steel."

Diehl and Kurtz went to their desks, grabbed their things, and left to spend the rest of the day with their families.

We were getting ready to leave ourselves when something on the muted television in the squad room caught my eye. Under the words BREAKING NEWS was a photo of a pretty, older blond woman. The chyron below read LOCAL REAL ESTATE AGENT STRANGLED. POLICE SEEK PUBLIC'S HELP.

Sampson left to use the men's room. I unmuted the TV. The screen jumped to a young reporter standing near a strip of yellow police tape with officers behind him going to and from a house on a tree-lined street.

"Fairfax County detectives are telling us that Brenda Miles, a longtime real estate agent in Northern Virginia, was found strangled to death late yesterday by a friend who'd become concerned when she missed a dinner date Saturday evening and didn't answer her door on Sunday.

"Miles, fifty-two, had held an open house here in Groveton shortly before she was murdered. Witnesses reported seeing a tall, slightly stooped man wearing a green coverall, running shoes, and a ball cap and carrying a toolbox leaving the scene.

"He drove away in an older white panel van with no markings on it. Detectives are asking anyone who may have seen the suspect or the white panel van in the Groveton area on Saturday night to call the Fairfax County Sheriff's Office."

I stared at the screen, then muted it when the broadcast turned to other news. Sampson came back and said, "Ready?"

"Give me five minutes," I said, and called the Fairfax County Sheriff's Office.

Dispatch patched me through to Detective Deb Angelis, the lead detective on the case, who was still on the scene.

"Angelis," she said, sounding tired.

I identified myself and said, "I know you're swamped, Detective, but did your witnesses get the license plate on the white van?"

"No. The light above the rear plate was conveniently out."

"Not even the state?"

There was a pause before she said, "We're withholding that for the moment."

"Let me take a wild guess. Pennsylvania?"

After another pause, Angelis said, "How did you know that?"

I pumped my fist. "We had a van like that around the area where Conrad Talbot, the lacrosse player from Alexandria, was shot. We have footage of it."

"That I would like to see, Detective Cross. Thank you."

"Would you mind if my partner and I came and looked at the scene? We'll share whatever we've got."

"Sure," she said. "Body's long gone, but we'll be here a few more hours."

I hung up, looked at Sampson. "The white van is in play. We better tell Pittman."

The chief groaned when we told him. "C'mon, there have to be a thousand panel vans like that in the greater metro area."

"But not near murder scenes with broken lights over Pennsylvania plates," I said.

The chief began to knead his temples. "So he's no longer impersonating Berkowitz, is that what you're telling me? After I went out on a limb to support your theory?"

I held up my hands. "I'm just following a common denominator, a beat-up white van with a faulty light above Pennsylvania plates. Shouldn't we at least go and take a look, sir?"

The chief chewed on that a moment, then flicked his hand at us. "Go. But you're not on department time. You're on your own."

CHAPTER

46

FAIRFAX COUNTY SHERIFF'S DETECTIVE Deb Angelis was in her forties, a little locomotive of a woman with tawny hair and a way of chopping at the air when she got worked up about something.

"I can give you twenty minutes, then I have to leave," Detective Angelis said as we stood on the porch outside the crime scene putting on hairnets, latex gloves, and booties.

"We appreciate it," Sampson said.

"Can you tell us what's solid so far?" I asked.

"A couple from Chevy Chase were the last people to see Brenda Miles alive. They said they saw a workman on his way in as they left. A plumber, they thought," Angelis said. She gestured down the street. "After the murder, two neighbors who were driving by reported seeing a man carrying a toolbox and wearing a green coverall and booties like these cross the street and go to a white panel van."

A woman who'd been out walking her dog said she saw the van pull out fast.

"She said the rear plate wasn't illuminated, but there was enough daylight left and she was close enough to see that the plates were gold and blue, like Pennsylvania plates."

"She didn't see any numbers at all?"

"She's seventy-seven. We're lucky she caught the colors. No one else got a good look at either his face *or* the plates."

Sampson asked, "What about the headlights on the van? Was one missing?"

"No one mentioned that."

That didn't help us, but it didn't rule out the van either. He could have fixed it.

We went inside. Angelis showed us the chalk outline where Brenda Miles had been found. A table and lamp were turned over. The floor runner had been kicked aside. Faux pearls from a broken necklace lay where they'd fallen. A crime scene photographer documented their locations.

Sampson said, "She fought him."

The detective nodded. "Her fingernails were broken and so was one of her heels. But he had to have surprised her to begin with. The medical examiner said he used a rope from behind, crushed her larynx."

Angelis said the ME believed the body had been moved postmortem, after the rope was taken from her neck.

"Then she was turned prone, and her slacks and panties were pulled to her knees," the detective said. "He sexually abused her with a wooden spoon that he left in her."

Sampson said, "He leave anything on her?"

"Nothing obvious. But her clothes haven't been processed yet."

"No other sign of sexual contact?"

She shook her head. "From the timeline we've put together, he was in and out of here in ten, fifteen minutes. No more. The couple said he came up the walk at roughly five minutes to five. The older lady with the dog thought it was no later than ten after five when he squealed out of his parking spot. Pretty brazen."

This was wildly different from the Talbot and Beltsville shootings. I tried to imagine the same suspect doing this. Aside from the white van, nothing seemed connected.

Detective Angelis looked at me. "I read about your theory that the shooter in those other cases was imitating Berkowitz. You're a profiler, right?"

I nodded. "I wrote my PhD dissertation on serial killers and mass murderers."

Sampson said, "It's gonna be published. The man's got insight."

She raised her eyebrows. "Okay, for the sake of argument, let's say my white van is your white van, and this same guy is responsible for five attacks, four dead bodies. Tell me who we're looking for here, aside from the physical descriptions we've got."

I thought about it for a few moments. "With the Bulldog shootings, there was a sense of randomness, that maybe those were crimes of opportunity. He might have seen people drive out to Bear Island and gone there knowing he'd find targets. Same thing with the two hospital techs.

"But if this is the same white Ford Econoline van, then the killer is more than just an opportunist, and we'd have to rethink. Similarities to Berkowitz's MO aside, if we assume it's the same perp, we can note he always kills up close, first with the forty-four and now with the rope. This suggests that it's satisfying to him to be in proximity to his victim. He gets his jollies from being right there."

I theorized that this seemed like an escalation, that the killer had probably enjoyed strangling Brenda Miles more than he had the close-range shootings. It likely excited him, sent his adrenaline surging.

"You described him earlier as brazen, Detective," I went on. "But unless he's an out-and-out homicidal maniac, he's a thinker and a thorough planner, and that's what allows him to act so brazenly."

She crossed her arms. "Explain."

"Think about it. Whether or not our guy personally knew Brenda Miles, he clearly knew how real estate open houses worked. The choice to come in at the last minute, dressed as a workman, carrying the toolbox? He had reason to believe that approach would allow him to get close to the victim."

"At least get him in the door," Sampson agreed. "But how'd he know she'd be solo?"

"No clue. But, and I'm speculating here, he could have just taken a chance that she'd be alone. Or he could have scouted the place, watched her earlier in the day."

Angelis asked, "What does he get out of this?"

"Aside from the rush? He's living out his fantasies, certainly. Maybe he became fixated on the Son of Sam murders and decided to copy them. And then he wanted a more intimate experience and picked up the rope."

"Assuming it is the same van and the same driver," Sampson said, "why did he leave the scene so quickly when there was still some daylight? Do you think he *wanted* to be seen?"

"Maybe. Or maybe he is completely unstable and does not care," I said.

Angelis shook her head. "This guy cared. Sounds like he was intentionally hiding his face. Witnesses said he was carrying the toolbox up on his right shoulder and holding his left arm and hand across the other side, like he was shielding himself from the headlight glare. Totally blocked anyone's view of his face."

Sampson said, "So maybe he wanted to be partially seen leaving the house, crossing the street to the van, and driving away fast. What's the motivation for that?"

Sampson was looking at me. I threw up my hands. "Even with my doctorate in the psychology of criminal minds, John, I have no good answer for that."

CHAPTER

47

WITHIN MINUTES OF MEETING Charles Pendleton Little, Gary Soneji pegged him as one of those scrubbed, preening, and entitled guys he used to see walking around Princeton when he was growing up, young men of practiced cheer and false camaraderie, the sort who threw around references to their pedigrees, education, and wealth as proof of their innate superiority.

"My ancestors were among the first Jamestown colonists," the headmaster of the Washington Day School told Soneji, settling into a leather chair behind a neatly organized desk in his office. "Six generations of my family have attended William and Mary, my alma mater. I'm blessed to have that kind of tradition and history behind me, despite not following my father or brother into the family banking business. I believe, however, that my background has given me a unique perspective on the value of constancy, rigor, and growth, all of which are at the heart of the Washington Day School experience and tradition."

Soneji had sailed through an initial interview with a vice principal, reveling in openly using his Gary Soneji pseudonym for the first time while honing a somewhat nerdy but affable persona, like Peter O'Toole's beloved Mr. Chips from the old film.

Wearing the toupee with the bald spot, the facial prosthetics, the green contact lenses, and the English-schoolboy glasses—a look that aged him by at least ten years—Soneji brightened. "Your reputation precedes you, Mr. Little. And this school is remarkable. I would be thrilled to be a part of the faculty here," he said. After purposely hesitating, he added, "Though it's only fair for me to let you know that I'm also interviewing at other high-caliber schools in the area."

Soneji saw the light of competition spark in Little's eyes. *Gotcha*. He demurred politely when the headmaster pressed for more details, feigning embarrassment for even bringing up the specter of a counteroffer.

A trim man in his fifties with a full head of silver hair slicked back, Little reminded Soneji of one of those bronzed Ralph Lauren male models of a certain age, instantly at home on a golf course or on a tennis court or in Bimini, the kind of guy who breezes through life with nary a whisper of effort. He was unused to being denied once he decided to acquire something.

After some persuasive back-and-forth—in which Soneji manipulated the headmaster into increasing his pay and decreasing his hours—they came to an agreement, with Soneji agreeing to decline his other (fictitious) offers.

"Excellent," Little said, pushing a piece of paper across the desk. "Now, I'm sure you are aware that among our student body are children whose parents are politically powerful, titans of finance, or celebrities."

"I am," Soneji said, feeling a little rush.

"That's a nondisclosure agreement barring you from ever talking publicly about the students, with significant penalties if the contract is broken. Please date and sign, and I'll take you on a little tour and introduce you to Mrs. Ravisky, whom you'll be substituting for when she goes on maternity leave."

Soneji scanned the document and signed it. He had no issue with keeping the students' private lives private.

"Well, Mr. Soneji," Little said, taking the paper and extending his hand, "welcome to the Washington Day family. You'll be here Tuesdays and Thursdays starting this Thursday, with a full schedule of classes."

With his best country-club grin, Soneji pumped the headmaster's hand. "I'm delighted."

Little led him on a tour of the facilities, which covered almost four acres in Georgetown, a campus of brick buildings, green lawns, and stately elms. As they walked, Headmaster Little praised Washington Day's excellent academics, athletics, art, and theater.

A bell rang as they entered one of the larger buildings that Little said held classrooms for grades nine through twelve. With the sea of students suddenly surging around them, Soneji tried to pay attention to all that Little was saying, but he found himself glancing at various teens, wondering who their parents were and whether they were famous.

Soneji had long been fascinated by fame. His mother and grandmother always had issues of *People* magazine around the house, and they talked about celebrities and royalty as if they were all on a first-name basis.

He thought about the Lindbergh case again and felt a thrill surge inside him. He remembered feeling like this after snatching Joyce Adams and bringing her to the old cabin in the Pine Barrens. He remembered how he felt when he overheard Conrad Talbot's plans in a school hallway and formulated his own.

Committing murder was often short and sweet, Soneji thought as he trailed Little up a staircase. But taking a captive—well, that was different, especially if you could grab a child of a high-profile parent. That would be the stuff of legend. That would mean fame of his own.

"Mr. Soneji?"

Soneji startled at the casual sound of his assumed name and realized they'd stopped outside a classroom.

"Right here, sir," he said and grinned at the headmaster, who was frowning.

"This will be your classroom," Little said. "Let's meet Mrs. Ravisky, then I'll leave you two to sort out your transition into Washington Day life."

Soneji increased the wattage on his smile one more time. "Nothing could make me happier, Mr. Little. Nothing."

CHAPTER 48

FOR SEVERAL DAYS, I felt like we'd hit a stone wall on both the shootings and our investigation into Patrice Prince and his gang. About the only real progress was made by Detective Angelis in Fairfax County.

Or, rather, by Virginia's state crime lab on behalf of Angelis. An analysis of nylon fibers found in Brenda Miles's neck abrasions had definitively identified the item used to strangle her as an MFP utility rope. Oddly, the rope analysis had also picked up blood traces that didn't belong to the murdered real estate agent or to any other human. It was deer blood.

When we told Chief Pittman about the lack of progress at our midweek staff meeting, he told us to shift our focus and put heat on Prince's cousin Valentine Rodolpho in a way that would signal to the gang leader that we were not easing up on him or his crew.

When we reminded the chief that undercover officer Nancy Donovan had asked us to lay off Rodolpho, Pittman said, "I have a little bit more experience than she does. I think you guys following him and hassling him a little could very well cause him to open up to her more. Or am I wrong on the psychology of this, Dr. Cross?"

I thought about it. "You're not wrong, Chief."

"There you go. Let's see how Valentine responds to a little flame to the tush."

A half an hour later, we were in a squad car down the street from Rodolpho's row house.

Sampson was irritated. "Flame to the tush?" he said. "I don't know about the chief sometimes."

"He has solid instincts and ten times more experience than both of us."

"Yeah, I get it. It'll be two hours until Valentino shows. I'm going to grab a nap."

"Not this morning," I said, gesturing toward the row house where Rodolpho was holding tight to the banister and limping down the stairs.

A black Lincoln Town Car rolled up, and we were after him again. Only this time, there was no trip to the Haitian coffee shop or the warehouse in Maryland.

The car took him to a known open-air drug market in Southeast DC, where we watched Rodolpho speak to a number of young guys who seemed to know him. He talked to them for fifteen minutes before getting back in the car and leaving.

"I didn't see any money or drugs changing hands," Sampson said as I put the car in gear to follow.

"Neither did I," I said.

Over the course of the next two hours, Rodolpho visited three more areas known for drug dealing and had several more brief conversations with various young men and women. Again, no drugs or money appeared to change hands.

"I say we put a little flame to his tush," I said when Prince's cousin got out of the car for the fifth time and limped toward a group of young men outside a housing project in Gaithersburg, Maryland.

"Let's," Sampson said, opening his door as soon as I'd parked.

We rolled toward them, coats open, badges displayed on our belts. Rodolpho had his back to us, but his young friends saw us coming.

One of them said something I didn't catch, and they all bolted. Prince's cousin turned and smiled, revealing a gold upper incisor.

"Ah," he said after glancing at our badges.

"Why'd they run?"

"A learned response," he said in a thick Haitian accent.

"Why didn't you run, Valentino?" Sampson said.

Valentine," Rodolpho said, his eyes going cold. "And I cannot run."

"We noticed that," I said. "We also noticed you've spent the morning doing a whirlwind tour of known areas where hard drugs are sold."

"Did you?" Rodolpho said.

"We did," Sampson said. "What's up with that, Valentino?"

Rodolpho's nostrils flared. "It is my give-back. I talk with the troubled youth, try to get them out of trouble before they are in bigger trouble."

I squinted at him skeptically. "You're telling us you're running some kind of street ministry?"

"If you want to call it that."

John said, "We're not buying it, Valentino. You tell your cousin that despite his humanitarian work and your street ministry, we are not letting go of this. We know that you and Patrice were involved in the murders of Tony Miller and Shay Mansion, and no matter how long it takes, we are going to prove it."

If Rodolpho felt threatened, he did not show it. "Good luck, because I do not know who those people are. Unless we have further business, I will go — my ride is here. Do not bother to follow me. Next stop is for the physical therapy."

CHAPTER 49

WE FOLLOWED VALENTINE RODOLPHO anyway. He did go to physical therapy, spent an hour there, then returned to his row house. We called off the surveillance at midnight and went home.

We were back in the morning in time to see Rodolpho go to his favorite café, where he stayed for an hour. We watched a visibly angry Nancy Donovan leave the café first, followed fifteen minutes later by an even angrier Rodolpho, who gave us the finger as he hailed a taxi.

This went on for two mind-numbing days. Rodolpho continued his daily trips to the café, though we did not see Officer Donovan again. By Saturday, figuring Rodolpho and Prince had gotten our message, we called off the stakeout.

It was time to enlist the public's help.

That evening, Maria, Damon, and I had a nice dinner at an

Italian place on Capitol Hill. The next morning, we met Sampson and Nana Mama before Mass.

According to Nana Mama, ten o'clock Mass on Sunday at St. Anthony's was always the best attended service of the week. While Maria, Damon, and Nana found seats, Sampson and I went to see Father Nathan Barry back in the vestibule. We admitted to Father Barry that we were making little headway on the investigation into Tony's murder and I asked if I could appeal directly to the congregation for aid.

Father Barry agreed, and before the parish announcements at the end of Mass, he called me up and introduced me: "Alex Cross, a longtime parishioner and now a detective with Metro PD."

"Thank you, Father," I said as I stood behind the lectern. "As Father Barry said, I grew up attending this church, as did my partner, John Sampson."

I paused and saw many heads nodding. I pressed on with my plea.

"Because we're from here and because we still live here, we have taken the investigation into the murders of Tony Miller and Shay Mansion as a deeply personal mission. We have been working hard to solve these murders, but to be honest, we have not made the kind of progress we would like. We need your help.

"As devastating as these killings were to the families of Tony and Shay, we have all been damaged by their murders. Two of our own young men were taken by what we believe was gang violence. For the mothers of these boys to get some kind of peace, their sons' killers must be brought to justice. I believe this community needs that too.

"If you know anything, please call me or John Sampson through the Metro main number. If you wish to remain anonymous, you can leave your information on the department's tip line. Thank you."

I nodded to the parishioners and to Father Barry, then went back to my seat. Maria took my hand. Nana Mama whispered, "Well said."

Damon had fallen asleep in my grandmother's arms. I winked at her and squeezed my wife's hand, hoping my words had been enough to shake something loose. When the service was over, we left the church.

I carried a still sleepy Damon down the church steps as many parishioners we'd known for years promised to help us in any way they could. Maria strolled over to my right to talk with Father Barry. Nana Mama was on my left, chatting with several old friends.

"Think it was enough?" I said to Sampson as I shifted Damon in my arms.

"Yeah," he said, his head slowly craning around. "If someone in there knew something, I think we'll hear about—"

He stared past me, his eyes widening. "Gun!" he whispered. "Eleven o'clock on the street and coming at us, Alex!"

I snapped my head around, saw a black Suburban heading our way. The rear passenger-side window was down, and a rifle barrel was sticking out.

"Gun!" Sampson roared. "Everybody, down!"

The gunman in the Suburban opened up, firing in bursts. Damon began to scream. A woman next to Sampson was hit, and panic took over.

Ignoring my son's screams, the shooting, and the people running, I took two steps, tackled Nana Mama to the ground, and used my body to shield her and Damon as bullets pinged off the concrete all around us. Then I heard shots coming from much closer, and I looked up to see Sampson squared off in a horse stance and pouring lead at the open rear window of the Suburban before it screeched off up the street.

"You okay, Nana?" I gasped over Damon's screeches.

"If you get off me, I will be!"

Maria!

I jumped up with Damon still in my arms and looked around frantically. Sampson was gone, and several people who'd been standing close to us now lay bleeding on the sidewalk in front of the church.

"Alex!"

My terrified wife rushed toward me, blood spattered on her face and down the front of her maternity dress. She ran into my arms, sobbing. "They shot Father Barry! Right next to me. He's dead!"

The three of us stood there shaking, arms wrapped around each other.

"I go home, Mama?" Damon cried. "I go home, Daddy?"

"Soon, buddy," I said to my son, feeling more vulnerable than I ever had. To my wife, I said, "We need to help the wounded. We can cry afterward. Okay?"

Maria shuddered, then nodded and pulled away. I handed her Damon, whose crying had eased.

Sirens wailed toward us as the first of the ambulances arrived. Sampson returned.

"What the hell was that about?" I asked.

"I think Prince got our message and decided to reply," Sampson said.

"You think we were the targets?"

"Yeah, Alex, I do."

CHAPTER

50

HURRYING BACK DOWNTOWN TO headquarters later that afternoon, I knew I was late for a briefing with chief of detectives George Pittman, who had been horrified to hear that a Catholic priest had been gunned down in front of his own church and outraged that Sampson and I might have been the true targets.

While Pittman attended a sit-down with the chief of Metro about everything, I'd taken a walk with Ellen Bovers, the FBI agent who'd gotten us the CCTV footage of the white van.

When I returned, Sampson was already at his desk. "Where you been?"

"Out talking to my FBI friend. She tells me they're becoming interested in Prince too."

"Good, because we've got a big problem."

I felt like we'd been constantly bombarded with big problems, one after another. The gang killings of two teens, the Bulldog murders, the drive-by shooting—and the slaying of Father Barry. How close my wife, my son, and my grandmother had all come to dying. How close *I'd* come.

"Tell me," I said wearily.

"Donovan? The undercover officer? She's missed her last few check-ins."

"She could be deep into something and unable to communicate."

"Or Rodolpho figured her out. Or Prince."

We were in Pittman's office five minutes later. Kurtz and Diehl were there too, as was Lieutenant Stacey Lindahl, Donovan's narcotics commander.

"Shut the door," Pittman said. "I want this kept quiet. I mean, if they'll gun down a priest, they'll do anything. Lieutenant? Can you bring us up to speed?"

Lindahl nodded, looking deeply concerned. "Donovan last checked in three days ago. She is supposed to be in contact once every twenty-four hours."

"We saw her four days ago," Sampson said. "At that café Rodolpho goes to all the time."

I nodded. "She seemed upset."

The lieutenant nodded. "She was angry that day when she checked in. She'd asked you to back off and yet you didn't. Rodolpho told her you were following him."

Pittman held up his hands. "That was my call, Lieutenant. We wanted to send Prince a message that we were not giving up on the Miller and Mansion murders."

"I understand, Chief, but Donovan didn't. She said she'd been getting closer to Rodolpho, but the surveillance spooked him. He'd gotten pissed with her and told her to leave."

"Like I said, my call," Pittman said. "But now I'm asking, how do we handle this?"

Lindahl said, "I'm concerned. But my gut says give her another day. She might be somewhere she can't communicate from. Or she's on the verge of something big and trying not to do anything to jeopardize it."

Detective Kurtz said, "With all due respect, Lieutenant, you could also assume Donovan's cover is blown, haul in every known member of LMC Fifty-One, and put the squeeze on them, bottom up, until we find her."

Diehl said, "I agree. There's a cop involved. They know the penalties. Someone will talk."

Pittman thought for several moments. "I spoke with the commissioner right before I came here. He knows she's missing and said that we were to prioritize her welfare, not the undercover operation."

Lindahl looked somewhat unhappy about that but agreed. "Okay, there it is, then. I'll get you a list of all known members of LMC Fifty-One in the greater DC area, along with last known addresses and aliases."

I said, "Can I make a suggestion? Before you start hauling them in, put a few teams outside Rodolpho's, at that café, at the crab-boil place Prince loves in Chesapeake Beach, and at the warehouse in Davidsonville."

"Good idea, Cross," Kurtz said. "Be in position if the rats start abandoning ship."

Sampson raised his hand, said, "Since we found the place, we'd like to be in Davidsonville. See what they're doing in there."

Pittman thought about that. "I don't know if we have enough to warrant a search."

Diehl said, "Really? They tried to kill two of our people, they murdered a priest, they've done God knows what to Donovan, and it's not enough?"

The chief said, "Problem is, Detective, no witnesses saw who was behind the gun at St. Anthony's, and the car with the license plate Sampson reported had been stolen."

John said, "That Suburban will have at least three of my bullets in it."

"I'm sure," Pittman said. "But until we know for certain that LMC Fifty-One was behind the shooting or Donovan's disappearance or both, best we can do is put surveillance teams in place and start bringing them in. Let's build the pressure fast until something pops."

PART FOUR
Revenge Is a Dish Best Served Cold

CHAPTER 51

EARLY IN THE EVENING on Monday, three days before he was to start his new job at Washington Day School, Gary Soneji could not take it anymore. The hunger, the desperate need, had been building in him ever since his big fight with Missy.

The two of them had argued bitterly all weekend over everything from the wedding to finances to Roni's day care.

Part of him wanted to just divorce Missy—or kill her—but another part of him acknowledged that his marriage to Missy gave him valuable cover, cover he was sure he would need in the future. But another fight like that and who knew what he might do to her.

Leaving home that morning, he'd decided to give in to the hunger. He was now two hours south of Washington, DC, waiting to sate his appetite. He wore the workman's coverall and sat in the battered white panel van, a black balaclava rolled up on his forehead. He'd parked the van in a dirt lot across the street from a strip club called Tillie's, a low, gray cinder-block affair with a garish neon sign on a lonely route just north of Richmond near the town of Short Pump.

Two summers ago, when he was working to drum up new heating-oil business in the region, Soneji had often visited Tillie's. He'd been obsessed with a dancer there named Bunny Maddox. Lean physique, large breasts, and wild mane of auburn hair.

He'd not only thought about taking Bunny to the Pine Barrens; he'd planned it all out, knew just how he'd grab her. Now he was going to put his plan into action.

Soneji sat there in the van, hoping that Bunny still worked the early shift. She tried to clock out by eight thirty so she could be home for her kid.

The boy had to be — what, five? Six? Not that he really cared. He remembered Bunny telling him that half the time, her kid lived down in Florida with her mom and older sister.

"I get anxious," Bunny had told him, running scarlet fingernails down his cheek the last time he'd paid her to dance for him. "Which makes me want to get high or drink or both. Which gets me in trouble. Makes me a shitty mom sometimes."

Soneji wondered if that was still true as he watched a dancer leave through the employee door at ten past eight. Then five more women from the day shift came out and drove away. He didn't want to go inside the strip club and risk showing up on a security camera.

At eight fifteen, Bunny was still a no-show. Eight twenty, same thing.

At eight twenty-eight, he was thinking that it might be time to head north. He'd actually started the van when Bunny Maddox came out the door and stumbled slightly as she crossed the lot.

"Still has problems," Soneji said, smiling. He felt a little breathless as he watched Bunny climb into a Ford Galaxie that had seen far better days.

Soneji waited until she'd pulled out of the parking lot and swung onto the county road heading toward Richmond. His heart beat faster. He put the van in gear and drove after her at a distance, telling himself to breathe deeply and slowly against the anticipation swelling in him.

There was no room for any sloppiness.

As Soneji had seen her do repeatedly during his scouting trips in years past, Bunny drove from the club to the closest Virginia state liquor store, where he knew she'd buy her usual pint (or quart) of vodka. Anticipating that she'd continue her typical pattern, Soneji drove ahead to her next stop, a Winn-Dixie about a mile away.

He parked the van and waited patiently with a panoramic view of the rest of the lot. Bunny's Galaxie came rumbling in ten minutes later. After parking, the dancer ducked down where she could not be seen, probably so she could take a swig off her newest bottle.

The second he saw Bunny leave her car and wobble her way to the grocery store entrance, Soneji felt a sense of overwhelming confidence. If he stuck to his plan, took every precaution, and avoided sloppiness, Bunny Maddox was his.

CHAPTER

52

WHILE BUNNY WAS IN the Winn-Dixie, Soneji drove west on Route 6 toward Maidens, Virginia. He took the Crozier exit and drove into a checkerboard of farmland and small wooded lots.

He liked rural areas. There weren't a lot of people around, and residences were scattered and often isolated, making situations far easier to control here than they were in urban environments.

Bunny lived with her brother and a male cousin and, at times, their girlfriends. The presence of so many people would ordinarily have all but eliminated the dancer as a target in Soneji's mind, and it certainly would have if she'd lived in a city. But Bunny's house was well off a county road and largely blocked from sight by a kudzu infestation that crawled up the trunks of the pine and oak trees and hung down from their limbs like so much green drapery.

He saw the mailbox and slowed. Rain began to sprinkle as he lowered his window and peered down the drive into the kudzu and pines. He saw rusted gate posts set to either side about thirty yards in from the road.

Everything was as he remembered it.

Soneji drove over a rise in the road, pulled the van onto the shoulder where Bunny wouldn't see it, and turned off his headlights. Then he tugged down the black balaclava, put on a headlamp and a second layer of latex gloves, and stepped out of the van. He shut the door softly and turned on the red bulb on his headlamp.

As he trotted back down the road, he peered south for headlights approaching but saw none before reaching the drive. He walked fast up the shallow grassy ditch and tiptoed across the gravel to the open gate.

Soneji swung the gate shut and wrapped the chain around the post just a few moments before he heard the growl of Bunny's car coming. The rain was falling harder. He ignored the drops in his eyes, walked fifteen feet toward the road, pressed himself back into the kudzu, and turned off his headlamp.

The Galaxie came closer. Soneji retrieved the Bulldog pistol from his right pocket. He tugged a ragged two-inch strip of flannel fabric out of his left pocket and pushed it into the vegetation behind him.

Headlights slashed the county road, then flooded the drive as Bunny pulled in. Her tires crunched across the gravel and the car slammed to a halt a few feet from the closed gate. She threw the car in park and heaved open her door, which squealed on its hinges.

"Assholes," Bunny slurred. She slammed her door shut and started forward. "Close the gate? Calvin, what the—"

She had no chance to finish the expletive because she had stepped in front of Soneji, so close he merely had to raise his free left hand to clamp it across her mouth. He jammed the muzzle of the Bulldog against the side of her head.

"Scream and you die, Bunny," he said, seeing her eyes, wide and terrified. "You're not going to scream, are you? You want a chance at a long life, don't you? Another chance to see that son of yours?"

The dancer was trembling, but she nodded.

"Good," Soneji said. "Now, back up with me."

He stepped from the kudzu. He guided her backward several steps and told her to open the Galaxie's door. When she did, he saw groceries in the back and a quart of vodka on the passenger seat beside her purse.

"Lean in," he said. "Turn off the headlights. Turn off the engine. Leave the keys, your purse, and your groceries. Take the bottle if it'll help."

The dancer hesitated when he lowered the gloved hand from her mouth. He pressed the pistol muzzle harder against her temple and she did as he'd asked. The driveway went dark and quiet save for the rain and the ticking of the Galaxie's engine.

He turned on the red light of his headlamp as she straightened up, gripping the liquor bottle, and turned to face him.

Bunny was crying. "Who are you? Why are you doing this?"

"I'm going to tell you everything, Bunny," he said. "Just come along quietly and I promise you'll hear all about it, and you'll be seeing your son before you know it."

CHAPTER

53

AT NINE THIRTY ON Monday evening in late October, a bank of chill, dank fog rolled in off the Chesapeake Bay. It swept, curled, and misted slowly through the oaks and pines overlooking the west side of the razor wire and chain-link fence that surrounded the construction equipment, the supplies, and the big steel-sided warehouse out of which Patrice Prince supposedly ran his import/export business.

We thought we'd come prepared, wearing winter clothes over our body armor and carrying wool blankets, radios, a thermos of hot coffee, binoculars, and a Tupperware with sandwiches. I had all the warm stuff on, but the fog wormed its way through the clothes, making me shiver as I adjusted an earphone and mic connected to my radio.

Two police-issue combat shotguns rested against a nearby tree. We were perched in cover on the bluff above the fence and inner compound.

Sampson checked his watch, murmured into his mic, "Any second now they're going to start knocking on doors and bringing in the first Haitian gangbangers."

"You'd think there'd be a delayed effect," I said. "We probably won't see any kind of real reaction for a few hours, maybe not till close to midnight."

He nodded. "If Prince knows he's under assault, he'll come here."

"Or, if he's here already, he'll leave," I said. I had my binoculars up and was looking over the fence. "We've got two more sets of guards coming from the north side of the complex with a pair of Malinois attack dogs."

"I see 'em, going by the backhoe and the bulldozers," Sampson said, peering through his own binoculars. "That complicates things."

"Only if we need to go in there," I said.

"Well, I'm hoping that's the eventual plan, search warrant or no search warrant, so we better figure out the canine situation."

For the next forty-five minutes, we stood and stamped our feet in the fog and the cold, shivering in the shadows and trying to monitor the radio chatter as Metro detectives moved in to take various members of LMC 51 into custody. Kurtz and Diehl evidently rapped on Valentine Rodolpho's front door but got no answer, and his row house was dark. They remained in position, watching his place.

The coffee shop Rodolpho liked and the crab-boil shack in Chesapeake Beach his cousin loved had long since closed for the day. Teams had left those locations with plans to return in the morning.

The other officers assigned to find the members of LMC 51 were also coming up short. It was as if the gang had disappeared from all their usual haunts.

I said, "Wish the hell we knew where Prince lives full-time."

"You think Donovan might have found out?"

"If she found out in the wrong way, it could explain her disappearance."

"It could," he said, "but I—"

We both heard vehicles approaching and tires crunching on the driveway into the warehouse. A few moments later, two black Chevy Suburbans rolled up to the gate, which the armed guards opened.

As they drove in and parked near the second loading dock, John double-clicked the radio, said, "Chief Pittman, this is John Sampson. We've got action here in Davidsonville. Two vehicles. One of them could be the Suburban used in the drive-by."

Pittman came back immediately: "You've got that confirmed, Sampson? Can you see your bullet holes?"

"Negative. Too far and there's fog, but stand by. Doors are opening and—"

"I've got Rodolpho coming out of the first Suburban," I said. "Three guys with him, all armed, heading toward the first loading dock door."

"And here's Prince from the back of the second Suburban," Sampson said. "Three other armed men with him are going to the rear of the vehicle."

One of the gunmen opened the back door and pulled out Officer Donovan. She was blindfolded and gagged with her wrists tied behind her.

"We've got Donovan," both of us said at the same time.

"That's confirmed?" Pittman demanded.

Sampson said, "Yes. They're taking her inside in restraints, blindfolded, and gagged."

"Hold your position," Pittman came back. "I'm notifying the Maryland state police and everyone else with jurisdiction out there. Repeat: Unless you believe Donovan's life is being threatened, hold your position until we've got the kind of team we need to contain and breach the place safely."

"ETA on that, Chief?"

"Two hours, maybe?"

"And if they try to leave with her in the meantime, sir?" I asked.

"Then you stop them, Detective Cross."

"Roger that," I said. "We're standing by."

"Don't send sirens or flashing lights," Sampson said.

"Roger that," Pittman said.

Two minutes later, we heard a diesel engine rumbling and then gravel crunching. An eighteen-wheeler emerged from the fog and the trees and pulled up to the gate.

The guards seemed to recognize the driver and opened the gates. The rig rolled forward and hard to the right of the two Suburbans and backed up to the third loading dock. The overhead door rose, revealing four more armed men in the bay.

"Looks like something important is getting delivered," Sampson said.

"Yeah," I said. "This is starting to get—"

Out in the fog near the far northwest corner of the fence, an explosive device detonated in a dull flash and blast that, even at a distance, boxed our ears and pulsed through our chests.

CHAPTER 54

WE'D NO SOONER RECOVERED from the shock of the blast than the wind shifted, intensified, and cleared away ribbons of fog. We saw many of Prince's men racing through the construction equipment and piles of supplies toward the site of the explosion.

Sampson triggered his mic. "Chief, we just had a bomb go off at Davidsonville."

"What? Repeat!"

Before John could, the wind blew another clear lane through the fog, revealing a heavily armed force of at least eight attackers in black hoods entering through a hole in the fence in the northwest corner of the complex. They spread out behind a bulldozer and a dump truck and began firing at the LMC 51 gunmen, who released their dogs.

Pittman yelled, "Sampson, Cross, repeat!"

Over the flash and rattling of the small-arms fire and the pinging of bullets ricocheting, I triggered my mic, said, "Davidsonville site is under attack by armed men. Firefight in progress. Donovan is inside. Send reinforcements! Now!"

"Jesus Christ. Roger that!"

I put up my binoculars and got glimpses of the combat through the ribbons of fog, seeing the dogs race toward the attackers as if I were watching through a lazy strobe. Three of the hooded men went to their knees, held up canisters, and waited until the Malinois were all but on them and sprayed the dogs with some kind of high-strength pepper spray.

The dogs fell down, screeching, whining, coughing, and pawing at their muzzles, and the emboldened attackers moved past the machines and piles of supplies in coordinated fashion, covering each other, firing when they could. One gunman went down, and another was hit hard; LMC 51 reinforcements began pouring out of the open loading docks.

Carrying automatic weapons, Valentine Rodolpho and Patrice Prince appeared at the first dock's door, the one closest to the Suburbans.

"They're gonna try to make a run for it," Sampson said. He spun around and grabbed one of our shotguns.

"What are we doing?" I said as I grabbed the other shotgun.

"You heard the chief. If they try to get out before the cavalry gets here, we're supposed to stop them."

"He said if Donovan was threatened."

"She and everyone in there is under attack!"

He took off before I could reply. I followed, running along the spine of the high ground that paralleled the fence, heading toward the gate.

Inside the fence, gunfire was near constant, a full-on war in a porous fog.

Prince's men were fighting ferociously and seemed to outnumber the gunmen of the attacking force. Even the gang leader and his limping cousin were forced to move away from the SUVs. They disappeared into the fog and joined the fray.

We reached the gate, now unguarded. Sampson was right, I decided. We needed to get to Donovan before the fight got to her.

Just as Sampson reached through the gap to raise the bar holding the gate shut, six more hooded attackers jumped out of the back of the eighteen-wheeler that had arrived before the explosion.

"It's a Trojan Horse!" I yelled and pulled Sampson down. They opened fire as a group, sweeping their guns left to right, catching Prince, Rodolpho, and the rest of the attacking gunmen in a crossfire somewhere in the fog.

CHAPTER 55

THE SIX NEW ATTACKERS split up and sprinted past us into the swirling mist and the roaring gunfight.

Sampson jumped up when the second wave of attackers were out of sight, threw up the gate bar, and said, "Let's get Donovan out of there."

He pushed open the gates, crouched down, and sprinted toward the second of the two loading docks, and I was right behind him. Bullets cracked through the air, slapped the pavement, and pinged off the Suburbans, forcing us to take cover behind them even as their windows shattered and safety glass rained down on us.

There was a lull in the shooting but not in the shouting. I heard French, Spanish, and English. John and I eased ourselves up, looked through the blown-out windows of the nearby

Suburban, and saw Prince darting up the stairs to the first of the three loading docks, Rodolpho covering him from the open dock door. He shot two hooded attackers, who spun and fell.

I had the gang leader's cousin square in my sights, but at seventy yards away, he was too far for me to hit with the shotgun or my pistol. Prince and his cousin disappeared into the warehouse.

The fog swirled. The gunfire to our north started once more, fiercer than ever.

"Let's go in at another angle," Sampson said. "Third bay. Wait. I'll cover you."

He hunched over and ran away from the vehicle and the gunfight and toward the rear of the semi. I took one more look in the direction of the gun battle.

Through the fog, I spotted a hooded attacker in full body armor clubbing the skull of one of Prince's men with the butt of his weapon. When the man went down, he sprinted toward the open second loading dock.

Sampson whistled.

I ran to him, keeping low.

We climbed into the building, the gunfire outside now echoing behind us. In the far distance, the first sirens wailed.

Dodging pallets of concrete mix stacked on both sides of the inner dock, we went to a set of double doors and looked through a porthole window into a large, high-ceilinged space filled with towering steel shelves, some heavily loaded, some empty.

"We've got company in here," I whispered. "Hooded dude went in the first dock chasing Prince and Rodolpho."

"I think the cousins are going for Donovan," Sampson said.

A figure sprinted toward us from the stacks. We both stepped back and to either side of the double doors.

When the man, one of Prince's armed guards, barged through,

he found the muzzles of two shotguns pressed to the back of his head.

"Police," Sampson said. "Drop the gun."

He dropped his weapon.

"Where's the woman?" I said. "The one they just brought in here."

He said nothing.

"Tell us," Sampson said. "She's a cop. If he kills her, you'll go down for it too."

The man answered in a thick Haitian accent, his voice shaking. "Other side of the warehouse. Prince's office."

"Who's attacking?"

"No idea. Prince, he got many enemies."

Sampson spun his shotgun and clipped the guy right behind the ear with the side of the stock, knocking him out cold. He dropped in his tracks.

"No time for niceties," he said to me. He kicked open the double doors and entered the warehouse.

CHAPTER 56

I'D KNOWN JOHN SAMPSON since elementary school. I'd met him shortly after I moved to Washington, DC, to live with my grandmother.

As we grew older, I'd seen him handle himself remarkably well in a couple of fights. And I was well aware of his training with the U.S. Army and of the years he spent on patrol with Metro before becoming a detective.

But I had never seen the man who blew through those doors, intent on rescuing Officer Nancy Donovan. Low, aware, with his attention sweeping three hundred degrees left and right, he raced forward into the relative protection of the stacks. I was right behind him.

Sampson slowed to a stop, held up his hand, and listened. We could still hear shooting outside, but it was distant and sporadic.

Then, far ahead of us and to our left, toward the northeast

corner of the building, we heard muffled, frantic voices. Sampson nodded to me, gestured in that direction, then turned into a stalker.

He moved quickly through the stacks, staying right in our aisle, and slowed again when we could see the far wall. Then he stopped and listened once more.

We could hear male voices arguing in Haitian Creole. They were closer and almost directly ahead of us now.

Sampson slipped off his shoes. I did the same, and we crept in the direction of the voices, shotguns shouldered, ready.

When we were some fifty yards away, we heard the argument growing more intense. There were at least three male voices. And then we heard Nancy Donovan.

"You do this, Patrice, and you are guaranteeing yourself a death sentence," she said.

A slap. "Shut up, bitch," Prince said. "We have other things to think about."

We crossed another aisle in the stacks of shelves. They were no more than three aisles away now, to our two o'clock.

A young male voice said, "We need to leave, Patrice. Back door. Cops are coming."

"Cops are here!" Sampson roared, stepping out to face Prince and the younger man, who were a good twenty yards away. They stood on either side of Officer Donovan, who was in a chair by a desk, still blindfolded, her wrists tied behind her. "Drop your weapons! Now!"

Both men were armed with pistols. Prince let his go. It clattered onto the floor.

When the second guy dropped his gun, John moved forward with me right behind him. "Step away from her and get down on your bellies," he told them.

They complied. The sirens outside were close now and the shooting was dying down.

Sampson and I were almost to Donovan and the crisis was almost over when Rodolpho appeared from the shadows at our five o'clock with an automatic weapon aimed at our heads.

"Drop your guns!" he shouted. "Or Valentine kills you now!"

CHAPTER

57

VALENTINE RODOLPHO HAD US.

We had no choice but to set the shotguns down on the concrete floor. He limped around in front of us, slowly waving the barrel of his weapon in our faces.

"We should kill them and go out the back door," Rodolpho said to his cousin. "All three of them, Patrice."

I spoke to Prince. "Kill three cops? I'm sorry, but any way you look at that, it is a bad, bad, bad idea."

"Three cops gets you a one-way ticket to the gas chamber," Sampson said.

"They're right, Patrice!" Donovan said.

Outside, sirens were drowning out the sporadic shooting. The head of LMC 51 turned his head a split second before four quick, brilliant flashes and flat cracks came from somewhere deep in the stacks.

The first round hit Rodolpho, shattering his right wrist. He let go of his AR and spun around as it clattered to the floor, grabbing wildly at his wrist and screaming.

The second shot caught the Haitian gangbanger guarding Nancy Donovan between the eyes. He crumpled.

Prince almost got his own pistol up before the third round hit him in the front of his thigh. He howled and grabbed for his leg, then went down hard.

The fourth and last round hit Rodolpho in the buttocks and he fell over, screaming gibberish.

"What's happening?" blindfolded Officer Donovan yelled as Sampson started to reach for his shotgun and Prince tried to raise his pistol.

The buff dude in the body armor and black hood stepped into the space, shouldering an automatic rifle.

"Toss the gun, Prince!" he shouted. "And don't do it, Detective. I do not miss."

Prince slid the gun away. Sampson straightened up, raised his arms.

Outside, the shooting had all but stopped, but the symphony of sirens and bullhorns was building.

"You're surrounded," I said to the hooded man.

"That's fine," he said, his attention sweeping from me to Valentine, who was panting and heaving with pain, and then to Prince, who had taken off his belt and was shaking as he tried to wrap it around his upper thigh.

"Stop," the gunman said.

"I bleed. I feel it."

"Why would I care?" the man said.

He pulled off his hood. The Haitian gang leader stared in surprise and then open hatred at Guillermo Costa, disgraced Marine, former leader of Los Lobos, ex-con who'd supposedly learned his lesson and gone straight.

Costa said, "Who did that to my nephew Shay Mansion? Who strung him up like that?"

Prince shook his head. "I don't know what you're—"

Costa shot. Donovan jerked in her chair. The round pinged off the concrete next to the Haitian, who looked terrified as he raised his hands.

"Next one takes off your cojones," Costa said. "Who did that to Shay?"

Prince swallowed and gestured with his head toward his cousin. "Valentine. It was his idea. He saw it through."

"Wait!" Rodolpho screamed and put up his hands when Costa stepped his way, aiming at point-blank range.

"You killed my nephew and destroyed my cousin," Costa said. He shot Rodolpho dead and swung his attention and weapon back to Prince, who had gotten the belt around his upper thigh and was tightening it.

Costa nodded at us. "Tell them where the heroin is, Patrice. They'll find it anyway."

The Haitian frowned.

"Your cojones?"

Prince angrily gestured with his chin. "South side of the warehouse. The blue fifty-five-gallon drums marked 'Dust-Control Liquids.'"

"And the other kid?" Sampson said. "Tony Miller?"

The Haitian looked puzzled.

I said, "The kid who was tipping off our narcotics division about the location of your street sellers."

Sampson said, "The kid who was stabbed multiple times and tossed in the Potomac."

Prince hesitated as if considering his options, then relaxed and pointed at his cousin's corpse. "Valentine's idea too."

"I don't believe you," Costa growled. "And even if it was his idea, you damn sure brought in the heroin that killed Shay's father, my cousin's husband. In every way, the world will be a better place without you, Patrice."

Prince had a moment of panic, a moment to shrink from his fate. Costa showed no mercy and shot him in the heart, then stood there, watching impassively, as the Haitian gang leader slumped and died, his eyes dulling.

It had all unfolded so fast, I did not realize how deep into fight-or-flight I was until Costa dropped the clip on his rifle, cleared the bullet in the chamber, and put everything down on the floor. He stepped over Rodolpho's body and took a seat on a folding chair by Officer Donovan, who was bent over, weeping.

He looked at us. "Sorry about all this, Detectives. It had to happen. You just got in Costa's way."

Costa patted Donovan on the shoulder and said softly, "You're going to be okay, lady, whoever you are. Let's get you free."

CHAPTER

58

BY NINE TEN ON Monday evening, Gary Soneji had Bunny Maddox in the van, liquored up, doped up, and bound with duct tape. He was driving northeast by nine fifteen.

On an ordinary day, the trip from Richmond to the Pine Barrens might have taken him five hours, tops. But shortly after he got back on I-95 north heading toward the nation's capital, he heard on the radio that a massive three-way gunfight was going on between police and two warring gangs in Davidsonville, Maryland, and roadblocks were being set up there and on the Beltway to prevent participants from escaping.

To give the area a wide berth, Soneji drove for hours through thick fog, sticking to state highways and dark county roads. It was shortly before dawn when he finally reached his isolated cabin. He pulled the van forward to the mouth of an old logging road that wound toward the rear of his property and the boundary with the state forest.

When he got out, a cold wind gnawed at him. He went around the back and opened the van. Bunny Maddox lay on her side in the trash and the leaves, eyes closed, wrists, ankles, and mouth duct-taped.

He shook the bottom of one red Chuck Taylor sneaker.

Bunny's eyelids fluttered. She groaned, tried to sit up, but couldn't; she closed her eyes again, probably still high from the barbiturates and vodka he'd made her ingest before putting her in restraints.

"C'mon, Bunny," he said. "Time to wake up, my friend."

Bunny opened her eyes groggily and made confused whining noises when he pulled her toward him by the ankles. She shrank when he reached for the tape across her mouth.

"Do you want to be able to speak or not?" Soneji asked.

The stripper stared at him, still dazed, puzzled. Then she nodded, shivering.

Soneji slowly peeled the tape off her mouth.

"There now," he said. "Let's get you inside by a nice warm fire. Poor thing. Scooch forward a little more so I can undo your ankles."

He knew what he was doing. He'd read about how captives' minds could be turned, controlled even.

Bunny's teeth were starting to chatter when she slid toward him through the leaves and trash. He tore the tape from her ankles and wrists and supported her by the elbow when she tried to stand up.

"Easy," he said. "I think someone overserved you last night."

Soneji led her toward the cabin. Bunny blinked slowly, as if trying to remember something. As they neared the porch, she slurred, "Where are we?"

"My cabin," Soneji said. "I told you all about it, Bunny. You said you wanted to see it. Don't you remember?"

She shook her head, yawning, but continued to shuffle along as he led her up to the porch. "Tired."

"I'm sure you are," he said, fishing in his pocket for the key. He slid it in the lock, opened the door, and brought her inside. "But then again, I told you about this place more than two years ago. It's no wonder you forgot."

She looked bewildered as he brought her to a couch. It was then he took note of the sleek ring she wore on her left fourth finger, two small rectangular diamonds flanking a larger emerald-cut diamond in an unusual setting.

"You engaged, Bunny?" he asked after she plopped down on the couch.

"Yeah. Billy's at sea."

"Nice ring."

"Isn't it something? Billy says it's art deco style or something like that. Diamonds are real. Platinum is too. His grandmother got it made in the 1920s."

"Real nice," he said. "Billy a navy man, then?"

"No," she said, still sounding dazed. "Merchant marine. I gotta pee."

"Oh, of course," he said. He led her through the kitchen and out the back door to the outhouse. "I'll wait right here for you."

After a moment, she opened the door to the outhouse and went in. Soneji kept it spotless. He knew she'd approve.

But when she came back out a few minutes later, she gazed at him with eyes that were less confused than they'd been before.

"Why am I here?"

"You wanted to see my place," he said.

"No, you put a gun to my head in my driveway. You made me eat those pills and drink the rest of that bottle."

"A gun?" he said and managed a chuckle. "Me? Not a chance. And I *made* you? No, you gulped that down all on your own. But you must be hungry, Bunny. Thirsty."

He could tell she did not want to admit it, but she bobbed her head.

"Then let's go inside and cook you up some eggs and bacon and toast. Maybe a cup of coffee with a little hair of the dog in it?"

"God, yes," Bunny said and she let him lead her back inside. He sat her down in front of a Formica table in one of the two ladder-back chairs that still had intact wicker seats.

"Do I need to retape your ankles?" Soneji asked. "I mean, you're not going to try to run, are you?"

"With my knees?" Bunny said and snorted. "After ten years of field hockey and nine dancing on platforms? You don't have a cigarette by any chance, do you?"

"Your favorite kind, as a matter of fact," Soneji said.

He retrieved a fresh pack of Winston menthols from his jacket and a lighter from a drawer by the sink. He opened the pack and slid a cigarette and an ashtray to her across the table, past an antique snow globe. He came around and lit the cigarette, which she held with trembling fingers.

Bunny took a drag, then exhaled, and seemed to swoon a bit. She gestured at the metal and glass snow globe with her cigarette. "That for me too?"

Soneji smiled as he went to the refrigerator. "I remember you collected them."

He brought out bacon, eggs, and a package of ground coffee. "I'll get the coffee going first. You look like you could use some."

Bunny cocked her head, her eyes glassy but focused. "I remember you now."

"Do you?"

"Yeah. You're that brainiac guy who used to come to the club and have me dance. Gary, right?"

"I'm flattered you remembered," Soneji said, knowing that this changed things; sped up timelines, certainly. But he tried not to alter his tone of concern as he said, "How do you like your eggs?"

"Scrambled, like my brain," she said, and laughed. "You said something about hair of the dog?"

Soneji smiled. "Let me get a pot brewing and I'll show you what I've got on hand."

Bunny took another deep drag off the cigarette. "That what this is all about? You want me to dance for you in private, Gary?"

"Maybe a little later," he said, winking as he took the coffeepot off the stove and turned toward the sink to fill it.

Soneji heard her chair squeak and the hush of fabric rustling just before something heavy and hard smashed into the back of his head.

He lurched and heard glass shattering before his left cheek struck the counter edge. He landed on his back, his awareness swirling toward black.

CHAPTER

59

AS GARY SONEJI CAME around, he heard the rear screen door slam shut.

He forced himself over onto his hands and knees, cutting his palms on the shattered glass of the snow globe. More blood dripped from a gash on his left cheek.

His head was pounding, a sound like waves crashing.

"Help!" he heard Bunny scream outside. "Help me!"

The inner voice that had always guided Soneji returned with a vengeance. He'd been sloppy. He'd been an idiot to think he could control her with words alone.

And now all his plans and dreams were threatened.

Rage tried to seize him. But he'd already made too many mistakes to go off half-cocked. Not now. Not when his freedom and his future were at stake.

Soneji lurched to his feet, felt like he was going to vomit, but swallowed against it and went to the broom closet in the corner. He pulled out his uncle's old loaded .308, ran the bolt action on the rifle, and went outside onto the porch.

It was hunting season. No one would question hearing a shot or two this deep into the Pine Barrens.

"Please!" he heard Bunny shriek from the woods beyond the van. "Help me!"

Realizing she'd mistaken the old logging two-track for the drive out to the county road, Soneji went cold. He'd planned to play with Bunny for several days at least before things came to a head.

But he had no choice now. Feeling clearer, as he hurried past the van he reached up and felt the tender raised bruise where the glass globe had hit him.

"Help!" Bunny yelled, sounding farther away.

Soneji broke into a jog. He wasn't worried about her screams. She would have to go more than two miles before she'd cross another road, and it was another half mile beyond that to the nearest cabins, summer places on a small lake that were most likely closed up for winter.

It occurred to him that he could cut her off if he was willing to gamble. The two-track trail she was on headed northeast through the state forest for a mile then jogged back to the northwest another solid mile before meeting a gravel road.

He left the trail and bushwhacked through the woods straight north.

It began to drizzle as he dodged trees, jumped over logs, and forced his way through thorns and bracken. Every fifty yards he paused to listen, hearing Bunny off to his right, three, maybe four hundred yards out, still calling.

It made her easy to track and goaded him into an all-out sprint through stands of beech and scrub pine.

The drizzle became a steady rain, which deadened sound, including Bunny's calls for aid. Soneji was soaked when he finally reached the base of the forested ridge he'd been navigating toward. He didn't care. He'd rest and dry off later.

He charged up the back of the ridge, ignoring the cuts on his hands, grabbing saplings and brush to keep from falling into the slick dead leaves. None of it mattered.

He at last reached the rim of a forested bowl on the back of the ridge and looked down through the trees to where the two-track crossed a flat about one hundred and fifty yards below.

Soneji went over to a tree stump about three feet tall, lay the .308 across the top, hunched down, and practiced aiming through the gun's ancient peep sight. He kept both eyes open as he did, catching movement to his right, close to where the two-track left a pine thicket.

He lifted his head, looked to where he thought he'd seen the movement, and caught a flicker of motion, then another. Two deer had broken from the pines and were stiff-legging across his line of sight.

Bunny had to be pushing them ahead of her. He adjusted his position and pointed the gun toward the two-track where it exited the pines.

"Help!" Soneji heard her calling faintly over the drumming of the rain. "Please!"

He pushed the rifle's safety forward. He had no choice. He had to protect himself. Nothing else mattered.

And here was Bunny, running out from the pines, checking behind her a second, then forging on, looking anguished, wiping at the rain on her face.

There's nothing wrong with her knees, Soneji thought as he swung the .308 along with her stride. Cheek tight to the stock, head down, both eyes open, he kept pace with her, seeing the peep and the front bead in his right eye track across the back of her jean jacket, her left shoulder, the front of...

He squeezed the trigger.

The rifle barked. Bunny hunched and fell to her hands and knees.

Soneji sprinted down the hill through the trees to the two-track. Bunny was moaning, trying to crawl down the trail, still calling for help.

She glanced over her shoulder when she heard him coming and was instantly terrified. Seeing how close he was, she stopped crawling and began sobbing.

"Please, Gary! I never did anything to you! I'm engaged! I'm gonna be married. And I have a son! You remember, I have a little boy!"

"Face it, Bunny, you were never much of a mom," he said. "And you're not exactly marriage material. Plus you lied to me. You said you wouldn't run. Too bad. We could have had fun, you and me."

Before she could reply, he threw the .308 to his shoulder and shot her dead.

CHAPTER

60

STANDING INSIDE THE DOOR of our house around ten on Tuesday morning, Maria held Damon in her arms and peered up into my eyes. "After what you went through last night, Alex, why are you going in to work at all?"

I shrugged wearily, feeling a little daunted by the prospect myself.

"John and I are on temporary leave because we were in a gunfight and people died. We have to make statements, write reports, and explain what happened from our perspective before some other narrative can take over."

Maria didn't like it, but she nodded. "You'll be talking to someone? A counselor?"

"Only way I can go back on duty," I said. I kissed her forehead and then Damon's. He was sucking his thumb, a habit he'd gone back to after the terror of the shooting outside the church.

Maria hugged me tight. "When you're done making statements, will you please come get me at work? I've got enough overtime I can leave when I want."

"I promise," I said and kissed her again before leaving.

It was drizzling and I didn't feel like driving or taking the Metro, so I hailed a taxi on Independence Avenue. At headquarters, a phalanx of satellite trucks and reporters was already gathered in response to the gunfight in Davidsonville. I'd known it was going to be a zoo, so I'd told the driver to take me to the garage entrance.

I was under orders not to talk, and I understood why.

The story had made all the network morning shows and dominated the local papers and news programs, though they had few angles other than what chief of detectives George Pittman had fed them at an impromptu midnight press conference near the entrance to Patrice Prince's property. I had to admit that Pittman was a master of communication—he dispensed only the information he wanted them to have and locked down the rest.

As of now, all the media knew was that a gun battle had taken place between LMC 51 and Los Lobos Rojos and gone on to involve an interdepartmental law enforcement detail assigned to round up members of the Haitian gang for interrogation.

The media had also been informed that twenty-one men had died, eleven had been wounded, and seven others were in custody.

They did not know, however, that there had been an undercover officer trying to infiltrate the Haitian gang or that she had been taken hostage. And they had zero inkling of Guillermo Costa's vengeful motivation for the attack or of his role in Officer

Nancy Donovan's rescue—and mine and Sampson's, for that matter.

But that would change. These things would come out in court.

I knocked on Pittman's doorjamb, and he told me to come in. "Costa and the others arrested at the scene will be arraigned later this morning after their transfer to federal court," Chief Pittman said, tossing a pen on his desk in frustration.

"Why federal?"

"Because kidnapping Donovan and bringing her across state and District lines immediately makes it FBI," Pittman grumbled. "The nature and number of weapons involved brings in the ATF. And the gangs attract Immigration like flies. The feds have got their claws in this now. We're there to assist and nothing more. It's been taken out of our hands, even though *we* were the ones who decided to lean on LMC in the first place."

I could see it was gnawing at Pittman that he'd lost control of the investigation and the story of the battle. An event of this magnitude should have had him in front of the cameras for the next three news cycles at least.

He sighed. "At least Donovan's okay. They've got her at GW running tests, but other than the trauma of being held hostage, it seems like she's going to be okay. And you and Sampson are good. So, you know what? I'm good."

I realized that I'd been a bit cynical in my thinking about Pittman. The chief clearly liked the attention, but I could tell that he actually cared about us. I saw it in the way his eyes glazed with emotion as he swiveled to get a folder from the credenza behind him.

"There are a few things that are not entirely out of our hands, Chief," I said.

Pittman turned back. "Like what?"

"Even though it all came out under extreme duress, we now know that it was Patrice Prince and Valentine Rodolpho who killed Tony Miller and Shay Mansion, and we know why. The FBI can't and won't stop you from announcing that."

He brightened. "That's a very good idea."

I smiled. "I do have good ideas now and then."

Pittman studied me. "I was your biggest supporter and yet I still managed to underestimate you, Dr. Cross. And Detective Sampson."

It was the first time he'd called me Dr. Cross without a hint of sarcasm, and I nodded. "We aim to please, Chief."

"Go make your statements to the FBI and I'll let you know when we're going to talk to the mothers of Shay Mansion and Tony Miller. I want you and John there. You've both got three weeks paid leave coming your way until Internal Affairs and the department shrink say you're good to go, so enjoy yourself. You earned it."

CHAPTER 61

ON THURSDAY MORNING, WHEN Gary Soneji left the Dupont Circle Metro station and headed to Georgetown and his first day at Washington Day School, he still felt like he'd been beaten to a pulp.

He was relatively athletic, but he'd never had to drag a dead body through the woods for almost two miles. Soneji had dug graves in the past, of course, but it was tough digging in the sand and shale soil he'd encountered trying to bury Bunny Maddox near Joyce Adams's final resting place. The rain had made it worse, and so did his cut hands. It took him hours with a pick and shovel.

When the chore was finally done and he'd covered Bunny's grave with forest duff, he returned to the cabin, took a long, hot shower, dressed his wounds, and went to sleep. He'd woken up nearly fourteen hours later.

All day Wednesday, Soneji had been focused on where else he might have been sloppy, his inner voice goading him about everything he had to do to be clean and confident.

He returned to the ridge where he'd first shot at Bunny and retrieved his shell casing. He went back to Bunny's grave and threw more forest debris on it. He cleaned up the shards of the snow globe. He used bleach to wipe dried blood off the rifle stock and the shovel and the pick handles. He burned the clothes he'd been wearing.

Soneji had finally left the cabin late Wednesday afternoon in the white van. He looped to the interstate, dropped south, and, under cover of darkness, returned the van to the shed on Diggs's grandmother's farm and retrieved his black Saab.

Then, after driving to a motel in Takoma Park, Maryland, where he often stayed when he was in the DC area, he'd broken his rule about mixing drugs and alcohol. He drank seven shots of bourbon, took two Vicodin, and passed out cold.

But not before he'd set the alarm. When it whooped at him at five that morning, Soneji roused himself enough to stand under a cold shower until he could almost believe he was sober, then put on his frumpy teacher disguise.

Now, sipping black coffee and getting closer to Washington Day with every step, he felt almost normal enough to play the affable, nerdy Gary Soneji, math and computer science teacher.

Half a block shy of the school, he saw a pay phone and looked at his watch. He still had twenty minutes. He decided he'd better check in with Missy.

Soneji called collect. Missy answered on the fourth ring.

"Hey, Missy," Soneji said after she'd accepted the charges. "I know I've been a shit lately. But I just called to say I love you. And I love Roni."

There was a long silence on the other end. "Don't you think it's time you showed us, and the world, exactly how much you love us?"

He knew what she was referring to—the wedding—but he said, "Tell you what, I'll be home for dinner tomorrow. I'd like to give you something very special."

"Okay?"

"Missy," he said. "I guarantee it's going to make you happy."

"You're sure?"

"I am," he said. "Kiss Roni for me. I've got an early appointment. Love you."

After another pause, Missy said, "I love you too, Gary."

He hung up and hurried to the Washington Day campus, showed his ID to the security guard, and went to Bright Hall, where the computer lab occupied a large room on the third floor.

Heading up the stairs, Soneji felt blessed to be there. The school was wall to wall with scions of wealth, of power, of fame. From here, he could—

"Mr. Soneji?"

He pivoted to find the Washington Day headmaster, Charles Pendleton Little, coming up behind him, grinning. "Big day," the headmaster said, sticking out his hand.

Soneji's own hands were bandaged, but he took Little's hand and shook it loosely.

"What happened to you?" Little asked.

Soneji tried to act sheepish. "I went over the front of my mountain bike and cartwheeled a few times down a steep trail the day before yesterday."

Little's eyebrows went up. "Ouch."

"Tell me about it." He sighed. "Could've been worse. I was lucky."

"Yes, you were," Little said. "By the way, I wanted to let you know we have a new student joining our seventh-grade class today. Cheryl Lynn Wise. She's the daughter of the president's new chief of staff."

Soneji flashed on the Lindbergh kidnapping. *The daughter of the White House chief of staff. Well, that would certainly do it, wouldn't it? All the fame you could ever want for snatching someone like that, and she'll be right there in my class.*

"I very much look forward to welcoming Cheryl Lynn to Washington Day."

"Cheryl Lynn will be accompanied initially by our in-house U.S. Secret Service agent. Her name is Jezzie Flanagan."

Soneji had to force his enthusiasm this time. "Wonderful. I can't wait to meet Agent Flanagan as well."

CHAPTER 62

GARY SONEJI HAD SPENT the day getting to know his students at Washington Day, including dear Cheryl Lynn Wise, a little string bean of a girl, and Special Agent Jezzie Flanagan, a stunning blonde who was built like a swimmer and seemed to know everything about him already—everything he'd submitted to Headmaster Little, anyway.

He'd also gotten up to speed on Sandy Ravisky's lesson plans for the various grades that came to the computer lab. All in all, Soneji thought his first day had gone smashingly well, and he returned to the motel in Takoma Park with a bag of Chinese takeout feeling like a barracuda that's discovered a bay filled with yummy fish.

He spent Friday out of disguise, tending to his list of heating-oil clients and landing two new companies that wanted Atlantic

Heating as their bulk fuel supplier. That made his brother-in-law Marty very happy. He'd called him with the contract particulars before he drove home.

Soneji reached the Colonial gingerbread house just as it was getting dark. He went inside carrying his suitcase and a stuffed bunny for Roni.

I can play Fun Daddy, he thought as he scooped his daughter up and gave her the toy along with a dozen loud cheek kisses that made Roni laugh with delight. Missy watched from the kitchen, her arms folded, her expression fixed.

"I have to give Mommy something too," he told Roni loudly. He kissed her again, returned to the Saab, and retrieved a bouquet of roses, a bottle of champagne, and a box of Missy's favorite dark chocolates.

"What's going on here?" his wife said suspiciously when Soneji came through the door with the presents. "It's not Valentine's Day."

"Every day's Valentine's Day when you're in love with a beautiful woman," Soneji said. He kissed Missy and gave her the flowers.

She took them but still regarded him warily. "What's come over you, Gary Murphy?"

He shrugged and set the chocolates and the champagne on the counter. "I've had time to think about things the past couple of days on the road. I guess it finally dawned on me just how good I have it. With my job. With Roni. And, mostly, with you. I'm sorry if I haven't been too pleasant to be around while I've been figuring all this out."

Missy squinted. "Yeah, it hasn't been pleasant, Gary."

"I know," he said, holding his still-bandaged palms out toward her. "And I promise I'll make it up to you. Later, after Roni's gone to bed. In the meantime, I'm going to play with my daughter and read her a story or two before dinner."

His wife finally softened a little. "That would be nice. She'd like that."

"And if the weather holds, maybe tomorrow we can all go for a hike in that park you're always trying to get me to go to. Maybe catch the last of the fall foliage."

"That would be nice too," she said, softening a little more. "I'll finish dinner."

For the first time in a long while, Soneji was as good as his word. He got down on his hands and knees and played with Roni while telling her the story of the Magic Kingdom of Miss Bunny Maddox, a fantastical tale of a rabbit and a unicorn. It mesmerized his daughter even more than the two Dr. Seuss books he read to her before they were both called to the table.

Missy had made a nice meal of salmon, little red potatoes, and Caesar salad. It really was great, and he made sure to say so multiple times. Soneji insisted on doing the dishes, giving Roni her bath, and reading one more book to her after she was tucked in her little bed.

"Good night, Daddy," Roni said. "I love you."

Her eyes were glistening. To his surprise, it touched him a little. "I love you too, little girl." He kissed her on the cheek, got up, and turned to find Missy standing in the doorway, tears welling in her eyes as well.

"Good night, Mommy," Roni said.

His wife went to their daughter and kissed her good night. When they were out in the hallway with the door shut, Missy said in a voice hoarse with emotion, "Thank you for that."

"What?"

Tears streamed down her cheeks. "All of it. Everything she's been missing."

"And you've been missing," Soneji said, wiping a tear off her cheek. "Now, come along, Miss Missy. I've got champagne and one more special present that I think is going to be an answer to all your prayers."

Soneji had Missy sit in her favorite chair in the family room while he popped the champagne and poured them each a glass. He brought the flutes out and handed one to her. "A toast," he said, raising his glass.

"What are we toasting?" Missy asked.

"A new beginning," he said. "A restart."

Then he put his glass on the table beside her, fished in his pocket, and pulled out a ring box. He went down on one knee and opened the box to reveal a beautiful, sleek, art deco–style ring with two small rectangular diamonds flanking a larger emerald-cut diamond. Missy gasped.

"You always said you wanted a real engagement ring," Soneji said. "So when I saw this unusual ring at a shop down in Virginia, I thought, *Now,* this *is a ring gorgeous enough for my bride to wear as long as we both shall live.*"

"Oh, Gary," Missy said, tearing up again.

"Wait, I'm not done yet," he said, grinning at her. "I've been practicing. Missy Kasajian Murphy, will you do me the honor of marrying me again and having a real proper wedding and reception this time?"

"Oh my God, yes," she cried. She broke down sobbing when he slipped the ring on her finger. It fit perfectly.

Later, after they'd finished the champagne and made love with more passion than they had in years, Missy admired her ring. "Wherever did you find this?" she asked.

"A guy who deals in fine estate jewelry down in Roanoke, Virginia," Soneji said. "That's art deco style from the 1920s and evidently someone's grandmother had it commissioned."

CHAPTER 63

THREE WEEKS PASSED QUICKLY, and we were in mid-November.

After I'd made my statements about the firefight at Prince's warehouse, John Sampson, Chief Pittman, and I visited Rosalina Mansion and then Maxine Miller to announce that we'd solved the murders of their sons. Both moms thanked us, though they admitted that the knowledge was bittersweet. Knowing what happened helped, but it didn't undo the pain or bring their children back.

In the spirit of realizing that life was short, I convinced Maria to take a few days off for a mini-vacation before we got too close to our second child's due date. She, Damon, and I headed south in the old Mercedes diesel I'd bought before graduate school. It had almost a hundred thousand miles on it, but I figured I could get at least a hundred thousand more from it.

We made it to Roanoke Rapids, North Carolina, before we stopped at a Motel Six. The next day we drove all the way to Savannah before we called it quits for the day.

Damon was fussy after spending so many hours in the car, and Maria was complaining as well. I wondered whether this had been a good idea.

"We wanted some warm weather," I reminded Maria. "And your doc said you can't fly."

"I know," she said, holding her back. "I guess I didn't think it through. And the way the baby's kicking, we've got an athlete or something. Mark my words."

"We can head back if it's too much."

"That's worse than going forward. We can't be far from real heat."

We weren't. Temperatures were in the eighties in Jacksonville. We rented a room at a motel near the beach and spent a couple of days staring at the ocean and playing with Damon.

He and I built sandcastles and played in the little waves, which he loved. Maria spent hours floating on her back in the water because she said it was the only time she got any relief. Floating made her feel weightless. Even the baby seemed to love it. Maria said the incessant kicking had stopped.

When mom and toddler napped in the shade of an umbrella, I stared at the ocean, still conflicted over Guillermo Costa.

I knew he was a killer. I'd watched him kill two men in cold blood. However, neither Sampson nor Donovan nor I would be alive now if Costa had not intervened, extracted confessions from the guilty, and exacted his revenge. And Prince's heroin trade would probably still be flourishing.

I'd made several statements to that effect to FBI special agent Mark Lane, the man who was overseeing the investigation into the gun battle. So had Sampson. Evidently, so had Officer Donovan, though we had not seen her since that bloody night. Still, we had no idea if a judge and jury would find enough mitigating factors in Costa's rescue of Donovan and mercy toward us to prevent him from going to jail for the rest of his life.

During the day, I paid little attention to my memories of that night. But twice I had crazed dreams reliving Costa's execution of Rodolpho and Prince and woke up sweating hard and shaking from the experience.

I knew—and the department psychologist I saw after we'd returned home confirmed—that nightmares were common after someone endured such a traumatic event. Other than the dreams, I told the psychologist, I felt at peace with what had happened, and after my twenty-one days of forced leave were over, she approved my return to duty.

I admitted to no one except Maria and Sampson that I didn't really know how I would handle a situation like that again.

"I understand," Sampson said as we headed back to work after three weeks. "I do. But that's where training comes in, Alex. The department has advanced courses where you're exposed to all kinds of scenarios with a weapon in your hand. It's amazing how quickly you get better at assessing situations and responding correctly."

"You mean not shooting innocent civilians," I said.

"Among other things."

"Would you have shot Costa if you'd had a chance? To save Rodolpho or Prince, I mean."

"I don't know," Sampson said. "They meant to kill us, Alex. And Donovan."

"I know. I really do. I guess I'm just confused as to how to think about Costa."

Sampson shrugged. "I think of him as a guy who made some bad choices in his past but tried to live the right way. And who was willing to sacrifice his own freedom to avenge his nephew's murder and end the Haitian heroin trade."

"But—"

"Think about it, Alex," Sampson said. "Costa could easily have decided to kill us too, so there would be no witnesses. Instead, he surrendered. His job was done. I'll never say this in court, but I admire the guy in a Dirty Harry kind of way."

"Maybe," I said as we arrived at headquarters. I didn't know exactly how to feel about it. We knew who'd killed the two boys, and we knew why. But the killers had received vigilante justice, and I remained conflicted about that.

To our surprise, when we entered the squad room, Detectives Diehl and Kurtz rose and began clapping. Chief Pittman came in and joined them. Soon the entire room of detectives was clapping.

For the first time, I felt fully accepted as a member of that elite investigative team, and I was deeply humbled.

CHAPTER 64

"WELCOME BACK," CHIEF PITTMAN said when the applause died down. He shook our hands and gestured to the stacks of reports that had accumulated in our absence. "Pick up your open cases for now. Miller and Mansion are officially closed."

I sat down at my desk and considered the pile of documents. I began to sort through the reports and quickly found forensics results from both of the Bulldog murder scenes and a copy of an extensive Fairfax County Sheriff's Office report on the Brenda Miles crime scene, all of which had come in over the past few days. I set these aside for deeper study and forged on, looking over various leads and tips.

Several pertained to the now-closed Miller and Mansion cases. I scanned them but saw nothing to change my understanding of those murders. Halfway through the stack, I found a note from eight days ago asking me to call Kelsey Girard, a detective with the sheriff's office in Goochland County, Virginia.

Subject: POSSIBLE KIDNAPPING/OLDER WHITE VAN.

I quickly picked up the phone and punched in the number.

A pleasant Southern voice answered on the fourth ring. "This is Detective Girard."

I identified myself and apologized for not calling her back sooner. Girard said, "I've been reading all about you, Detective, and I know why you haven't returned my call."

"Just got back today," I confirmed. "So, you had an older white van involved in a suspected kidnapping?"

"Correct," she said. "A white van was seen in the vicinity of what we are investigating as a possible kidnapping down here. When I did some research, I came across notices of a similar white van suspected of belonging to your Berkowitz copycat, so I called you."

I started taking notes fast as Girard laid out the story of her case. Within five minutes, I'd heard enough to want to know more.

"Can my partner and I drive down and visit the scene?" I asked. "Talk to the witness about what he saw?"

"I guess that would be okay," the detective said after a moment. "When would you like to come?"

"We can be there in two and a half hours, tops."

"That works," she said. "I'll give you the address and meet you there."

CHAPTER

65

DETECTIVE KELSEY GIRARD OF the Goochland County Sheriff's Office was sitting on the hood of an unmarked squad car looking at the contents of a manila file when John Sampson and I pulled up on the gravel road off State Route 634.

Even in mid-November the vegetation on both sides of the road was so dense, we didn't see the driveway snaking off until we were almost blocking its entrance.

"You might want to back your vehicle up twenty or thirty yards so I can better explain what all was found and not found," said Girard, a lanky Black woman in her early forties.

Sampson backed up our car, and we got out and walked over to her. "Where was the van seen?" Sampson asked.

"All in due time," she said.

"What about the witness?"

"In due time for him too," she said, closing the file, hopping off the hood, and reaching out to shake our hands.

The sheriff's detective opened her file to show us photos taken from different angles and at different times of day, all featuring an older model Ford Galaxie in front of a farm gate. She said the vehicle belonged to thirty-three-year-old Elizabeth "Bunny" Maddox, a stripper with a minor rap sheet and a long history of alcohol and drug abuse.

"Bunny, I have been told, has always been something of a wounded soul who cannot cope with life," Girard said. "She had her kid taken away from her a few times because of it. He's currently living down in Florida with her mom. Bunny lives up the drive there with her brother Calvin and a cousin of theirs named William Mars. Maddox and Mars are both carpenters. Clean sheets. No history with the police. And they both say that Bunny has been mostly clean since getting together with a merchant mariner named Billy Gallivan."

Sampson said, "I sense a twist coming."

She tensed a little. "Yeah, so, anyway, Calvin calls the sheriff's office and says he's not sure if his sister Bunny 'has been kidnapped or just gone off the wagon with another guy who had cocaine.' That's a direct quote."

"So?" I said.

"So we did not pay it much attention for about three days because Calvin was high and shitfaced at the time and admitted on the first call that prior to her engagement, Bunny had been known to occasionally disappear on benders with guys she'd just met," Girard said. "But then Calvin calls back three days later, stone sober, and says Bunny has now missed two ship-to-shore calls from Billy and another with the social services worker monitoring her custody case. He said his sister lived for Billy's calls and that, drunk or high, she would never miss a call that involved her son, and now she had missed both."

Girard said she'd finally driven out to meet Calvin. By that time he'd moved the Galaxie because he and his cousin needed to use the drive.

But Bunny's brother had thought ahead enough to take photographs on the night of his sister's disappearance and again the following morning.

"What about the van?" Sampson asked as an older maroon Dodge pickup in need of a muffler job came around the corner from the south.

"I'll let Calvin tell you himself."

The truck rolled to a stop and the engine was mercifully silenced. Calvin Maddox, a lean, rawboned man in his thirties, climbed out. He had sawdust on his Carhartt pants and denim shirt, and his hands were calloused and strong when he shook ours.

"Wish you all had come out when I said to in the first place," Maddox said, taking a step to one side and spitting out the chew he had in his cheek.

"We went over this, Mr. Maddox," Detective Girard warned.

"Yeah, yeah, I know it didn't seem high priority or nothing. Bunny's only a stripper, an unfit mother, and an addict. No priority there. No humans involved."

The detective said, "We're here, Calvin. I've been here ever since Bunny missed her custody call."

"Yeah, but not for three days," he said, staring at the ground. "Anyway, what do you all want to know now?"

I said, "You saw the van?"

Calvin nodded, gestured north toward a rise in the gravel road. "Over the knob there, just as it was pulling out."

"Start at the beginning," Detective Girard said softly.

Maddox still wouldn't look at her, but he told us how his sister had pretty much quit cocaine after her last rehab. She usually left her shift at the strip club, headed for a liquor store, bought food for dinner, and came home. The night of her disappearance, she'd called him right before leaving work to ask if he wanted her to pick up ham or chicken for dinner.

"She usually comes straight on in from there," Maddox said. "She was still drinking, but trying to keep it under control, and she didn't want to be driving, you know?"

We shrugged.

Bunny's brother went on. "Anyway, I was watching the Monday night football game with our cousin and noticed Bunny wasn't back yet. I went out on the porch and saw there were headlights shining up the drive and then there weren't."

He had grabbed a beer and walked down the drive in the rain. He saw Bunny's car in front of the gate. But the gate was closed, which was strange, because he knew he had left it open ninety minutes earlier when he'd returned from work.

He'd walked over and looked in through the Galaxie's window and seen Bunny's purse and groceries, and the keys were in the ignition.

"That's when I heard an engine idling over the knob there," Maddox said, walking in that direction. We followed him until he stopped at the crest of the rise.

He pointed sixty yards downhill to the lowest spot before the next rise. "Old, banged-up white van was down there, parked just off the road on the shoulder. I don't know if the driver saw me or what, but when I started to jog down the hill, the van pulled out and drove off fast, spitting gravel."

Sampson said, "You see the license plate?"

"Nope. But my old game-trap camera up the road did."

"Game-trap camera?" Detective Girard said angrily. "You didn't tell me that, Calvin."

"Honestly, I didn't think to look till just last night 'cause I thought the batteries in it were dead. I went to put new ones in last evening and there was a full roll of used film. But because the batteries were low, the camera triggered on a delay and caught only the back end of the van at a weird angle. Pennsylvania plate, beginning *TN*."

CHAPTER

66

CALVIN MADDOX WENT TO his truck and retrieved a print of the image his game camera had taken. It was slightly blurry due to the weak batteries and the speed of the van and showed only the left rear quarter of the vehicle, including part of a Pennsylvania plate with the letters *TN*.

But we also had decent images of two large scrapes on the left rear quarter panel and a serious dent on the back bumper, enough that we felt sure we'd be able to identify the van if we came upon it, even if there was no damage to the front left headlight. Bunny's brother had to return to his job but said he was working only a couple of miles away if we needed him.

We planned to request a search of Pennsylvania DMV records for an older white Ford Econoline panel van with a license plate that began with *TN* as soon as we returned to our offices. But first, Sampson, Detective Girard, and I looked at the printed photographs Maddox had taken shortly after his sister disappeared. The photographs were glary and showed raindrops beaded on Bunny's Galaxie and clinging to the grass and the walls of kudzu growing on either side of the drive.

In the daylight shots, the rain had dried, but we could see where some of the grass and weeds in the little ditches along the drive were pressed down. I walked over and looked at the ditch, then held up one of the pictures taken at night.

"See how the grass is different here, darker?" I said. "I think someone walked up the ditch that night."

"Why?" Sampson said.

"My guess? To shut the gate. To stop Bunny."

Detective Girard said, "And get her out of the car."

"So he could get her into his van"—Sampson continued the thought.

"Definitely," I said. "Which means this was an ambush. Which means he hid somewhere, waiting for her."

"Which means he knew her," Girard said.

"Knew her habits, anyway," I said.

Sampson gestured to trees across the road. "I'm betting he hid over there so he could come up behind her."

"Check it out," I said. I asked Girard for the night and day pictures Calvin had shot. She found them and laid them on the hood of her car. He'd stood a couple of feet away from the Galaxie with his lens aimed from the front right bumper diagonally across the vehicle to the left rear quarter panel. I didn't know what I was looking for at first, but then Girard pointed at the night picture, beyond the brilliant reflection of the camera flash showing on the Galaxie's windshield, to the wall of kudzu on the other side of the car. "What's this shadow here?"

I squinted to better see what she was showing me. I could kind of make it out, but I could not see it at all in the daylight shot.

Girard returned to her car and came out with a large magnifying glass she said her partner gave to her when he retired.

"It comes in handier than you'd expect," she said and began poring over the nighttime picture. "You can see part of Calvin's reflection on the windshield along with the flash, and there's that big shadow. You look."

I took the magnifying glass from her and studied the area she was pointing to.

"Definitely looks darker, and there are no raindrops on a lot of the leaves and vines," I said, shifting the magnifying glass to the same spot in the picture shot the morning after Bunny disappeared. "Okay, now. Look at that. Good call, Detective."

Sampson walked over. "What call?"

I handed him the magnifying glass and pointed at the kudzu beyond the Galaxie in the daylight photograph. "There are snapped branches and vines and places where the vegetation has been pressed back."

"If he hid there," Girard said, "he would have been right on top of her when she got out of the car."

"Or just in front of her," Sampson said, nodding. "Either way, she gets out of the car, shuts the door, takes a few steps, and he's right there."

I took the daytime photograph and walked down the drive toward the open gate with Sampson and Girard following until I found the spot where Calvin Maddox had taken the photographs. We all agreed on the angle, then walked the fifteen feet or so to the thick wall of greenery there teeming with new growth even in mid-November.

The sheriff's detective peered in. "Kudzu grows so fast, I don't know if we'll…" she began. "Wait, there's one of those broken vines, right there. And here's a couple more."

"I see them," Sampson said.

I said, "He could easily have been standing right there, hidden."

"Depending on how he was dressed, she wouldn't have been able to see him before he grabbed her," Girard said. "Hold on, I'm going to photograph this." She hurried back to her car.

Sampson pulled out a mini-flashlight and shone it into the foliage, low behind the broken branches and vines where we believed the kidnapper had stood.

The Goochland County detective came back carrying a Nikon camera with a big flash attachment and a tape measure. John was inspecting the vegetation at roughly waist height when he said, "I got something here. Reddish."

Girard took out her own flashlight and trained it where Sampson had his focused. "Looks like fabric got caught up on the thorns there." She methodically photographed the broken vines and crushed plants using the tape measure to give scale and perspective to the pictures. Each time she moved something, she took another photograph to ensure that the recovery would be well documented.

"Probably won't be admissible because so much time has passed since Bunny disappeared, but it's still good to try," she said. "Wish I'd picked up on it sooner."

About ten minutes later, Sampson and I held back the foliage as Girard reached in with a long pair of tweezers. She got hold of the fabric and gently pulled it from the thorns.

The detective held it up for us. "Looks like flannel. Old, faded flannel."

Sampson said, "Like maybe his shirt got hung up in there on the thorns while he was hiding, waiting for Bunny, and it tore when he stepped out."

I grinned as Girard slipped the fabric into a plastic sleeve.

John said, "You're suddenly the happy guy, Alex."

"I am the happy guy," I said. "I think our perp has made a real mistake for the first time since we started chasing him."

CHAPTER 67

DETECTIVE KELSEY GIRARD HAD to leave for a court appearance in Richmond that afternoon, but she left us with a promise to keep in close touch, and we all shared the certainty that the kidnapper had screwed up.

Before returning to DC, Sampson and I decided to track Bunny Maddox's known whereabouts backward from the time her brother saw her car lights.

At the Winn-Dixie, where she'd bought fried chicken and potato salad for dinner, we were able to review security footage from the night of her disappearance. We picked the stripper up on both interior and parking-lot security cams.

We also spotted a white van enter the far end of the supermarket lot and park in the shadows several minutes before Bunny's arrival and leave eight minutes before she did. We couldn't know if this was the same white van, but it seemed likely.

"More than enough time for him to set up his ambush," Sampson said, "if he knew where Bunny was going. And he sure does seem to anticipate her routine."

"But still no good look at the driver or the license plate," I said.

"Yeah, but we can have stills from this blown up. The more we can say about the exterior of that van, the more likely we are to match it."

"True that," I said, and thanked the guard who'd given us access to the footage.

We were also able to review the feeds from the security cameras outside the Virginia state liquor store and Tillie's, the bar where Bunny danced.

An exterior liquor-store camera facing the parking lot and the highway picked up a white van passing slowly as the stripper exited her vehicle and then rolling out of frame without giving a clear view of the driver or the plates.

At the strip club, a camera facing diagonally across the parking lot to the road picked up Bunny Maddox leaving work the day of her disappearance and heading north toward the liquor store roughly two miles away; a white van pulled out of an overflow lot across the street and followed her.

We got lucky. The camera caught the van just as the headlights of a pickup truck coming from the south lit it up from behind for several seconds.

"Definitely Pennsylvania plates," Sampson said. "And that third letter is a *Z* or an *S*."

I nodded, feeling like we were breaking through. "Definitely *TNZ* or *TNS*. And then maybe a three or an eight after it?"

"We're going to get this guy now," John said, grinning as we left the club with the security footage.

"I feel like it's only a matter of time."

"So do I. But let's try to speed things up."

Before we drove back to DC, Sampson called Tommy French, an old army buddy of his who was now an investigator for the Pennsylvania police.

"Can you have someone run a Pennsylvania license plate search for us?" Sampson asked after greeting his friend.

"Sure, what do you got, John?" French said.

"Pennsylvania *TNZ* or *TNS* and either a three or an eight after it. That's all we can see."

"Vehicle make and color?"

"White Ford Econoline van. Older. Rough shape."

"And urgency?"

"We think the driver may have killed four people, attempted to murder another two, and potentially kidnapped or killed a seventh."

"I'll see what our records team can find and get back to you," French said, and hung up.

CHAPTER 68

GARY SONEJI SMILED AND nodded to many of the students in his seventh- and eighth-grade computer science class as they filed into his room for the last course of the day. But he intentionally avoided eye contact with young Cheryl Lynn Wise when she entered and walked to her seat.

Not that Cheryl Lynn paid much attention to Soneji anyway, and that's how he liked it. Especially when Secret Service agent Jezzie Flanagan was around, as she was that day.

Tall, fit, late twenties, attractive but with an imposing presence, Agent Flanagan had paid more attention to Soneji than he wanted. But at least she had stopped sitting in the back of his classroom whenever Cheryl Lynn was there, scrutinizing his every move.

Flanagan actually stopped in the hall outside his doorway that afternoon, let Cheryl Lynn enter, and then motioned to him. Soneji strolled over without hesitation and greeted her politely.

"Agent Flanagan," he said. "Nice to see you."

"You as well, Mr. Soneji," Flanagan said quietly. "What's the initial report on Cheryl? Her dad asked."

"Academically? Cheryl Lynn is very bright and seems to fully grasp the binary system underlying computer coding."

"Starting to fit in?"

"She strikes me as a little shy, but yes."

"She'll come out of her shell eventually. It will help that a friend of hers is transferring here next week."

"I heard that," Soneji said. "You'll be overseeing her security as well?"

"Her grandma's a sitting cabinet member," Flanagan said.

"That will do it."

At first, he had not understood exactly why a Secret Service agent was in the school. But Flanagan had explained that so many children of politicians attended Washington Day, an interdepartmental decision had been made several years before to put the Secret Service in charge of overall security. Flanagan and two other agents rotated in and out of the school on a monthly basis.

"I'll let you know how she's doing every week?" Soneji asked.

"I think her dad would like that. See you at the end of the day."

He forced a smile. "Enjoy your coffee, Agent Flanagan."

"Believe me, I will," Flanagan said, and strode away.

Soneji walked back into his class. An inner voice told him that he was flirting with disaster, being this close to a Secret Service agent. So far, though, Flanagan seemed unaware of his dark side.

Then again, he had done everything he could think of to keep the lives of Gary Soneji and Gary Murphy separate. He flashed on an image of Missy admiring Bunny Maddox's engagement ring and felt perverse pleasure. The memory of Bunny bound and drugged in the back of the van made him yearn to do it again.

He allowed himself a glance at Cheryl Lynn, who was chatting with a girl across the aisle. She was right there. And she was famous. Her father was, anyway.

Before the fantasy of taking the daughter of the White House chief of staff to the Pine Barrens could completely seize his attention, the interior warning voice told Soneji to slow down, that his cover needed to be deeper and broader before he took that kind of risk.

For a second, Soneji was confused as to how to deepen and strengthen his cover. And then he wasn't. He just needed time and patience and a—

"Mr. Soneji?" one of his students called. "Are you okay?"

Soneji realized many of his students were watching him.

"Just thinking about a dear friend of mine," he said, and laughed as he picked up a stick of chalk and turned to the blackboard. "Let's continue with another look at how an operating system works."

CHAPTER 69

TEN DAYS LATER, THE Tuesday before Thanksgiving, Sampson and I finally got a return call from Pennsylvania police detective Tommy French.

We were at our desks, and John put the call on speaker. "Anything good, Tommy?"

"I asked folks in the DMV in every county in the commonwealth to look in their files for Pennsylvania plates beginning with *TNZ* or *TNS*," French said. "Right now we've got forty-two with the *Z* and one hundred and seventeen with the *S*. We have nine that have a three behind both variations and sixty plates that have an eight. Not one of them is registered to an older white Ford Econoline van."

"So it sounds like the plates were stolen," I said, feeling one of our leads dying.

"I thought of that," French said. "And I had them all cross-reference plates reported as stolen with my list. Struck out again."

Sampson said, "Is it possible that the plates aren't stolen? That maybe he's taking them off one vehicle and putting them on the van when he's using it?"

"Very possible," French said.

We thanked the detective and went in to update Chief Pittman about our trip south last week and the video clips of the white van present at the sites of multiple crimes in the DC and Richmond area. We also told him about the issue with the plates.

The chief thought about that for several moments before saying, "Call French back. Ask him if it's possible to search expired plates with those letters against old registrations."

"See if a white van pops up," I said. "Can't hurt."

Sampson nodded. "I suppose if we're theorizing that he'd be willing to steal plates and drive around, why wouldn't he also be willing to use expired plates?"

Pittman said, "No one would even know as long as he slapped on an up-to-date expiration sticker."

It was nearly six in the evening, but Sampson tried French again and got him just before he was about to leave.

When we told him Chief Pittman's idea, the detective balked. "I'll ask, but I wouldn't count on this happening quickly."

I said, "We've got a lot of bodies down here, Tommy."

"As long as it happens eventually, we're good," Sampson said.

He sighed. "Where should I begin?"

"Start ten years ago and work your way back."

French wasn't exactly thrilled, but he agreed to make the request in the morning.

When I reached home, I found Maria and Damon on the

couch watching TV. My son had his head on his mom's lap but shot upright when he saw me.

"The baby kicks, Daddy!" Damon said. "The baby kicks!"

Maria started laughing. "That's all this baby does these days."

"Like you said, maybe it's a sign we're gonna have a little athlete. A soccer star or maybe a runner," I said, going to embrace them both.

"A marathoner, at this rate." My wife kissed me and then groaned and rubbed at her side. "My lower ribs are all sore."

Damon frowned. "Mommy hurt boo-boo?"

She smiled at him. "Mommy a little hurt boo-boo, D-man."

He put his hand on her belly and leaned in close, still frowning, very serious. "Stop that, baby. No kicks. No hurt Mommy little boo-boo."

For some reason, Maria and I both found that hilarious, and we laughed until we had tears coming down our faces.

"I love being that little boy's mom," she said later after Damon had gone down for the night and we'd laughed again about him lecturing his little sibling in utero.

"I love being his dad," I said. "And your husband."

"Aww," Maria said, and kissed me. The baby kicked again.

"Wow, even I felt that," I said.

"Baby wants out," Maria said. "I predict this little one will be coming any day."

PART FIVE
Deeper Cover and Renewal

CHAPTER

70

CLASSES AT WASHINGTON DAY School formally ended at noon on the Tuesday before Thanksgiving.

Getting in his Saab, Gary Soneji felt grateful to be leaving the city and heading north before the traffic that would snarl the highways up and down the East Coast in the next twenty-four hours started. He'd packed last night and put his things in the trunk this morning. The short academic day meant Soneji had not had a chance to see Cheryl Lynn Wise before the vacation. But that was fine.

If he got too close too soon, he'd risk suspicion, and his interest in the chief of staff's daughter might swell to uncontrollable obsession.

This was for the best. He had five free days now to not only widen his cover but thicken it to the point he'd be all but invisible to the police.

He drove north on I-95 until he reached an exit he'd circled on his map, near the Maryland-Delaware line. He drove east and then across the border, looking for the address of an abandoned farm he'd found in a real estate listing.

His experience with Bunny had made him realize how fortunate he was to have the cabin in the Pine Barrens. It had also made him aware of his remote property's rareness and fragility. He could not make it a constant center of his quiet activities.

He had to use it as a frugal man might a treasure.

And Diggs's grandmother's place was out of the question. Soneji planned never to set foot on that property again. Which meant he needed a new place, one he could explore and develop before he welcomed dear Cheryl Lynn or whoever it was he decided to snatch.

When he arrived at the farm from the listing, however, he dismissed it as a possibility, given the property's open nature. He wanted no view of the house or barns from any road or hillside.

Over the next two hours, he drove to two more farms for sale. The first one, also in Delaware, was another disappointment. The second was in New Jersey, fifteen miles north of the border. Instead of heading east toward his place in the Pine Barrens, Soneji went west in search of the elusive, secluded, and abandoned farm of his fantasies.

At first glance, the third property seemed the perfect spot: one hundred and sixty acres, forty of it overgrown CRP fields, none of it tilled in three years. And the farmhouse, barn, and yard were all well shielded from the road.

Driving by the entrance to the property, he got a glimpse of the yellow farmhouse far down a lane flanked on both sides by mature ornamental spruce trees. He also saw a FOR SALE sign with a real estate agent's picture, name, and number.

That alone made Soneji nervous. When he swung the Saab around and drove past the property again, his instincts were confirmed and then amplified.

A maroon Chevy Blazer came down the road toward him, slowed, and turned into the drive. A magnetic sign advertising the same real estate agent clung to the driver's-side door.

Soneji considered following the car and asking to see the place, but that would be sloppy. Besides, the agent at the wheel was a big guy. And there was a client in the passenger seat.

Too risky. He went back toward the interstate, telling himself that he had to be patient. He would find the right place. He flat-out knew it.

By the time he reached his home in Wilmington, dusk was falling. Roni greeted him at the door. He swept her up in his arms and tickled and kissed her.

"Daddy home!" she cried and ran into the kitchen. "Mama, Daddy home! Gamma, Daddy home!"

Soneji followed his daughter, chuckling. She really was a ball of energy.

He went inside and found Missy, her sister, Trish, and his mother-in-law, Christiana, sitting at the kitchen table with several large open three-ring binders between them. Trish had three kids of her own under five and looked like she could use a nap. As always, Missy's mother was very polished and put together.

"Trish," Soneji said. "Get some sleep."

"In about five years," Missy's sister said.

"Christiana," Soneji said to his mother-in-law. "I love the new hairdo and nails. How are things?"

Christiana smiled at him, but it felt forced. He wondered how much Missy confided in her mother and sister and started to feel as if he were being closely observed. He hated that.

He and Christiana had not gotten off to a good start. But after her husband died and she saw just how much business he was bringing into the Atlantic Heating Company, she'd warmed to him. Somewhat.

"Gary," his mother-in-law said, nodding. "We are as good as we can be with five weeks to plan a wedding reception."

"Five weeks?" he said, taken aback. He'd figured the following summer at the earliest.

"Christmas Eve, hon," Missy said.

"You want to get married on Christmas Eve?"

"Perfect timing," Trish said. "Everyone's in a great mood, ready to party."

"And it's the only time of year my entire family is guaranteed to be in the area," Missy said, looking at him hopefully.

"And just as important," Christiana said, "my brother, Missy's uncle Ari, has a barn he rents out for events. It's available on Christmas Eve and he's agreed to let us have it."

"It's decided," Trish said, nodding.

Very close to the top of all things Soneji most despised was being at the whim of others, being under someone else's thumb. It was bad when men forced him into things. It was worse when women told him what to do or made decisions about his life.

He felt anger building like lava in his brain and he had to summon every bit of control not to blow his top.

"Christmas Eve it is, then," Soneji said finally and made himself grin as he picked up his daughter. "We'll have a grand old time, and Roni will be our flower girl, and Missy will make me the luckiest man alive a second time."

CHAPTER 71

THE AFTERNOON BEFORE THANKSGIVING, after more than a week of failing to get another line on the killer in the white van, Pennsylvania state police detective Tommy French called me. His friends at the DMV had compiled the results of the search Chief Pittman requested.

"They got a hit on an old registration," French said. "A 1977 White Ford Econoline van, license plate TNS eight five four. It was last registered to a Michael and LeeAnne Lawton of Oxford, Pennsylvania. Both are now deceased. I'll fax you the VIN and the address. You'll have to take it from there. I'm headed home to my family for the holiday."

"We're right behind you, Tommy," I said. "And we owe you."

"Maybe," the detective said. "You might want to check land records in Chester County, see who owns the Lawtons' place now."

I called the Chester County Recorder's office after we hung up but got a message saying they were closed for the holiday and wouldn't reopen until Friday morning.

"We're shut down for now," I said, getting up from my chair and grabbing my coat.

"Everyone with a brain has gone home," Sampson said, putting his things away.

"You're suggesting we're brainless?" I chuckled.

"Sometimes," he said, grinning at me. "What time tomorrow?"

"Nana Mama wants everyone there around two thirty. Dinner at four."

"I'm fasting tonight so I can pack it away tomorrow."

"Really?"

"Nah. I don't do fasts."

"I didn't think so."

Forty minutes later, I was home and down on the floor playing with Damon while Maria watched over us and we waited for an order of Chinese food to be delivered. I told her about Sampson's fasting claim, which cracked her up.

"That man eats six meals a day," she said. "He'd collapse if he fasted."

"Right?" I tickled Damon, who squealed with laughter and ran away. "Another runner."

Maria patted her belly. "Not like this one."

"Still kicking?"

"I think baby's doing a Jazzercise routine in there."

I got up, came over, and put my hand on her belly. I could feel the movements immediately. "What a squirmer!"

"I told you," Maria said.

The baby continued to dance around the next morning, which

we spent helping my grandmother prepare for twelve guests. They started to arrive promptly at two thirty.

Sampson showed up last, around three.

"You're late," Nana Mama told him.

"Still on daylight saving time."

"Shouldn't you be early, then?"

"I'm a slow learner," John said.

The rest of the day went on like that, with lots of laughter and stories and too much good food. Everyone brought something, but the crowning glory went to Nana's turkey, which she deep-fried outside in a gizmo she'd bought for the occasion.

The skin was like crispy thin bacon. The meat was extraordinarily tender and juicy. I ate so much, I fell asleep with Damon crashed in my lap while watching the Detroit Lions game.

Maria had to wake me up to head home, and I was thinking about bed for the night as soon as we had Damon down.

"You going to work tomorrow?" she asked.

"I'm actually off, but I think I'll make a couple of phone calls from here and then spend the rest of the day with you and D."

She smiled. "We'd like that."

The next morning I let Maria sleep in and took care of Damon, changing his diaper and feeding him breakfast, after which I called the office of the Chester County Recorder of Deeds.

A woman answered on the second ring. "Shaina Watson, recorder's office."

I told her who I was and gave Ms. Watson the address I was interested in.

"LeeAnne and Michael Lawton used to own that place," she said immediately.

"You know it?"

"Mmm-hmm," the woman said. "Off the north side of the Chrome Barrens, big untouched area up there."

"You know who owns it now?"

Her voice got tighter. "I know who inherited it. LeeAnne's grandson, Eamon."

"Eamon Lawton?" I said, scribbling it down.

"Eamon Diggs," she said, sounding disgusted. "Heard of him?"

"Can't say that I have," I said.

"Look the creep up. He did time for rape."

CHAPTER 72

SUDDENLY I NO LONGER had the day off.

"I have to go," I told Maria when she got out of the shower.

"Alex." She groaned. "You said you'd spend the day with us. I need you here."

"I know, and I'm sorry," I said. "But I have a very strong feeling that we just got him, the Bulldog killer, the guy in the white van. There's a potential suspect we've just unearthed who was previously convicted for multiple rapes."

Maria looked discouraged, maybe a little abandoned, as she sat on the edge of the bed. "Can't wait until Monday, I suppose?"

"I don't know if I could live with myself if we waited and—"

Maria held up her hands in surrender. "You're right. You're right. Go. I'll see if Nana Mama can come over and give me a hand with a few things."

"You're sure?"

"Go. I won't be responsible for someone else dying."

I was out the door ten minutes later. Sampson picked me up in a squad car, and as soon as we were on I-95 heading north, we radioed and got patched through to Tommy French's home phone.

"You guys are overstaying your welcome," he grumbled by way of greeting. "I'm about to go out Christmas shopping with my daughters."

"We apologize, Tommy," Sampson said. "But a name's come up in association with the registered owners of that van. You know anything about a guy named Eamon Diggs?"

There was a silence long enough for us to hear one of his daughters complaining in the background. French said quietly, "John, listen to me, that is one bad dude, so bad I can't talk about the specifics at the moment. How did he come up?"

I said, "Turns out he's the grandson of the van owner and inherited the farm near Oxford, Pennsylvania, where our Ford Econoline was last registered."

There was another long silence. French said, "Where are you now?"

"On our way to that farm," Sampson said. "Gonna look around."

"You've got no jurisdiction and no cause to go in there, John," French said firmly.

Before we could protest, the state police detective said, "But I do."

"Two and a half hours?"

"Do me a favor?"

"Sure."

"Stop and get a coffee and a cruller on the way. I'll finish up this episode of 'Daddy the Grinch Goes Christmas Shopping' and meet you at the Mobil station in Oxford in, say, three hours?"

"Half past noon," Sampson said. "We'll be there."

"Good. We won't be but ten miles to that farm from there and not twenty to Kirkwood, where Diggs is living now."

CHAPTER 73

A SHINY BLUE FORD F-150 rolled into the Mobil station in Oxford, Pennsylvania, about ten minutes after we did. Tommy French jumped out of the pickup.

The detective was a short, stocky man with a bull neck and a buzz cut he must've had since his days as a U.S. Army MP. He took off his aviator glasses and shook Sampson's hand and then mine.

"I checked with Diggs's parole officer, and he confirmed the Kirkwood address but said he had no record of Eamon owning any property."

"Chester County Recorder confirmed ownership," I said.

"I know," French said. "I double-checked, and because Diggs did not declare it, we have ample just cause to go in and take a look around to see if he is in violation of his parole."

French said that due to the recent rain, the way into the farm that Diggs inherited was likely to be very muddy. He suggested we leave our squad car outside town and ride in his truck with him to the farm.

We put on our body armor and got in. Sampson sat up front and was immediately enamored of the truck.

"I like this, Alex. You're up here, king of the road. This new, Tommy?"

The detective smiled, said, "Got it last month. More practical than anything for the way I live."

"I want one."

"Could be tough to park in DC, John."

"I'd learn."

I said, "Tell us about Diggs."

French visibly stiffened at the wheel. "Diabolical. Smart. Played mind games with the women he violated. Made them think he was going to kill them at any moment."

"Sadistic control," I said.

"That's Eamon Diggs through and through."

"How'd he get out after only twelve years?"

"Like I said, Diggs is very sharp. Once he figured out the game at the penitentiary, he played it. Zero infractions. Model prisoner. Went through counseling. Found Jesus. All that bullshit. But you know how it is with those guys. They never change."

"Some do," I said. "But it is rare for them to keep their urges bottled up for good."

"Exactly," French said. "I've been waiting ever since he got out for a report to surface that matched his MO."

Sampson said, "Which was what, exactly?"

"Young woman gets taken, drugged, assaulted, sometimes repeatedly, scoured clean, and then dumped alive in a rural area."

"Alive. That's surprising," I said.

"He was also a suspect in two murder-rapes, but we could never make them stick."

"So you wouldn't put homicide past him," Sampson said.

"Not a chance."

Within ten minutes we were taking a left at where the preserve began, and French was explaining how the property was managed with fire in adherence with American Indian practices. Indeed, over the next few miles, we saw several long wide strips of grassland that had been burned and now awaited the regrowth of spring.

"Here we go," French said and turned at a dilapidated mailbox that was leaning so far right, it defied gravity.

The cornfields to our left had been harvested; the odd stalk stuck up out of the dirt here and there. There were several rows of mature pines on our right, which French said had probably been planted as a windbreak.

We had almost reached the farmyard when we bounced through a muddy rut.

One hundred and fifty feet ahead of French's pickup, dead center on the gravel drive, thunder clapped.

A fireball erupted, blowing a column fifteen feet high.

The truck's windshield shattered.

CHAPTER

74

WITH GRAVEL, ROCKS, AND mud raining down on his truck, Tommy French roared, "He's booby-trapped the place!"

The detective rammed his pickup into reverse and floored the gas. The Ford F-150 slid and swung in the wet dirt, throwing clods of greasy mud around as Sampson and I dug for our service weapons.

When we were all the way back to the road, French slammed on the brakes and threw the truck in park, panting as he looked through the filthy, spiderwebbed remnants of his windshield toward the flames at the far end of the drive.

"We need backup, Tommy," Sampson said at last.

"We need more than that, John," French said, picking up his police radio with shaking hands, which made me realize my own hands were trembling. "Goddamn it, this was my dream truck!"

The police detective got patched through to the Chester County dispatcher, identified himself, and reported the explosion. "I need enough manpower to seal off the road on the south side of the barrens ASAP. And the east side of the old Lawton place. No one crosses until we know what we're dealing with." He went on barking orders, calling for a helicopter, a special emergency response team, and a team from the hazardous devices and explosives unit.

By that point, I'd regained enough of my composure and strength to climb out of the truck. The case was now out of our control.

Squirrels chattered in the pines. Crows cawed somewhere behind me. Falling leaves from the scattered oaks floated on the chill breeze.

If I hadn't noticed the last of the fireball dying at the other end of the drive, I might have called it an idyllic scene. Instead, my nerves twitched at every sound.

Sampson climbed out. French still had the dispatcher on the line.

"He's calling in an army," John said.

"He should. We don't know what we're facing here."

French got out, the radio receiver still held to one ear. In the far distance, from back toward Oxford, we could hear the first sirens.

He told the dispatcher we were going to take a walk to the explosion site. Then he hung up and walked around his truck, looking at all the dings and pockmarks from the blast and shaking his head. Finally, he shrugged. "Chopper won't be here for forty minutes. Let's do a little recon before the cavalry comes."

"And set off another bomb?" Sampson asked.

"No, just up the drive, past that rut we hit before the explosion, so SERT has some idea what we're dealing with."

The drive was torn up. There was mud all over from our skidding retreat, even in the leaves and pine needles we now crept across with weapons drawn.

The rut in the drive turned out to be a water bar that was supposed to drain the drive, put rain into the ditches. On the right side, Sampson found a thin cable that snaked to a pine tree ten yards into the woods. Some kind of remote device was linked to the cable and taped to the trunk.

"There's got to be a pressure plate or something there under all that mud," John said. "When we drove across it, the trigger was tripped."

I said, "Kind of a long way from the trigger to the actual bomb."

"Fifty yards?" French murmured.

"Far enough to make you wonder whether it was meant to kill or warn."

"I think we're fair to call it attempted murder," French said, and continued past the water bar, stopping every few feet to examine the way ahead.

"Look for fishing line, trip wire, or another cable," Sampson whispered to me.

"What if there's another pressure plate?" I asked, suddenly feeling very uncomfortable about what we were doing. "Under the leaves, I mean."

That stopped John for a moment. But not French, who kept on going to the charred bomb crater, which was about twenty inches deep and just as wide.

"Smells more like gasoline than cordite or C-four," French said when we arrived beside him.

"I'll let your bomb guys figure that out," Sampson said.

We scanned the surface of the drive ahead but saw no fresh tracks in the thirty yards before it opened up into an overgrown field, turned to the right, and vanished. The police sirens were getting close now.

French said, "Let's see what's what in that field before we head back to the road."

He eased forward and we followed, eyes searching the ground and the trees ahead for signs of a second triggering device, but we found none. We reached the last big pine standing sentinel above the drive.

French eased left around the tree trunk and took a peek. When he pulled back, he murmured, "House is about seventy out. Place looks dead. Roof's ready to cave in."

I was standing to his right and moved aside several of the lower pine boughs on the opposite side of the tree. It gave me a different angle and a new perspective on the field that cut back toward the road.

In the deep pocket of the field, there was a long, low, open-front shed of sorts with a metal roof and pigeons fluttering about.

One of the Chester County Sheriff's cruisers was close now, siren whooping, almost to French's truck.

"Let's head back, Alex," Sampson said behind me. "Cavalry's here."

But I stepped forward another foot and pushed aside the last brushy tree limb blocking my view of the far end of that shed. I took in the scene for a long moment, enough time to be sure that my heart was slamming in my chest for good reason.

"Cross!" French called.

I pivoted, stepped back around the tree, and grinned at them, feeling victorious.

"What's going on?" Sampson said.

"I just spotted an old white van half under a tarp in a shed not a hundred yards from us. I think we've got our killer."

CHAPTER 75

IT TOOK ALMOST THREE hours for the Pennsylvania police SERT and bomb squad to arrive to sweep the area. They'd had to wait until a helicopter with infrared showed no one was on the property.

Sampson and I argued that we should be spending our time finding Eamon Diggs so we could place him under arrest. But French wanted to look at the van first.

Neither the SERT nor the hazardous devices and explosives commanders were happy to learn we had gone all the way to the edge of the farmyard; they didn't let us in until after they'd cleared the driveway, the farmyard, the farmhouse, and the shed.

After they cleared the locations, they came back and told us that the entire place was empty, with no evidence that anyone had lived there for a long time. And they took photographs of the van and the ground around it before they made sure it was not booby-trapped.

"Both teams said the dirt floor looked as if it had been raked before the leaves and whatnot got blown in there," French said as we donned latex gloves and booties to walk over to the van along a lane of white butcher paper that had been laid down to prevent further contamination of the site.

"Definitely the right rig," Sampson said, gesturing to the van's left rear quarter panel, which was scraped exactly as we'd seen in earlier security videos. "New headlight bulb cover on the left. See how it's different from the right."

"I see it."

"New tires," Sampson said. "Different treads."

"I see them too."

The van's rear double doors were hanging ajar when we reached them. A bomb team member had found keys to the van on a shelf.

French opened the two doors fully. We were hit with a blast of mustiness coupled with the scent of things rotting somewhere in the old trash, moldering leaves, and God only knew what else covering the van floor.

We stood by as the forensics techs began to pick apart the chaos. They found several latex gloves similar to the ones we wore.

"How old are those?" I asked.

"There isn't a lot of mold growing on them," said Helen Mathers, the lead forensics officer on the scene. She was dressed in a blue hazmat suit minus the full headgear. "I'd say they're recent, but we'll know better back at the lab."

"Let me check something," I said. "Can I use the keys a second?"

Mathers frowned but nodded. I went up front and asked Javier

Cruz, the tech working on the driver's seat, to give me a moment. Then I leaned in, put the key in the ignition, and turned it to accessory. The dashboard glowed enough for me to read the mileage. I turned the key to start, and the engine coughed to life. I quickly shut it down, thanked Cruz, and went back to Sampson and French.

"It started right up," I said. "It's been driven recently."

French gestured to a plastic evidence bag. "They just found a length of rope buried in there. It's got blood and skin traces on it."

Sampson said, "Could be the rope that strangled the real estate agent, Brenda Miles."

I picked up the bag and looked at the cord. I said, "I'm betting MFP utility grade."

Mathers climbed into the back of the van and crouched over the right wheel well, sifting through the debris with a trim paintbrush.

"This is going to take a long time," Sampson said.

"Not today," Mathers said over her shoulder. "We'll bag it all, then dissect and test everything back in the lab. I'm looking for the obvious at this point."

"Helen?" said Cruz from the front seat. "I have a shell casing. It's a forty-four caliber."

John and I gave each other high fives.

"Helen?" Cruz called again.

"That's good, Javier," she said, staring down. "Real good."

She set her brush aside, took several photographs of whatever was in front of her, and retrieved a large pair of forceps from her pocket. She reached down somewhere we couldn't see.

A moment later, she came up with a two-by-three-inch shriveled piece of dark gristle clenched in the forceps jaw.

"What'd you find, Helen?" French asked.

Mathers said soberly, "From the hairs growing out of it, I'd say part of a human scalp, Tommy."

Sampson grimaced, said, "Could be from Alice Ways, one of the shooting victims. We know that a piece of her scalp is missing."

"That's more than enough now, Tommy," I said. "We need to get Diggs into custody."

French nodded. "Let's go find Eamon."

CHAPTER 76

SHORTLY AFTER FOUR THAT afternoon, the three of us took the squad car to the gate of the Keegan's Granite quarry, where Eamon Diggs's parole officer said Diggs had worked since leaving prison.

We showed our badges and drove to the operation's headquarters. The office manager, a nice lady named Judy, confirmed that Diggs did indeed work at the pit but had taken the day off to hunt with a bow and arrow before the rifle deer season started on Monday.

"His creepy little friend's with him, I think," Judy said and gave a little shiver.

"Who's that?" French asked.

"Harold Beech," she said and shivered again. "He took the day off too."

French seemed to know the name.

I said, "By any chance, do you guys use dynamite in the quarry?"

"All the time. Why?"

"Just interested," Sampson said. "You keep it on-site? The dynamite?"

The office manager squinted. "Yes, in a moisture-and-temperature-controlled vault that is inspected by the Bureau of Alcohol, Tobacco, and Firearms every year. You'd have to talk to Jack Stark, the operations manager, about the vault. But he's gone until Tuesday afternoon, up at his brother's place in the boondocks west of Wilkes-Barre."

French asked, "He have a pager or beeper or anything?"

She snorted. "No, Jack's too cheap for that. He checks in when he wants to."

We were turning to leave when she said, "What'd he do? Diggs."

"It's unclear if he's done anything, actually," I said. "We just want to talk to him."

"Well, whatever it is, you can bet your patootie that Beech is involved. Thick as thieves, those two."

Before we headed back to the squad car, the police detective called his office and asked them to look up a Harold Beech, see if he had a sheet. Not five minutes later, he got a response.

After listening for several moments, French said, "Why doesn't that surprise me?" He hung up and told us, "Beech did eleven years for assault, kidnapping, and forcible penetration with foreign objects. Victims were two sixteen-year-old girls."

"Birds of a feather," Sampson said.

"Wait a second," I said. "Foreign objects?"

"That's what the man said."

"Brenda Miles, the real estate agent, was found with a wooden spoon in her vagina."

"You're thinking Beech is involved?"

"Spoon fits his MO. *Beech* could be the strangler."

Sampson said, "Think we need SERT with us?"

French said, "Not unless Eamon knows his bomb went off. Otherwise, we're just dropping by for a chat. But if I see something I don't like, I'll get them up here pronto."

We piled back into the squad car and drove toward Diggs's residence. A mile or so down the road, we passed a woman walking an Airedale, then we pulled into Diggs's yard. An older Chevy pickup with plates that matched Diggs's DMV records was parked to the right of the double-wide. Next to it sat a blue beater Subaru with cardboard duct-taped where the rear window should have been.

We got out and went to the front door. French knocked while Sampson and I kept our hands on the grips of our service weapons.

No answer. Then a dog whined behind us.

A woman said softly, "Hey, if you're looking for the pervs, they're not in there."

CHAPTER 77

THE LADY WALKING THE Airedale had come up to what passed for a lawn in front of Diggs's double-wide. She was a tired-looking brunette in her late forties.

"Where are they?" I asked just as quietly.

"Sit, Bernie," she said, and the dog sat smartly at her side. She pointed to woods diagonally across the street. "It's state land. They've got a blind back in there off the logging road. Bernie and I don't go in there during hunting season, and we try to avoid them at all costs."

"Them?"

"Diggs and his friend. My brother Jimmy's a criminal lawyer. Knew all about them when they moved in here. Both of them convicted perverts."

"We know."

"Once I found that out, I had double bolts put on every door and an alarm on every window in my place. Bought a twelve-gauge too. And I wait until they're at work or off in the woods before I take Bernie out in this direction."

French gestured toward the woods. "How far is this blind?"

She shrugged. "Go down the logging road to the roundabout, then there's three trails off it. I can't remember which one is theirs. Bernie and I like to go for tramps off the path when we can, but anyway, it's another sixty yards or so off that roundabout. You can't miss it even with all the brush and branches they put on top of it."

We thanked her, got her name — Penelope Harris — and started toward the woods and the entrance to the logging road. Halfway there, I noticed a two-by-eight board fixed high between two large pine trees.

A rope passed through a pulley bolted into the crossbar.

I pointed to it, muttered to Sampson and French, "What are the odds that's a MFP utility-grade rope?"

"I'm thinking high," John said as we headed for the opening where the logging road began.

The weeds and grass growing in the lane had withered and browned after a recent frost. The maple and oak trees were already bare.

The leaves underfoot were damp and quiet. Rain began to patter down. The wind picked up. A gloomy light seized the woods.

Sampson had his hand on his pistol. So did I. So did French.

We reached the place Ms. Harris had described about two hundred yards into the forest. The logging road dead-ended in a circle of sorts with three trails running off it at ten o'clock, twelve, and two.

The police detective whispered, "We each take one. Sneak in. Second you see this blind, get out of sight and squawk like a crow. We'll come to you."

I said, "I'll take the trail on the right."

Sampson gestured at the path straight ahead, and French went toward the one at ten o'clock. I saw him take out his pistol before he entered the trees.

I did the same, holding the pistol loosely at my side as I tried to make as little noise as possible with each step in those soft wet leaves and the pattering of the rain. Several small branches popped beneath my shoes about twenty yards in, and I paused.

I scanned the woods ahead for a mound of branches, saw nothing, and kept going. About fifty yards down the trail, I heard a crow caw to my far left.

French, I thought, and started to turn.

From high and back over my left shoulder came a soft, two-toned whistle.

I paused and looked up and behind me into the treetops. I saw a camouflaged Eamon Diggs on a metal tree stand about twenty-five feet in the air and twenty yards away. He was holding a bow and aiming a nasty-looking broadhead arrow right at me.

"Toss the gun, asshole," he growled.

My survival instincts told me to get my gun up and fire at him.

But his bow was at full draw, and I was holding my gun waist high, muzzle pointed down. Still looking at that broadhead, I tossed the gun and said, "I'm a cop, Eamon. Just wanted to talk—"

Diggs squinted. He made a shrugging motion with his right shoulder.

I caught a flash of yellow a split second before his arrow hit me square in the chest and sent me staggering. My feet got tangled and I fell.

The back of my head struck something hard, and everything went wavy and then black.

CHAPTER 78

I DON'T KNOW HOW long I was out. A minute? Ninety seconds?

All I know is when I came to, I felt like I'd been kicked by a mule. Eamon Diggs's arrow jutted from the low center of my chest, that nasty broadhead embedded in my body armor; the shaft and yellow vanes danced above me as I struggled for air.

"Goddamn it!" Diggs cursed. "Goddamn it to hell!"

I looked up to see him still twenty feet up but free of his safety line and getting off his stand, arms wrapped around the tree, his thighs and upper body scraping against the bark as his right foot groped for a climbing peg screwed into the trunk.

He found the steel step and came down the tree, still cursing, his bow hanging from a hook at his left hip.

I heard Maria's voice in my head: *He's going to kill you, Alex. The white-van psycho is going to come down and finish you off.*

Dazed, struggling to breathe, I knew I had to get to my gun. I started to roll over and get to my knees, but the nock of the arrow in my chest snagged the damp ground and hindered me.

I grunted against it, feeling the bruise building beneath my armor, and gasped against the pain; the aluminum shaft bent and I got to my knees. My head was too foggy for me to stand. I started crawling along the trail when Diggs was halfway down the tree.

I saw my pistol on the other side of the path, its handle sticking out from the leaves. The throbbing in my chest was so acute, I did not know if I could go on.

But then I saw Maria and Damon in my mind, and the pain was overwhelmed by my love for them and for my unborn child and the knowledge of how crushed they would be if I died here in the woods. I crawled faster, ignoring the arrow flopping and catching on the roots and sticks under me, my focus on my weapon, now fifteen feet away, and now ten.

I caught a flash of something in my peripheral vision and could not help but glance over. Diggs was almost at the bottom of his tree.

Get to the gun! Get to the gun, Alex! With Maria's voice screaming in my head, I scrambled forward and lunged for the pistol at the same time I heard the thud of Diggs's boots hitting the ground. I got hung up on the bent arrow for a second before it snapped.

But the holdup was enough to leave me four inches short of my weapon.

"Don't! Don't, goddamn it!" Diggs yelled. "I don't want to do this!"

I looked over and saw him standing there not fifteen feet from me, his bow raised and drawn, another nasty broadhead nocked and aimed right at me. I glanced back at my gun and knew I could not reach it before he shot.

This close, he could shoot me in the throat. No armor would save me there.

But before I could raise my hands, I heard John yell behind me, "Police, Diggs! Drop the bow, or I will shoot!"

Diggs glanced over. I peered back and saw Sampson in the trail about fifty feet away, crouched in a combat-shooting stance, weapon up, ready to fire.

"Goddamn police," Diggs said in a resigned voice. He lowered the bow and tossed it and the arrow aside.

He gazed at me and said, his voice shaking, "I swear to Jesus Hisself, man, I did not mean to shoot you."

CHAPTER 79

SAMPSON TOLD DIGGS TO lie facedown in the leaves, fingers laced behind his head. A beaten man, he complied.

Sampson hustled forward. He secured the ex-con's wrists and read him his Miranda rights, then came over to me. I'd struggled to a sitting position, breathing hard and hurting, adrenaline pumping, the sweat pouring off my forehead. The saliva at the back of my throat had a burned-aluminum taste that made me want to gag.

"Jesus, he did shoot you," Sampson said, looking at the stub of the arrow sticking out of the front of my shirt.

"Almost point-blank," I said, feeling dizzy. "Chest was hammered."

"I bet," he said. "You're lucky it wasn't a bullet at that distance."

Diggs, still facedown and restrained, yelled, "I did not mean to do that, man. I would never shoot a cop!"

"But you did, Mr. Diggs," Sampson snapped. He yelled, "Tommy!"

A second later, from off in the woods a good hundred yards, French yelled back, "I've got Beech in custody!"

"Call the sheriff! Call an ambulance! Diggs shot Cross with an arrow."

"What!"

"His armor stopped it. But he's shook up bad and I want him looked at."

"Done!"

By that point, I was trembling head to toe.

"I didn't have a chance, John," I said, hearing my voice wavering. "My gun was pointed down and I was looking for a blind on the ground, not up in a tree. I…"

"Doesn't matter," Sampson said. "You're going to be fine. You're going to go home, see Maria and Damon."

"Help me up."

"Not a good idea."

"I feel like I should get up, John."

He sighed, helped me to my feet. I stood there, my focus swirling, my balance off.

"I might have a mild concussion," I said, feeling a little nauseated as the egg throbbed at the back of my head.

Sampson said, "Which is why we're getting you checked out ASAP."

I reached over and put my hand against a young oak tree. "Agreed."

Sampson went back to Diggs. Before John hauled him to his feet, he scraped a square in the leaves around the bow and arrow.

"Let's go," John said.

"I want a lawyer," Diggs said.

"I bet you do." Sampson told him to walk out the path. "And don't run because I'd love nothing more than to shoot you in the ass."

"I told you, I didn't mean to do it!"

"And yet you did do it," John said. "Now, march."

Diggs appeared ready to cry but started down the trail slowly. Sampson offered me his arm, which I took.

I don't remember much of the walk out, but we were met in the turnaround on the old logging road by French and a small, scrawny man, presumably Beech. He was in cuffs and spitting mad.

"What is this?" Beech demanded. He nodded at the state police detective. "This shithead here won't tell me nothing. Just dragged me out of my blind."

"I read you your rights," French said. "First thing."

"For what?" Beech demanded. "We are allowed to own bows. They're not guns. And we are allowed to hunt."

"Not for humans, you aren't," Sampson said.

"For humans?" Beech said, losing color. "No, no, we've—"

"Shut up, Harry," Diggs said. "This is wrong, so until you talk to a lawyer, just shut the hell up."

His friend appeared to have been on the wrong end of a gut punch, which was how I still felt when the sheriff's cruiser and an ambulance met us in Diggs's front yard. French had Beech and Diggs transported to the state police barracks in Coatesville while an EMT checked me out.

I had a livid diamond-shaped bruise low over my sternum, that egg on the back of my head, and signs of a mild concussion. But I turned down the offer of a ride to the closest hospital.

"If I feel different in a half hour, you'll take me there," I said when Sampson protested. "I want to see what's in that trailer first."

French agreed. I sat outside when they went in. But although I had a colossal headache, my mind became less foggy with each passing minute, and soon I felt strong and clear enough to go inside and help with the search.

We combed through the double-wide and the yard around it for more than an hour. We did not find the .44 Bulldog pistol, but we had the rope from the deer pole. And we came across several items that were violations of Diggs's parole, including marijuana and cocaine.

But it wasn't until Sampson searched a shed in the back of Diggs's place that we knew we had him cold. John exited the small outbuilding wearing gloves and carrying a handful of blasting caps with tags that read PROPERTY OF KEEGAN'S GRANITE.

Tommy French saw them and broke into a toothy grin. "Well, well, well."

CHAPTER

80

TWO HOURS LATER, JOHN SAMPSON and I were at the Pennsylvania state police barracks in Coatesville, a long, low brick-faced affair surrounded by leafless bushes. John and I were on the phone with Chief Pittman while Tommy French was on another line with his supervisor.

"An arrow to the chest?" Pittman said. "That had to hurt, Cross."

I had thought he'd be angry that I'd been caught with my guard down. Relieved, I said, "I have a whopper of a bruise on my chest, and my ego's a bit crushed, but I'll be all right, sir."

"Good, good," Pittman said. "Are we ready to announce this? That we got the Bulldog killer and maybe the strangler? Or should we call them the white-van killers?"

Sampson said, "Give us a chance to talk to them first, sir. Both have lawyered up, but we're going to tell them what we found in the double-wide, see if that will pry something open."

"Anyone searching Beech's place?"

I said, "French sent a team right after we took him into custody."

"Keep me posted."

"We'll call as soon as we know something," John promised and hung up.

French finished his conversation, and a sergeant led us all to a hall outside an interrogation room. The sergeant knocked, leaned his head in. "Detectives would like to talk to you, Ms. Cox."

A few moments later, Emelie Cox, Diggs's public defender, exited the room and crossed her arms. "My client says he *accidentally* shot one of you."

"Me," I said. "For the record, he whistled at me and heard me identify myself as a cop before he shot me. It was no accident."

Cox, a petite redhead in her thirties, said, "Hear him out. To clear up whatever you think he's done, he says he'll answer your questions unless I tell him not to."

In the interrogation room, Diggs looked across the table at me with an agonized expression. "Look, man, I'm sorry. I did not mean to shoot you."

"But you did!" Sampson said, slamming his hand on the table. "You shot him. If it hadn't been for his vest, my partner would be dead now."

Diggs cringed like a kicked dog. "I admit I saw him coming through the woods. Saw the pistol. I did not know what to think. I came to full draw on a guy roaming around the woods with a pistol. Who knew what he wanted?"

He turned to me. "You got to understand that there are people out there who want to kill me for some of the things I've done in the past."

"I could see that," I said. "But why did you pull the trigger on me if you didn't mean to shoot me?"

His head bobbed. "See, that's the thing. There is no trigger. I had what's called target panic when I used a trigger release, so now I use a back-tension release. You had to have found it near my bow."

French said, "I'm sure we did. So what?"

Diggs said the back-tension release was a mechanical device with small jaws that attached to the nock of the bowstring. The system was engineered to release an arrow only after the shooter pushed hard enough against the bow handle with the left arm and pulled back hard enough with the muscles of the right shoulder to, in effect, pry open the jaws.

He stared at me. "Honest to God, when you said you were a cop, I remember thinking I'd better let down. So I shrugged, you know, like, *Okay, he's not a threat.* But then the bow just went off, man. I had no idea it would do that. I would never intentionally shoot a cop. Ever."

French was having none of it. "How about the bomb booby trap at your farm? How about all the pot and blow we found in your trailer? How about the blasting caps we found in your shed? Stolen from Keegan's Granite, along with dynamite, no doubt."

"What?" Diggs said, sounding frightened. "No. No, that's BS."

Cox, his lawyer, put her hand up in front of him. "No more, Mr. Diggs."

Sampson said, "We almost died earlier today when we triggered the bomb you set up on the dirt road to your grandmother's old place."

Diggs, ignoring his attorney, shook his head violently. "No. Absolutely not. I haven't even been down that way in months, and I sure as hell didn't booby-trap anything there. Is that what this is about? Is that why you were out looking for me?"

"You're here because of the murders you committed," French said.

Diggs said, "Murders? Me? No way."

Cox again put her hand in front of her client. "Don't say a thing, Mr. Diggs."

Sampson said, "We've got you, you puke. We've got your white Ford Econoline van out at the farm."

His attorney said, "What white van?"

Diggs squinted. "You mean my grandfather's old junker? Doesn't even run."

"Oh, yes, it does," I said. "And it's impounded. The best crime techs in Pennsylvania are all over it. We've already found the piece of scalp you cut off one of your victims and a shell casing from the forty-four-caliber bullet you put in her head."

Diggs said, "Hey, hey, man, I don't even own a gun. I can't own a gun. I am a convicted felon and the only thing I can have is a bow. That's all I have. And I don't know where the drugs and those blasting caps came from. Other guys at Keegan's, other ex-cons, lived there before me. Lots of guys just out of the stir."

"Mr. Diggs, please," his attorney said.

I said, "Okay, Eamon, let's say you're telling the truth. You never meant to stick an arrow in me, and you don't own a forty-four."

"Didn't and don't."

I nodded. "But what about your friend? What about Harold Beech? Did he know about the farm? The van?"

Cox stood up. "Detectives, we're done."

Diggs sighed, then said, "Why don't you ask Harry? On the advice of counsel, I'm shutting my yap."

CHAPTER 81

RYAN DAVIS, HAROLD BEECH'S public defender, was fresh out of law school. He was likely in his late twenties but looked fourteen. He had a wild shock of black hair and wore a disheveled suit and a semi-dazed expression that said he knew he was in way over his head. But when the three of us entered the second interrogation room he did his best to sound authoritative.

"My client's done nothing wrong, Detectives," Davis declared, pushing his glasses farther up the bridge of his nose. "He has no idea why he's here. Charge him or let him walk."

"He'll be sticking around for a while yet, Counselor," French said, taking a seat across from Beech, who was wringing his hands, lips twisted like he'd just tasted something rancid.

Beech had been wearing archery gloves when we encountered him in the woods. Now I noticed his palms. I reached over and pointed to the livid lines around a quarter of an inch wide that ran across both of them.

"Where did those come from, Mr. Beech?"

Beech looked at his attorney, who shrugged.

"Rope burns," Beech said. "Own fault. Wasn't wearing my gloves like I should have been last week when we took down Eamon's deer from the game pole."

"So your blood's on that rope?"

"Who knows? That's what happened."

I decided not to ask him about Brenda Miles yet. "You and Eamon Diggs good friends?"

"About the only one I got. We keep each other on the narrow, you know?"

French said, "Knew Eamon in prison, did you?"

"Of course," Beech said. "We met in an after-release program and got hired together at the quarry. One of the few places that will hire people like us. Fresh out, I mean."

John said, "What about his grandmother's farm, the one he inherited. Ever been there?"

He nodded. "We've shot our bows long-distance-like down there a couple of times, maybe three? I told him to sell the place, buy something where he could live nice, 'stead of renting."

"Why didn't he?" I asked.

Beech shrugged. "Can't let go, I guess. He said it was the only place where he was happy as a kid. With his grandparents."

"You see the white van at that farm?" French asked. "The one in the shed?"

He nodded. "Got inside and under the hood to see if there were salvageable parts."

"Were there any?" I asked.

"Engine, radiator, transmission weren't bad, and the quarter panels and doors weren't rusted at all 'cause of the van's being under the shed roof, but Eamon wouldn't let me scavenge it. Said it had sentimental value too."

"You see him drive it? The van?" French asked.

Beech snorted. "I didn't even think there was a key to it."

"There was one, and it does run," I said.

"News to me. What's the big deal?"

"The van was seen in the vicinity of several recent murders in the greater Washington, DC, area."

The sour look on Beech's face deepened, but he did not reply.

"Three were shot point-blank in their cars," Sampson said. "One was strangled with a rope exactly like the rope you say you burned your hands on, Harry."

I said, "And the strangled woman was found with a wooden spoon rammed in her vagina, Harry."

Beech licked his lips nervously but still said nothing.

French leaned across the table. "That was one of your favorite moves, wasn't it, Harry? Putting things like wooden spoons in the girls you drugged and assaulted?"

All the blood drained out of Beech's face. He said in a shaking, gasping voice, "I don't do that kind of thing no more. I was sick in the mind back then. I paid my debt to society and have my head on straight now. I been through behavior-modification therapy. I have!"

"I'll bet you have," French said. "Except it modified you from a deviant to a killer."

"No!"

"Mr. Beech," his young attorney finally said, "I think we should stop now."

"I didn't do nothing, man," he snarled at him. "Nothing."

Sampson asked Beech where he'd been on the evenings of the

Bulldog murders. Beech said probably where he always was, in his dump of an apartment or at Diggs's double-wide.

"I don't go out. I don't do nothing 'cept work and bow-hunt in the fall, fish for bass in the summer. Stay away from all women. Especially young ones."

"What about Diggs?" I asked.

Beech shook his head, struggling with something. "I don't know. I mean, I'm not paid to be the dude's keeper, am I? But I'll tell you what, and this is no lie: Eamon's been known to disappear now and then. And when I asked him where he'd got to, he told me I didn't want to know."

CHAPTER

82

ON THE SUNDAY AFTER Thanksgiving, Gary Soneji continued to act the part of the attentive husband, one who was sorry to soon be leaving his family yet again. He played with Roni outside in the leaves on the blustery fall day. He held Missy's hands as darkness approached and told her that he'd be back from the road on Friday evening and said how much he was looking forward to Christmas Eve.

"Can't you stay tonight and drive south first thing in the morning?" she asked. "The traffic will be heavy on the interstate."

That was true, but he had places to be. "I'm taking back roads to Philly. I'll spend the night there and drive the rest of the way to my first appointment in the morning. There's some company Marty wants me to pitch to in Spofford, Virginia."

Missy gave a faux pout. "We'll miss you, Gary. This new you."

"And the new Gary will miss you, Missy, and Roni. I promise I'll call every night."

As he was leaving a few minutes later, he looked up to see his wife holding Roni, who was in her cute pink sweatshirt, both of them waving. He waved back and quickly drove away.

As he almost always did after leaving, Soneji felt a weight come off his shoulders. But even a mantle of invisibility could be heavy, right?

Heading toward the interstate, he turned on the radio and searched for an all-news station. He found one on the AM dial, broadcasting out of Philadelphia.

He did not have to wait long before he heard what he wanted, an update on the big story in the region. He'd read about it briefly in the *Philadelphia Inquirer* that very morning, and he wanted to know more, much more.

The radio announcer said, "Police from three states and the District of Columbia as well as agents from the FBI and the BATF are still searching a remote farm in Chester County for clues to five homicides in the Washington, DC, area. Two felons convicted of sex crimes, forty-two-year-old Eamon Diggs and thirty-seven-year-old Harold Beech, have been arrested based on evidence gathered at the farm, including the remains of a booby trap that exploded when detectives began their search.

"Both men await arraignment and extradition hearings tomorrow in Chester County. WKW-AM will be there for the latest on these troubling crimes."

When the broadcast moved on to football coverage, Soneji turned the radio off, feeling pleased with himself. He'd questioned whether he'd gone over the top by booby-trapping the driveway, but it had worked to turn all investigative leads toward the rapists.

The police surely had the van by now. They had to be tearing that thing apart.

Driving south on I-95, past the exit that led toward the Pennsylvania border, Chester County, and the farm, Soneji went from smug to ecstatic. He'd created suspicions that were now pointing the investigation and prosecution in a direction entirely opposite from him. In his mind, Soneji was already the there-but-not-there man, easy to overlook.

The traffic on I-95 south wasn't as bad as he'd expected. When he approached the Beltway sometime later, he slowly came down off that euphoric high and allowed himself to cast his mind forward, to imagine his future both near and distant.

First, he saw himself getting through the whole wedding farce, of course. Then he saw himself snatching Cheryl Lynn Wise and bringing her to...

He shook his head, telling himself he could not bring the girl to his uncle's cabin. He had to take her to another place, a new place, one that had no connection to him. He couldn't just go off like Bruno Hauptmann, snatching the Lindbergh baby and murdering him within hours. That was unacceptable as far as Soneji was concerned. Besides, he had more important issues to address in the short term — and keeping his part-time teaching job at Washington Day School was one hundred percent his long-term plan.

There was no way he was leaving a place with so many opportunities to indulge his various hungers anytime soon.

CHAPTER 83

AT OUR STAFF MEETING the Monday morning after Thanksgiving, Chief Pittman loudly praised the work Sampson and I had done in bringing Eamon Diggs and Harold Beech to justice.

"Detective Sampson and Detective Cross went above and beyond the call of duty bringing these fiends in. And I mean that word, *fiends*," Pittman said. "As far as I'm concerned, mimicking serial killers like Son of Sam and the Boston Strangler is fiendish and incomprehensible behavior, a total distortion of human values."

He took a big breath, then said he was putting us both up for commendations for our "dogged work and commitment to solving the white-van murders."

There was a lot of congratulations. Even from Detectives

Edgar Kurtz and Corina Straub Diehl, though they came up to us afterward and told us not to get used to it.

"We're still top dogs around here," Kurtz said.

"Agreed," Sampson said. "Just don't piss on our ankles to prove it."

That made them both laugh, and they walked away.

We spent the day writing detailed reports of all that had transpired at the farm, in the woods near Eamon Diggs's home, in his double-wide, and at the state police barracks. I kept coming back to the photographic evidence gathered at the farm, specifically one picture that showed the rear of the white Ford Econoline van.

The shot, by the Pennsylvania state police forensics team, showed the interior of the van with both back doors flung wide. At a glance, it looked like a roadside dump strewn with an inch or two of dead leaves.

But below that light carpet of leaves, there seemed to have been little or no effort to hide what was found in the van: the chunk of scalp, the used latex gloves, and especially the spent .44-caliber-bullet casings. It was like they'd just been tossed in the back as an afterthought following each heinous crime.

Who does that? What kind of mind?

Keeping some sort of souvenir was not unusual. Many of the serial killers I'd interviewed for my doctoral dissertation had kept souvenirs of their victims. But those souvenirs had been safeguarded, at the least, and enshrined more often than not. Yet Diggs and Beech seemed to have been tossing their murder trophies into what was essentially a trash bin.

What was the psychology behind that?

I could not come up with a satisfactory explanation, so I asked Sampson.

"I don't know," John said. "Maybe Diggs's twisted psyche sees it as throwing his victims into the void."

I thought about that. "Maybe you should be sitting where I am."

"I'm good right over here, man," Sampson said and laughed.

Something about the case felt off, but by the time I made my way home, I'd managed to set thoughts of it aside.

Maria opened the front door and stepped way back so I could get past her belly.

"Damon's got a little sniffle," she said quietly, shutting the door behind me. "He fell asleep on the couch."

"How're you?" I whispered. I kissed her hello and put my hand on her belly. "How's our little runner?"

"Playing gymnast today," Maria said. "Doing cartwheels, I think. How about you? Doctor look at your chest?"

"She did, and I've got a bruise on my sternum, but I will be fine," I said, wanting to move on. She'd about flipped when she found out about the arrow.

I took off my coat and followed Maria into the kitchen, where she was preparing shrimp in a red sauce, another amazing recipe from her mother that filled the air with good smells and ordinarily gave me an intense desire to eat. But I was distracted.

Ever intuitive, Maria studied my face as she stirred the sauce. "What are you confused about, mister?"

"Whether we've got the right guys."

"You said the evidence looked ironclad."

"We're waiting for labs, but it did and does."

"So what's the problem?"

"Why would Diggs and Beech just dump all that stuff in the van like it meant nothing?"

"Maybe they didn't dump it all. Maybe you're finding traces of other victims back there. Alex, you need to be happy about this.

If the labs back you up, you're now batting one thousand on your murder cases. I think you need to bring that to Chief Pittman's attention before you're *not* batting one thousand."

"You're saying I'll screw up eventually?"

"We all do, baby. We all do."

CHAPTER 84

MID-DECEMBER TURNED DANK AND cold up and down the mid-Atlantic. But the foul weather did nothing to dampen Missy Murphy's enthusiasm for her and Gary's rapidly approaching wedding.

"Do you want to hear about the cutest napkins Mom found for the appetizer table?" she asked as Soneji stood shivering at an outdoor pay phone on a commercial strip in Lincolnia, Virginia. A wintry mix of rain and snow was falling in the fading afternoon light.

I'd rather suck a bullet, Soneji thought. "Tell me about them," he said.

"The napkins have little Santas officiating at weddings on them!" Missy cried. "Roni loves them. So do I!"

"That's hilarious," Soneji said. "Hey, babe?"

"What's that?"

"I'm in a phone booth freezing my ass off, and it's snowing and they're saying the DC area is going to get clobbered tonight. Can I go eat and call you later from my motel?"

There was a long pause before she sighed. "Okay, but promise to call after I get Roni to bed, okay? There are still many, many things we need to discuss."

"And I love you and I can't wait to hear them," he said, then hung up.

He got in the Saab, turned the heat on high, and moved his toes to restore circulation. Then he drove down a series of roads and parked up the street from an eggshell-blue, two-story Colonial.

Soneji turned off the Saab's ignition, checked his watch, and saw it was already past five. Movement would not be long in coming now.

At twenty past the hour, the lights of a Christmas tree went on in the Colonial's front room, casting a festive glow through the window and onto the lawn. At five forty-five, as she'd done every evening for the past three, a woman Soneji had met only once came out the front door.

Sandy Ravisky, the computer science teacher he was subbing for, got in a Chrysler minivan and backed out. An older woman, presumably Ravisky's mother, stood in the doorway holding her newborn grandchild. When her daughter was gone, she shut the door.

For the first time since he'd started watching the Ravisky family, Soneji did not follow Sandy. The woman was habitually late wherever she went and liked to drive fast, which made her difficult to tail.

Besides, he knew exactly where she was going: to pick up her husband, Peter, at work.

True to form, the Raviskys returned around six thirty and quickly went inside together. Sandy's mother left the house soon after, retreating to a mother-in-law's cottage in the backyard.

Soneji drove to Old Town, Alexandria, and had Greek food, no alcohol.

Tonight's work had to be mechanically flawless. He'd spent two weeks researching how best to achieve his aims and felt he understood the process cold.

At nine p.m., he called Missy from a warmer pay phone in the hallway near the restaurant. They talked about seating plans for obscure relatives he'd never met before and would probably never meet again.

By the time they got to flower arrangements, he'd had enough. "Sorry, Miss, but I have to be up early. Can we talk again before I head out?"

After a pause, she said, "That would be nice. Get a good sleep."

"You too," he said, and went outside to the Saab, which had about a half an inch of snow on the windshield.

He was back in his observation post down the street from the Raviskys' home at ten thirty. The snow was falling heavily now.

Soneji left the engine running, listening to the radio. The forecast was calling for as much as three inches overnight with plunging temperatures toward dawn, exactly why he'd chosen this evening to act.

The Raviskys' Christmas tree went dark at eleven p.m. The bedroom lights went off not long after. Soneji stayed put, waiting for the lights to go out in the mother-in-law's place, starting his car every half hour to warm his feet. The cottage finally went dark shortly after midnight. He kicked off his shoes, put on a second layer of wool socks, and slipped on low rubber galoshes.

He donned a black hood, a headlamp, and gloves, picked up a

small bag with the essential tools, and slipped outside. It was snowing steadily as he padded diagonally to the Raviskys' Chrysler minivan.

Soneji paused at the rear of the minivan for a long moment, studying the house and the mother-in-law's cottage, then lay down on his back in the snow building on the drive.

He wriggled beneath the vehicle, dragging his tool kit, ignoring the icy slurry that found its way under his collar. When he turned on his headlamp's red bulb, he could see the underbelly of the minivan well enough to identify the brake linkages.

Soneji opened his tool kit, found the correct sprocket wrench, and set about loosening the linkages until they would dance on a razor's edge before shearing.

CHAPTER

85

THE MORNING OF DECEMBER fifteenth, the nation's capital was a quintessential mess. Four inches of snow, sleet, and freezing rain had fallen and temperatures had plunged into the twenties with a howling wind behind them.

I almost hit the ground three times on the slick sidewalks between the Metro stop and work; and I called Maria when I got to the office to tell her not to go out at all and to reschedule her appointment with her obstetrician. Sampson did not make it to the office until after nine.

Diehl and Kurtz came in together at a quarter to ten.

"Nice brunch?" I asked.

"Yeah, I wish," Kurtz said. "Effing Beltway was a hockey rink."

"DC don't do ice," Diehl said, plopping down at her desk. "I don't do ice."

Kurtz said, "We made it in slowly, but we heard there were fifteen accidents this morning, including a bad one westbound on the Beltway. Chain-reaction pileup."

Diehl nodded grimly. "Ten cars. They're taking out survivors by chopper."

"Survivors?" Sampson said.

"I was told two dead in the first vehicle to crash. They expect the toll to rise."

Before we could comment on that sad state of affairs, Helen Mathers, with the Pennsylvania crime lab, called.

"Tommy French wanted me to say happy holidays to you and Detective Sampson and give you both an early gift," she said. "It wasn't easy because there was deer blood on the rope, but we got a match to Brenda Miles's blood type. Diggs's and Beech's blood are on the rope too."

Sampson grinned, sat back with his fingers laced behind his head. "We got them. No matter what, we've got those bastards."

"That's amazing, Helen," I said. "Really seals the deal."

"Oh, there's more."

Mathers said that her team had identified human hair in the debris removed from the back of the van. Auburn, probably female.

"Could belong to Bunny Maddox," I said. "We know she was in the back of that van."

"Bunny could be buried somewhere on Diggs's farm," Sampson said.

"Tommy French is going back with cadaver dogs once the weather clears," Mathers said. "Oh, and we have a blood type match from the scalp to Alice Ways as well."

We hung up, and suddenly it did feel a lot like Christmas. Whatever misgivings I might have had about Diggs and Beech's involvement in the Bulldog shootings and the strangling of Brenda Miles were a thing of the past.

For the next hour, we contacted the various detectives who'd helped us on the case, including Deb Angelis in Fairfax County and Kelsey Girard in Goochland County, and told them about the evidence linking both men to the strangling of Brenda Miles, the murder of Alice Ways, and the kidnapping and possible murder of Bunny Maddox.

"You want me to call Calvin, Bunny's brother?" I asked Detective Girard.

"No, thanks. That's on me."

Both detectives told us they were going to recommend that Diggs and Beech be charged and tried for capital murder in Virginia for Brenda Miles's death before Maryland and the District of Columbia had their chance, which worked for us because we had the pair sitting in the federal detention center in Alexandria awaiting disposition of trial venue.

The temperatures had risen throughout the morning, and the wind calmed. That afternoon, we drove over to the detention center and arranged to meet with Diggs and his new defender, a sharp-faced guy in his forties named Richard Conlon.

"Tell us about Brenda Miles," I said when they sat down.

"Never heard of her," Diggs growled.

"She was a real estate agent here in Alexandria."

"Still never heard of her."

"How about Bunny Maddox?"

"Nope."

"What is this all about?" Conlon demanded.

Sampson said, "Your client's blood was all over the rope that strangled Brenda Miles. Bunny Maddox, who is missing and presumed dead, left hair in your client's van, and hair and blood from known murder victim Alice Ways was found there as well. Mr. Diggs is looking to go down for at least two murders and maybe as many as six. And since it looks like he will be tried here in Virginia, he will face the death penalty."

Diggs turned beet red and furious. "I don't know anything about any of these women! I'm being framed! You guys are all either too stupid to see it or too corrupt to want to."

CHAPTER

86

AROUND NINE IN THE morning at Washington Day School, Gary Soneji was walking around his classroom, cup of coffee in hand. It had been a long day already for him as he tried to make up for yesterday's snow day.

His seventh- and eighth-grade students were tackling a simple coding sequence he'd introduced that morning, and he actually found himself happy with their progress. Most of them were getting the concept rapidly. Even dear Cheryl Lynn Wise, ordinarily not the sharpest of tacks, had completed the task on her second try.

A knock came at the door, and the headmaster, Charles Pendleton Little, poked his head inside. "Mr. Soneji, might I have a word, please?"

"Absolutely," he said. He put his coffee on his desk and told the class to try to reverse the coding sequence. "You should be able to get out of anything you get into, right?" he asked.

He hurried out into the hall to find Little and U.S. Secret Service agent Jezzie Flanagan looking stricken. When the door shut behind Soneji, the headmaster spoke in slow, whispered, and choking words.

"Agent Flanagan just heard that Washington Day has suffered a terrible tragedy, Mr. Soneji," Little said, and then he stopped, unable to go on.

Flanagan jumped in. "There was a ten-car pileup on the Beltway yesterday morning. Among the casualties were Sandy Ravisky, her husband, Peter, and their new baby, Irene."

"Wait, what?" Soneji gasped, his trembling hands going to his lips. "No. No, that's…oh my God."

The truth was, Soneji felt gutted.

He had prepared for everything but the baby's death. His reconnaissance had clearly shown Sandy's mother coming over daily to care for the baby while Sandy took Peter to work and then again in the evening when Sandy picked him up. Every time.

"Are they sure?" he asked, the sickening sensation growing.

"I confirmed with the state troopers," Flanagan said. "And the family."

Soneji took a step back and put his hand against the lockers to steady himself. "You're right, Mr. Little. This is terrible."

The headmaster said, "We're going to tell the rest of the faculty in person and then call an assembly for sixth period to inform the students."

"You okay with keeping this quiet until then, Mr. Soneji?" Flanagan asked.

Soneji smiled weakly. "I don't have much of a choice, but yes, I am okay."

"Then go back to her students," the headmaster said. "Though I guess they are your students now if you want the job."

"They're still Mrs. Ravisky's students for the moment," Soneji said, feeling acid churn his stomach. He glanced at Flanagan, then returned his gaze to Little. "Today, I'm still a stand-in for her, Mr. Little."

CHAPTER 87

GARY SONEJI WENT BACK into the classroom and saw his students as if through steam brewing up out of the sourness in his stomach. The kids seemed part of a dream he was observing; he was wholly separate from them, from everything now.

He went to his desk, needing to sit, though he still felt no remorse whatsoever about the loss of Sandy and Peter Ravisky. They were obstacles that had stood in the way of the job being his. No more. No less.

But the baby. The infant. What was her name? Iris? Irene.

She was not supposed to be in that van. Irene was supposed to be home with Grandma. But she was collateral damage.

Any way Soneji looked at it, he didn't feel regret.

That understanding cut some last cord inside him.

He was different now, stronger in a way. He told himself he

was more dangerous than Berkowitz. More deadly than DeSalvo and every other homicidal maniac he had ever studied, from Jack the Ripper to the Green River Killer. None of them had ever killed a baby. Not one.

He had gone beyond all of them.

He was—

"Mr. Soneji?"

Soneji startled when he realized that Cheryl Lynn Wise had come up to his desk. This was a first.

"I'm trying to do the retreat by flipping the code, but for some reason it's not working. Or at least, I don't think it's working."

"Let's take a look, shall we?" Soneji said. She handed the printout to him and came around the desk so they could look at it together.

It took every bit of his willpower not to focus on Cheryl Lynn being so close, not to smell her preteen odor, as he showed her how she could work toward the answer without the extra steps she'd added, which had cut her off from the solution.

"Thank you, Mr. Soneji," Cheryl Lynn said and laughed. "My mom says I always make things more difficult than they have to be."

"It's just a learning process, Ms. Wise," Soneji said. "Sometimes we have to go down blind alleys in the maze to find our way out."

He smiled, handed her the printout, then gazed at his desk as she walked back to her seat.

Soneji was his own monster now.

That lovely idea spawned another thought, a new one. It triggered a sudden bolt of power that spiraled up through him, triggering the new thought again and causing another surge of strength that became a dead certainty in his mind. He raised his head to watch Cheryl Lynn take her seat.

He was his own monster now.

And with monsters, anything was possible.

Absolutely anything.

CHAPTER 88

THE DEEPER WE GOT into December, the bigger and more uncomfortable Maria became and the more excited and boisterous Damon turned in anticipation of Christmas.

He'd caught on to the concept of presents at his last birthday and was using that word and the word *candy* more and more as we closed in on the twenty-fifth of the month.

Maria had officially started her maternity leave and wasn't sleeping well, which meant I wasn't sleeping well either. But I was still getting up to take care of Damon while she rested.

I was yawning and drinking a strong cup of coffee at my desk downtown on December 23 when John Sampson plopped another stack of files in front of me.

"More evidence against Diggs and Beech," he said.

Chief George Pittman had made his way into the squad room.

"It's a slam dunk now. Diggs is going to fry, and Beech? Who knows?"

"Chief—" I began.

"That's over for now, Cross. I have a new case for you and Sampson."

Pittman said he'd been contacted by the chief of homicide for NYPD in Brooklyn.

"They're dealing with a gangland slaying up there, an Italian Mob hit that might have ties down here," the chief said, putting a piece of paper with a phone number on it on my desk. "Detective's name is Slattery. He's waiting for your call."

I could tell it was an order, so I nodded, told Sampson to get on the same line, and punched in the NYPD detective's number on my desk phone.

"Damian Slattery, Homicide," said a harried voice.

"Alex Cross and John Sampson, DC Homicide," I said. "Our bosses thought we should talk."

"Yeah, that's affirmative, Detectives, and I appreciate the call back," Slattery said, and he gave us a brief intro to his case.

Late the afternoon before, Aldo Ricci, a lieutenant in the Capula crime family, had been found dead—beaten and skinned in places—near the back of a junkyard. The consensus among investigators was that the murder was the work of the rival Maggione syndicate.

"But no one's talking on either side, Capula or Maggione. Least of all to me, a mick."

Sampson said, "That's how it still goes up there?"

"Being Italian helps in certain circles; being Irish helps in others," he said matter-of-factly. "Which is why I don't think the killer was a Maggione soldier."

"Contract killer?" I said.

"A very specific one," Slattery said. "His name is Michael Sullivan, but he goes by a dozen aliases. In Ireland and at Scotland Yard, they call him 'the Butcher of Sligo.' Likes to leave a calling card like flaying skin off his victims before and after death."

Slattery said Sullivan was last known to be working in Europe, but the way Aldo Ricci was beaten and his skin taken off his back, the NYPD detective was fairly sure they were dealing with the Butcher.

"But you could help me nail that down by visiting Aldo's brother Emilio," Slattery said. "He lives in DC. He does not know that his brother is dead. We have not announced the killing yet."

"Give us an address," Sampson said, "and we're on our way."

CHAPTER 89

EMILIO FAZIO, A LEAN, intense man in his late thirties, lived by himself in a small condo complex near the Bethesda line. We caught him exiting his place dressed in running gear.

When he saw our badges, Fazio was initially hostile. "Whatever's going on, I had nothing to do with it and I intend to keep it that way."

"We're not here because of you, Mr. Fazio," I said. "It's your brother Aldo."

Fazio turned stony. "Aldo's my stepbrother, and I am not involved. Whatever Aldo's done now, I am not involved."

"I'm sorry to say that Aldo's dead, Mr. Fazio," Sampson said.

The news hit Fazio hard. He looked at the ground, shaking his head at the injustice.

"When?" he asked finally.

"He was found yesterday afternoon," I said. "We're waiting on time of death."

Fazio bobbed his head slowly. "How? Where?"

Sampson and I exchanged glances.

I said, "In a Brooklyn junkyard. Beaten to death."

The dead man's stepbrother took a long breath and let it out slowly. "I'm sorry to hear that. Aldo deserved something more... merciful. Just glad my mom's not around to know."

"Some skin was cut off his back," Sampson told him.

"His upper back?"

We nodded.

"The tattoo," Fazio said.

"He had a tattoo on his upper back?"

"Eagle wings," he said. "Got them when he was fifteen. Drove my mom nuts."

Fazio talked to us for an hour, describing how his widowed mother had married Aldo's divorced father. His stepfather had operated on the fringes of the Maggione family, running small bookie operations.

"Aldo and I, we were almost the same age," Fazio said. "At first, like when we were ten, it was good between us. But I did everything to stay out of the crime thing. And then Aldo got that tattoo and started hanging with guys from the Capula family just to piss his dad off."

Fazio said his life and Aldo's life had gone in separate directions.

"I went to Fordham at eighteen," he said. "Aldo boosted seven cars at eighteen, got caught, and went to Sing Sing for grand theft auto."

By the time his stepbrother was released, Emilio Fazio had a whole new life.

"I have a law degree and work for the Commerce Department, cover international trade issues," he said. "I've had nothing to do with Aldo for years."

"When's the last time you saw him?" I said.

Fazio looked uncomfortable. "Two Thanksgivings ago. So, a little over a year? My mom was sick, and she insisted we both come to her place in Queens."

"How'd that go?"

"Bad," Fazio said. "Aldo got drunk and started talking about all the women he was seeing, the money he was making, and the people who had it out for him."

"He mention any names?"

"Just that they were all with the Maggione family," he said, and frowned at some distant memory. "No, that's not true. He did mention someone specifically and seemed very unnerved when he did."

My pager buzzed. I took it out and saw it was my grandmother calling, which she never did when I was at work.

I walked away from Sampson and Fazio, found a pay phone, and called her. "Nana? Something wrong?"

"Everything's right," my grandmother said. "Maria's gone into labor. I've just come back from taking her to St. Anthony's. Go meet her there, and I'll stay here with Damon."

CHAPTER 90

MARIA'S FIRST DELIVERY HAD been slow, with Damon coming into our lives after fourteen hours of labor. But she'd dilated fast after her water broke at Nana Mama's house, and I almost missed this birth.

I literally skidded into Maria's room to find her sweating from head to toe, tended by two nurses and her obstetrician, Dr. Barbara Holmes, and very happy to see me.

"You made it for the grand finale," she said, grinning.

"Just made it," said Dr. Holmes. "We're going to push at the next contraction, okay?"

I took my wife's hand, and when the contraction came, Maria strained and screamed. At the end a nurse said, "Already starting to crown. Your baby's at the finish line!"

Twenty-five minutes later, the miracle that was Janelle "Jannie"

Cross slid from her mother. She immediately began taking heaving breaths of air that she expelled in cries and squawks. Maria and I broke down, grinning with joy through our tears.

"She's a big girl, got all her fingers and toes," Dr. Holmes announced, examining her. "Look at those legs. And listen to the set of lungs she's got!"

Indeed, Janelle squawked and wiggled and sputtered between deep breaths that visibly expanded her rib cage. We started laughing.

"No wonder it felt like she was fighting to get out," Maria said.

I said, "My little Janelle, my little Jannie, was ready for life. She *is* ready for life!"

I gazed at my daughter. Even though she was full of what Nana Mama would call piss and vinegar, it was love at first sight. The nurse laid Jannie on her mama's chest.

Jannie almost instantly stopped squawking, and Maria cooed. "Look at you, little one. Welcome to the world, Janelle."

I don't know if I've ever seen a more beautiful sight or had a better moment. I started tearing up again. The nurse took Jannie to check her vital signs, and the baby squawked again.

"You'll be right back, young lady, I promise," the nurse said.

She weighed and measured Jannie, then brought her back to Maria, who was being cleaned up, and laid our baby on her chest again, skin to skin. "Eight pounds and two ounces, twenty inches," she said. "Perfect APGAR score."

"Yay," Maria said softly, tiredly, stroking Jannie's back while the other nurse put a warm blanket over her little body.

I put my hand by Maria's on Janelle's back, and we basked in the grace of that for several minutes before Maria said, "You should make some calls, tell Damon he's got a baby sister."

"When do you think I can bring him in?" I asked Dr. Holmes.

"I think mom and baby will be ready to greet visitors in a few hours or so," she said. "Give Maria and Janelle time to rest."

I got home about two hours later. Damon was just waking up from his nap.

I went into his bedroom and said, "Santa brought you an early Christmas present."

That got him alert pronto. "Present?"

"Your baby sister was born!"

He seemed confused until I said that *Janelle* was the present, at which point he looked a little disappointed, but he cheered up when I asked him if he wanted to go with me and Nana to meet Jannie and see his mother.

We walked into Maria's hospital room soon after, with Nana Mama leading the way. Jannie was swaddled in Maria's arms and sound asleep.

"She's beautiful, Maria," my grandmother whispered.

"Isn't she?"

I carried Damon over to the bed. At first he frowned, as if he were unsure about this new thing taking his spot in his mother's arms.

"Isn't she pretty, Damon?" Maria asked.

Damon shrugged and held out his arms, whining, "Mommy."

"Mommy can't hold you right now. I have to hold your sister for a bit, just like I held you when you were born. But do you want a kiss?"

He nodded with a pout, and I lowered him until she could kiss him on the cheek. He laughed and said, "Kiss Jannie?"

"You want to?" Maria asked.

Damon nodded. We moved them close, and he kissed her forehead, which set off *Ahh*s in the room from the nurses on duty.

"Jannie pretty," Damon said when I shifted him to my hip.

"She's more than that, bud," I said and rubbed his head. "She's your little sister, and you always need to help and take care of her. Okay?"

"Okay," he said, and laid his head on my shoulder, and suddenly everything was perfect in my life.

CHAPTER

91

GARY SONEJI HAD TO admit it: Missy was right about the tuxedo. It fit him well and made him feel different, empowered even.

And her mother, Christiana, had been absolutely correct about her brother's heated barn being a wonderful venue for a wedding and reception, especially when it was lavishly decorated for Christmas Eve.

Fresh holly, laurel, and evergreen garlands wrapped the old posts, lower beams, and railings inside the barn. A string trio was softly playing Christmas tunes. The air was scented with spice from pots bubbling atop woodstoves burning in the corners.

Three large wood and electric-candle chandeliers were suspended over the central space, throwing a warm glow on the crowd of one hundred, all busily gabbing or drinking or nibbling cheese or finding assigned dinner seats at one of the long tables on the floor or up in one of the old haylofts.

It was all so wonderful that it unnerved Soneji a little as he moved through the crowd, sipping from his champagne glass, accepting congratulations, and feigning interest in the names of the perfect strangers who'd come at him in waves since Roni had toddled down the aisle with flowers, and he and Missy had exchanged their vows. By the time he crossed the room a second time, he was getting upset. How was he supposed to remember all these names?

"Gary!"

Soneji would not have turned if the call had come from behind him, but Missy's older brother, Marty, was coming right at him, his bow tie already undone and his collar open. A glass of whiskey neat was nestled in his paw of a hand.

"Marty," Soneji said, and prepared for the man-hug he knew was coming.

Built like a Greco-Roman wrestler, Marty Kasajian had huge, long arms that he wrapped around Soneji as he rubbed his dense, dark beard against Soneji's cheek. His breath stank of cigar smoke and liquor.

"You're true family now, Murph," Marty said when he broke the embrace. "A brother to me and to all who are gathered here for you and my baby sister and that precious Roni."

"That's kind and great," Soneji said, trying to sound pleased. "So great. Thank you, Marty."

"A drink!" Marty cried. "We must drink to this union, Gar, with a great bourbon!"

Soneji hated it when Marty called him Gar.

"I promise I'll share one with you later," he said. "I don't think Missy would want me sloppy drunk this early in the night."

Marty Kasajian closed one eye, pursed his lips, and nodded as he held out his glass. "And my sister would be right. She's always right. That's the thing about wives and sisters—they have a sixth sense about what's right, don't they?"

Soneji spotted Missy waving him to their table. "I'm learning that," he said. He left his brother-in-law and went to his bride's side.

"You look stunning in that dress," he said. "Really."

"Aww," Missy said. "Thank you. Mama says I got lucky."

"No, I'm the one who got lucky."

Beside Missy, Roni started clinking a glass with her spoon. Soon many in the barn were clinking. Soneji leaned in and kissed Missy and then Roni, which got a roar of approval.

Soneji raised his glass to the crowd, feeling once again that this was all happening to someone else. The sense of being an impostor in the constant center of attention intensified during dinner and with every spoon-clinking and kiss.

Halfway through his roast duck, claustrophobia began to set in. He needed air. He needed a few moments alone.

He excused himself and told Missy he'd be right back, then he went to the stall that served as a cloakroom and found his overcoat.

Soneji went outside. He walked away from the barn into the darkness, glad for the clear, cold night, glad to be free of the incessant chatter that constantly boiled out of his wife and everyone at the event. Couldn't they all just shut up once in a while?

He wasn't sure how long he stood there looking up at the night sky, but it was long enough that his fingers and toes felt numb when he turned back toward the barn and his future. He was confronted at the door by Missy, who whispered furiously, "I've been looking for you. We've all been looking for you."

"But Missy—" he began.

"Don't 'But Missy' me," she hissed. "You're embarrassing me. We were supposed to cut the cake with Roni, and you were nowhere to be found! And the band kept playing and saying, 'Where's the groom? Do we have a runner?'"

"I was looking at the stars on Christmas Eve at my wedding reception," he said wearily. "I suppose I could get angry at *you* for not being there. But I'm not."

"Let's cut the cake, shall we?" she said after a long pause. She took him by the hand and led him back into the barn. "He was out there freezing and looking at stars," Missy said in a voice loud and exasperated enough to make the crowd laugh. But he could see she wasn't amused as they cut the cake.

Soneji kept smiling as they pushed pieces of cake into each other's mouths, but Missy shoved a little too hard for his liking.

He kept smiling. He would let her get away with this kind of thing tonight, but not in the future. Missy would have to be taught not to diminish him in public. She would have to learn there were punishments for that.

The harsh fantasies that sparked in his brain then should have been enough to calm his anger. But when it was time for their first dance and Missy warned him against stepping on her hem and ruining everything, he had had enough.

As they danced, Soneji kept looking at his twice-bride's eyes and then down at her neck, thinking once again how satisfying it would be to strangle Missy with his bare hands and how perfect it would be when Cheryl Lynn Wise finally took her rightful place in his cruel loving arms.

CHAPTER

92

LATE CHRISTMAS AFTERNOON FOUND our family at Nana Mama's, where we'd spent the previous day and evening after Maria and Jannie's release from St. Anthony's.

Mom and newborn were upstairs nursing. My grandmother was baking a ham and making garlic potato pancakes, the delicious smell of which competed with the odor of the Fraser fir tree in the front room. On the TV was a football game.

I was on the floor with my back to the Christmas tree and the opened presents, paying little attention to the game and playing with Damon, his new Tonka dump truck, and the little figurines from his Lego set. He had a grandma in the cab at the wheel of the truck and the other five figures seated in the dump bed with a stuffed little Saint Bernard he was calling Tilly for reasons that were unclear.

"Tilly nice dog," Damon said.

"I can see that," I said. "Why is she named Tilly?"

Damon shrugged. "She Tilly, Dad."

That was about as logical as toddlers got, so I decided not to probe further. He got on his knees and began to push the toy truck around, making *vroom-vroom* noises. The doorbell rang.

The door opened and shut, and John Sampson peeked his head into the front room. "Merry Christmas!"

"Merry Christmas to you! Dinner in half an hour," I said.

My little boy popped to his feet as Sampson entered with several wrapped gifts.

"Presents?" Damon said.

"He's addicted," I explained.

"Isn't every kid on Christmas?" Sampson laughed and handed him a gift. "They're for you, Damon."

My son tore off the paper and looked puzzled for a second when the contents fell out. They looked like two large wool socks, but when he turned them over, he saw the faces of Big Bird and Cookie Monster and started giggling. "Puppets," he said.

"That's right," Sampson said. He knelt down to put Damon's hand into Cookie Monster's body. The puppet was a little big for his arm, and the head flopped, but my son did not care.

"Nana!" he yelled and headed off toward the kitchen. "Look! I Cookie!"

I started laughing. "I Cookie."

Sampson chuckled. "Where's the new baby?"

"Upstairs with Maria," I said. "They'll be down soon. By the way, what happened after I left you with Fazio? He was saying something about some guy his stepbrother was afraid of?"

John's eyebrows rose. "That's correct. He remembered the

guy being Irish, not Italian. A few minutes later, no prompting from me, he came up with a name, Sullivan, and said the guy owned a meat shop."

"Like a butcher," I said.

"Exactly," Sampson said.

"You tell the NYPD detective?"

"Called Slattery on the spot. He was pretty happy, said he knew it had to be the Butcher of Sligo's work."

CHAPTER 93

BEFORE I COULD RESPOND to John, Maria came down the stairs with Jannie swaddled in her arms. All thoughts of work went by the wayside. And Sampson got to hold his goddaughter for the first time.

As long a body as Janelle had for being a two-day-old, she looked like a peanut in the big man's arms.

"She's gorgeous," Sampson said. "Just a miracle, isn't she?"

Maria smiled. "She is."

"How you feeling?"

"Like my stomach got beaten by a two-by-four and I'm a whole lot tired," Maria said, yawning. "She didn't sleep well last night."

Nana Mama called us to dinner. Big Bird and Cookie Monster were not allowed on Damon's high chair, but my grandmother stopped his crying by propping up the puppets on the counter beside him.

She had used a Creole recipe on the Virginia ham that made it both sweet and a little fiery. Her potato and red onion pancakes came out perfectly crispy on the outside and savory on the inside. The green beans roasted with slab bacon chips were a vegan's nightmare and a carnivore's dream.

"That's the best Christmas dinner I've ever had," Sampson said, putting his napkin down after consuming a gargantuan quantity of food.

Nana Mama grinned. "Same thing you said last year and the year before that and the year before that."

"What can I say? You keep outdoing yourself."

"You do," Maria said.

I said, "Absolutely, Nana."

That pleased my grandmother even more.

"I have an announcement," Maria said as I helped serve pie and ice cream.

"You're not pregnant again already, are you?" Sampson said.

"Ha-ha," Maria said and gently punched his arm before looking at me. "I'm going to leave St. Anthony's when I'm ready to go back to work."

That was a big surprise to me, since she'd been working at the hospital since we'd met and always said she loved it.

"And go where?" I asked.

"There's a social work position open where I grew up, in Potomac Gardens."

Nana Mama winced. "That's a tougher place than you remember."

"Which is exactly why I'm needed there," Maria said, gazing

at me. "I think I can do more good in Potomac Gardens than I can at St. Anthony's."

I could see the conviction in her eyes and hear the passion in her voice. Feeling concern as much as pride over her decision, I said, "As long as there's ample security for you, I'm all for it."

Maria beamed at me. "The position doesn't start for another three months, and I'll make sure about the security."

"Perfect," I said, though again, there was hesitation in my thoughts. Potomac Gardens was one of the roughest projects in the District of Columbia.

After the dishes were cleared, we retreated to the front room and finished the football game. We watched *A Christmas Story* until Sampson had to leave.

Nana Mama went upstairs cackling after Santa told Ralphie that he'd shoot his eye out and then put his boot in the kid's face, her favorite scene.

Damon fell asleep in my lap during the scene about the Scott Farkus affair, Maria's favorite. She fell asleep on my shoulder with Jannie in her lap before Ralphie actually got his BB gun.

After watching all the way to the scene of the beheading of the roast duck during the Christmas dinner at the Chinese restaurant, I clicked off the TV with the remote. I sat and looked at the lights on the tree, feeling Damon shift in my lap and hearing Maria breathe with her mouth open. Jannie made fussy little newborn noises.

I felt tears come to my eyes as I gazed up at the angel ornament that always sat atop Nana Mama's Christmas tree.

"Thank you for my family," I whispered. "Keep them safe in the coming year."

CHAPTER 94

BY TEN A.M. ON New Year's Eve day, snow was falling steadily in the Pine Barrens. A couple of inches of it already coated the pines and the ground when Soneji drove his brother-in-law Marty's Dodge Ram pickup up the steep two-track to his house.

He stopped shy of the gate and the multiple NO TRESPASSING signs, looking ahead into the yard. Seeing no tracks and nothing out of place since his visit with Bunny Maddox, Soneji got out, unlocked the gate, and pushed it open, noticing that the length of rope he'd practiced with was still hanging around the post there and was clad in snow.

He got in the truck, pulled into the yard, backed up to the porch, and turned the engine off. He lowered the window. The gentle tapping of the snowflakes deadened all other sound.

Soneji closed his eyes a second, thankful for this peace and quiet after the wedding and their three-day honeymoon at Missy's cousin's condo in the Poconos. The sex aside, Missy had yammered so much about all the changes to be put into effect after their marriage restart that he'd thought about hitting her over the head with a hammer at one point and cutting her vocal cords at several more.

In the end, he said he had to help an old friend do some carpentry work on his lake house to satisfy a real estate agent who wanted to list the place. Marty offered him the truck, saying he could use his Cadillac in the meantime. And Soneji told Missy not to worry, that he'd be back long before the start of Trish's annual New Year's Eve party.

At the back of the pickup, he lifted the window on the cap and lowered the tailgate so he could get at the eight-foot lengths of two-by-four pine studs stacked on top of drywall sheets. Soneji got the lumber into the basement in four trips.

The drywall was trickier to handle and demanded a difficult negotiation of the steep staircase. But once he had the method down, he quickly got two more sheets into position and stepped out onto his porch for the final one.

"Halloo the house!"

Soneji stopped short, looked over the truck cap, and saw a woman puffing and trudging toward him in the snow. She was in her late forties, doughy, dowdy, and wore an old navy pea jacket over a peasant dress and boots.

A bright, multicolored knit wool cap sat on her head at an angle. A matching scarf hung loosely around her shoulders.

Holding up mittens in another riot of color, the perimenopausal hippie stopped about forty feet from his truck and said,

"So sorry to intrude, but I got myself stuck in the ditch a good way up from the bottom of your steep driveway."

"Why were you coming *up* my steep driveway?" Soneji asked. "There's a No Trespassing sign on each side."

CHAPTER

95

"MY MISTAKE! MY MISTAKE!" the woman said and then chuckled. "Had directions to my sister-in-law's place somewhere out here and I got turned around and saw your fresh tracks and started after them to ask directions. Do you know her? Lainey Dodge?"

"Can't say I do."

"Too bad. Anyway, I was wondering if you might help me get out of the ditch? Or let me use your phone to call a tow truck?"

"I don't have a phone yet," Soneji said, seeing new possibilities in this previously unwanted visit. "Let's go take a look at your predicament and I'll see if I can get you out."

He came down off the porch, strode up to her, grinning, and stuck out his gloved hand. "Gary Murphy."

She pushed back her hat, revealing sweaty hair, and shook his hand. "Cynthia Owens. My friends call me Cyn-Cyn."

"Okay, Cyn-Cyn, lead on."

Owens started back. "I'm clueless with maps and compasses and such. You?"

"Also terrible with navigation," he said, though that was far from true.

"Didn't help myself coming out here without better tires," Owens said, almost to the gate with Soneji a few yards behind now. "But I'm one of those folks just likes to dive right in once I decide. Lainey said at Christmas she had a place rented in the Pine Barrens for New Year's Eve, and I woke up early this morning, fed the cats, and thought, *Why not go?* Make it a surprise for my cousin that I actually showed up for once."

She chuckled and shook her head. Soneji sniffed something familiar floating off her and tried not to scowl. He hated cats. He hated the smell of cat people.

She passed through the gate and she shook her right rainbow mitten. "Typical Cyn-Cyn Owens move. If I'd been born a hundred fifty years ago, I'd have just jumped on a wagon train and headed west. Oregon trail, you know?"

Soneji couldn't believe it. He'd come in search of a little quiet time away from Missy, and here he'd traded one chatty Cathy for another.

Then he saw the practice rope there, looped over the gate post. He reached out and snagged the rope as he walked through the opening in the fence.

With all the newly fallen and still falling snow, it was almost too easy for him to move up quick and silent behind the woman as she jabbered on about people who were supposed to be at her sister-in-law's party.

Soneji no longer cared. He was set on sating a sudden and overwhelming need.

For the second time, Soneji felt the rush, the adrenaline, as he flipped the rope over the woman's foolish cap, nose, and chin. He felt it settle at her throat and yanked back viciously.

Owens made a gargling cry of alarm as her boots slid out from under her on the slippery drive. As she crashed down, her full weight came against the rope, choking her even more.

"Nnnnn-aaa!" she grunted. "Nnnnn-aaa!"

Soneji wrenched the rope tighter, smelling the feline stench all over her now.

"Nnnn-aa," she grunted again, weaker this time.

"What's that, Cyn-Cyn?" Soneji said. "Cat got your tongue?"

Her mittens flailed at her throat, and she made guttural noises in her windpipe for almost fifteen seconds. Then the sounds stopped. The mittens slowly sagged, followed by her shoulders, and finally her head.

Despite the cat smell, Soneji felt the thrill of strangulation, so close, so intimate, exploding through him as strong as it had when he'd throttled the real estate agent. He let loose his hold on the rope and allowed the cat lady's corpse to collapse into the snow.

Soneji stood there, chest heaving, as happy as he'd ever been.

Then he caught the scent of something fouler than cat and realized the woman had shit herself dying. That completely destroyed the mood, the elation, the celebration.

He needed to get rid of the body and its...stenches. He thought about going to get the truck, then decided to just drag her carcass by the rope already around her neck. He'd leave drag marks, but the snow was intensifying. The drag marks would be gone within the hour.

Once he had her inside the shed, he'd get the truck and pull her car out of the ditch, bring it up, and put it under tarps until he could move her vehicle where it would never be linked to the house.

"Ground's going to be tough to crack today, Cyn-Cyn," Soneji said, pulling hard on the rope, squeezing her neck, causing her head to loll and her damn hat to fall off.

He cursed and grabbed the hat, which reeked of cat and made him want to dry-heave, and stuck it back on her head. He took up the rope once more and slid the body across the snow, up the drive. "I'm probably going to need to use a pickax first."

That meant no progress on his secret room. Not today. He felt frustrated.

Then again, he had managed to get all the remaining building supplies for the room into the basement. That counted.

The cat woman walking into his life also counted. She had confirmed his love of strangulation. The feline and crap odors aside, he thought that choking her had almost felt better than the first time with the real estate agent.

As he dragged Owens's body through the gate and up the slight rise toward the shed and the house, he told himself that these kinds of one-off events, crimes of opportunity, just might be enough to check his hunger, his need to kill, while he took his sweet time learning about Cheryl Lynn Wise and the heavy security around her so he could execute the perfect kidnapping.

After all, Soneji was his own monster now.

He would no longer study and role-play the homicidal greats of yore.

"Let them study me," Soneji said and chortled. "Let them all study me now."

EPILOGUE

A Reckoning

Present Day

CHAPTER

96

I HEARD FOOTSTEPS COMING down the stairs, shaking me from the trance I'd been in, reading Soneji's kill diary inside his secret room in the Pine Barrens cabin.

I looked at the last line I'd read: *Let them all study me now.*

"Alex? You still in there?" Sampson called. "We've been outside three hours."

I shook my head, set *Profiles in Homicidal Genius* aside with a quarter of the pages still unread, and stood up. "Felt like weeks to me."

"The dogs have located more bodies," John said. "Going to be a chore identifying them."

I shook my head. "Probably not. In his book, he names several of the victims and describes where he buried them. There's probably more in the pages I didn't get to. One will be a woman named Cynthia Owens. And you don't want to know the names of two of them."

Sampson frowned. "What's that supposed to mean?"

I gazed around at the bins. "These are murder kits, John. Specific kits assembled so Soneji could practice the methods of serial killers he admired. *TBS* is the Boston Strangler. *NS* is the Night Stalker. *ZK* is the Zodiac Killer, *GRK* is the Green River Killer, *JWG* is John Wayne Gacy, and *SOS*—"

Mahoney came pounding down the stairs. "We've got another one, and I need all hands on deck."

Realizing I desperately needed fresh air, I took a last look at the bins, the macabre treasures, and Soneji's memoir. When I ducked out of the room, Mahoney and Sampson studied me.

"You look like you've seen a ghost," Ned said.

"I have, in a way. Quite a few, in fact," I said, jabbing my thumb over my shoulder. "It's all in there."

"All what?"

Sampson said, "The names and burial locations of Soneji's victims."

"And all the evidence against Soneji—and us," I said, feeling gutted again. I wanted to cry or rage at everything that had changed so completely inside the spider's nest.

"Evidence against *us?* Who is *us?*" Sampson demanded.

I gazed at John, then Ned. "A long time ago, Soneji duped the FBI, the Virginia state police, the Maryland state police, and the Pennsylvania state police. But most of all, he duped DC Metro's Homicide team, specifically me and John, when we were junior detectives on our earliest cases."

Sampson's expression turned hard. "I do not know what you're talking about, Alex."

"I'll explain it in full on the drive back to DC, but for now,

Ned, I don't think John and I should have anything further to do with this investigation."

Mahoney rubbed his jaw. "What? Why? Stop talking in opaque loops."

"We can't be a part of this because we are compromised," I said. I felt closed in and pushed past them, heading toward the stairs. "Like it or not, culpable or not, Sampson and I had a role in a lot of what happened in this cabin."

John came after me as I climbed up from the basement. "What in God's name are you talking about, Alex?" he yelled.

I ignored him, wanting cold air in my lungs and something in my stomach before I explained it all. He stayed right behind me, and Mahoney followed him. When we were all out on the front porch, I gazed across Soneji's yard with new and stunned eyes.

"We could have stopped him," I said. "A long time ago."

My anguish must have shown on my face because when Sampson spoke again, it was in a lower voice and with more empathy. "What did you mean when you said I didn't want to know the names of two of the people buried here? Please, brother, you're upsetting me."

"And me," Mahoney said.

"A nineteen-year-old named Joyce Adams was evidently the first to be tortured, killed, and buried here," I said.

"Joyce Adams?" Sampson said, squinting. "I have no idea who—"

"She was a freshman who disappeared from Princeton University a long time ago, more than a decade before Maggie Rose Dunne was kidnapped from the Washington Day School," I said. "Bunny Maddox is buried here too."

Sampson blinked and shook his head slowly as he turned from me. "No."

"Yes, John," I said firmly. "And I believe ballistics will prove that the forty-four-caliber Bulldog pistol down in that room fired the bullets that killed Conrad Talbot and the two hospital techs. The rope we found in the van? Soneji stole it from Diggs's game pole to use on Brenda Miles. It was all an elaborate frame job designed to ensure that evidence of Soneji's early killings pointed straight at Diggs and Beech."

Looking into the middle distance, my oldest friend shook his head again, then faced me. "Diggs kept telling us he was innocent."

"I remember."

"Everyone said the evidence against him was ironclad. Jury. Appeals courts. Everyone."

"Every single one," I replied.

Sampson's defenses broke down then. There was a tremor in his voice and a glassiness in his eyes when he choked out, "We helped put an innocent man…"

"We did," I said, and the damage to my reputation and my belief in the judicial system felt completely and utterly irrevocable.

CHAPTER

97

WE TOOK TURNS DRIVING back to Washington, both of us silent, the weight of what we'd done and hadn't done so long ago pressing in around us.

Eamon Diggs had proclaimed his innocence throughout his years on death row and all the way through the appeals process, or almost all the way. He'd been waiting to hear if the U.S. Supreme Court would hear his case when he was stabbed to death in a prison fight.

Afterward, Sampson and I told the relatives of his victims, including Bunny's brother and Conrad Talbot's parents, that in a savage way, justice had been served.

The memories made me sick. The memories made me question whether we had made other deadly mistakes in the years we'd been investigating homicides since the white-van murders.

I thought about how painstaking Soneji's framing of Diggs had been. I recalled his descriptions of how he'd hunted Bunny Maddox when she'd tried to escape, how he'd strangled Brenda Miles. How Cynthia Owens had died just because she'd had the bad luck to step into this psychopath's lair, and how he had planned to abduct Cheryl Lynn Wise long before he'd set his sights on nine-year-old Maggie Rose Dunne and her friend Michael "Shrimpie" Goldberg.

I thought back to that Christmas right after Jannie was born, remembered how Maria, Damon, and my infant daughter had all fallen asleep in my arms on the couch at Nana Mama's and how I'd looked at the angel on the tree's top and prayed for my family to be kept safe.

But that had not happened.

After a Virginia grand jury indicted Diggs and Beech for capital crimes, Sampson and I helped the NYPD and the FBI in the hunt for the Butcher of Sligo. Michael Sullivan had eventually come to our home and confronted me, looking for a woman who'd told Maria that the Butcher had raped her.

The following evening, I went to Potomac Gardens to pick up Maria, and as I hugged her hello after a long day's work, one of Sullivan's henchmen shot her. The love of my life and the mother of my two young kids died in my arms.

The children and I moved in with Nana Mama. She helped me raise Damon and Jannie.

But Maria's death sent me into a long, slow, haunted downward spiral.

I became obsessed with catching killers, and I put the hunt for them above everything else in my life. Eventually I became Metro PD's deputy chief of detectives and then a profiler for the

FBI, where I partnered with Ned Mahoney in the Behavioral Science Unit.

During those years, I am ashamed to admit that I neglected my kids too many times and I neglected myself all the time. Most nights I went to bed feeling like a hollow man, like I had little to live for outside of my work and providing for my children.

And now, as Sampson pulled up in front of my house on Fifth Street, I felt the same way, hollowed out, as if all the work I'd done since Maria's murder were tainted by my involvement in the wrongful conviction of Eamon Diggs and by my inability to see through the veils of deceit Soneji had hung.

Sampson said, "I feel like I've been mugged, hit over the head by this. I don't know what to say or do about it."

"I feel the same way, partner," I said, getting out. "I'll call you later."

I went into the house and found Bree watching the evening news and Nana Mama doing a crossword.

Bree said, "I thought you wouldn't be showing up until long after midnight."

"We had to leave the investigation. Turns out John and I are compromised."

"What?" my grandmother said, setting her puzzle aside.

"Compromised how?" my wife said.

"Hold that thought," I said. I went and got a beer, then sat down and told them.

When I finished, there were four empty beer cans on the coffee table, all of them mine, and shock and silence in the room.

"I don't know what to do to change things," I said. "To make it right."

"You can always make some good out of the worst situations," Nana Mama said.

"Diggs spent nearly twenty years in prison unjustly, and now he's dead," I said sharply. "There's no fixing that."

"I'm aware," she replied calmly. "But get outside your head and all this nonsense about the destruction of your reputation. It's tarnished a little, but that happens to the armor of any great knight. Go play some of your Gershwin. You'll figure out what to do."

Bree gazed at me with a degree of sadness. "That's probably not a bad idea, babe," she said. "A better one than having another beer, anyway."

I shrugged and walked, wobbling a little, through the house and out to the porch, where I sat at the piano and once again tried to play *An American in Paris*.

It was so bad, I almost gave up and went to the fridge for a fifth beer. But I knew in my heart that Bree was right, booze was not a good answer, so I kept playing.

Slowly, as sections of the piece came together, thoughts of Soneji, of Diggs, and of Maria slipped away until I was thinking of nothing but the music.

I don't know how long I sat there playing.

But when I came back to reality, I knew exactly what I had to do to start to remove the tarnish on my armor and fight the pull of the downward spiral that threatened to swallow me for the second time in my life.

CHAPTER

98

THREE DAYS AFTER LEAVING the Pine Barrens, John Sampson and I took a long drive to the southwestern tip of Virginia and the Red Onion State Prison.

One of the commonwealth's two supermax facilities, the Red Onion squatted in a large clearing in a forested unincorporated area near the town of Pound.

In aerial photos I'd seen, the prison was laid out in four repeating geometric patterns, like the design of an American Indian blanket. Seen from the parking area, the facility looked like what it was: a place for dangerous criminals to be caged for the safety of inmates in other correctional facilities.

"They've got the poor bastard with the worst of the worst these days," Sampson said when we climbed out of his new Ford F-150 into ungodly heat. He loved that truck.

Before I could reply, I heard a man say, "Dr. Cross? Detective Sampson?"

We turned and saw a sharp-suited man hurrying toward us with an awkward gait; he carried a briefcase and kept pushing a pair of heavy black-framed eyeglasses up the bridge of his nose. He was in his late forties and wore a nice suit, but that move with the glasses and his wild tousle of now-graying hair gave him away.

"Ryan Davis," I said, shaking his hand. "I'm glad you could come, Counselor."

"It's the least I could do," he said. "Except for a little gray at the temples, you guys look the same. I mean, it's kind of amazing. Like it all could have happened yesterday."

"Some ways, it feels like it did," I said. "Shall we?"

We went to the gate, showed our credentials, and turned over our weapons while Davis's briefcase was searched. Then we were led through six different security doors and gates before being met by Warden Daniel Celt, a tall whippet of a man in his fifties.

"Does he know we're coming?" Sampson asked.

"He has no idea," the warden replied.

I said, "And he's heard nothing from the outside world?"

"Been in solitary for breaking the rules," Celt said. "Twenty-three hours a day in his cell. One hour of exercise in the yard, which is where he'll be coming from."

Celt led us to an interior room with booths that faced bulletproof glass.

I said, "Given the circumstances, can we meet with him without the glass?"

The warden hesitated, then nodded and took us to a second room with a long table and benches made of concrete. Eyebolts jutted up out of the other side of the table and the floor.

The warden left through another door. A few minutes later, it opened.

A slight, older man in an orange jumpsuit with sweaty gray hair, glasses, and a furious expression shuffled in. An armed guard followed. A short chain linked the handcuffs he wore to a leather belt around his waist. A longer chain linked the cuffs around his ankles.

He sat, rage on his face, glasses fogged from coming out of the heat and into the air-conditioning. He said nothing as the guard connected his restraints to the eyebolts in the floor and on the other side of the table.

When the guard left, the inmate said angrily, "Can't see you for nothing. But I told the guard and the warden, I don't want to talk to no lawyer, much less three. Got no use for goddamned lawyers and I'm missing my fresh-air time."

"Mr. Beech," Ryan Davis said. "You probably don't remember me, but I was your attorney when you were held in the state police barracks in Coatesville."

"Here," I said, "let me clean your glasses before we go on. Is that okay?"

"Go ahead," Harold Beech said, sounding even more infuriated.

I took the glasses, wiped them clean, and put them back on his face.

Beech blinked, looked at Davis. "You're right. I don't remember you."

"How about us?" Sampson asked.

The inmate stared at each of us in turn and then nodded, stony. "Cross and Sampson. You put me here."

"We did," I said. "And now we're going to get you out."

CHAPTER 99

SHAKING HIS HEAD SLOWLY, Harold Beech glared at me, Sampson, and Davis, then snarled, "Don't you be effing with me now, giving me hope like that. I been effed on hope and every appeal for decades. I just can't—"

"It's different this time, Mr. Beech," Davis, the attorney, said.

Sampson said, "We've uncovered new and incontrovertible evidence that we believe exonerates you from the accessory-to-murder convictions in the deaths of Conrad Talbot, Selena DeMille, Alice Ways, Brenda Miles, and Bunny Maddox."

"It's going to take a little while for the old DNA samples to be matched to the bodies found recently in the Pine Barrens," Davis cautioned. "And I have to file motions based on the new evidence to get us a court hearing. But we are all confident that you will soon be a free man, Mr. Beech."

The anger began to leave the inmate's face, and tears welled in his eyes. "Is this real, man? Am I dreaming?"

"It's real, sir," I said. "No dream."

"I was framed. Isn't that right?"

"You were framed," Sampson said. "Clearly."

"You were caught in the web of a diabolical spider named Gary Soneji," I said. "We all were."

After we gave him all the nuts and bolts—who Soneji was and who he became and how he had slowly and meticulously planted the evidence that had sent him to prison for life—Beech swallowed hard and stared at us, the anger returning.

"Eamon," he said.

Both Sampson and I hung our heads. "We know," John said.

"He was innocent, just like he always said."

"He *was* innocent of the white-van killings," I said, hearing my own voice shake. "And we're never going to get over that, Mr. Beech. Never. We know our work helped lead to his wrongful imprisonment, which led to his murder. It's crushing to us."

"Beyond crushing," Sampson said. "Like buckshot in our hearts."

I said, "Soneji has been dead for years now, but it turns out he still has the power to inflict pain and suffering. And we want to end your pain and suffering by helping you get free."

Beech sat quietly for a moment, seemingly lost in thoughts of a different world.

"I been in a long time," he said hoarsely, emotion in his voice. "Spent more of my life behind bars than out."

"Yes, sir," I said.

"How do I learn to live outside prison?" he asked. "I'm too old and broken to work in a granite quarry. And I got nothing else to give."

Davis said, "You've given enough, Harry. Which is why Dr.

Cross and Detective Sampson contacted me. I haven't worked as a criminal defense lawyer in decades. I'm a private litigator in Philadelphia, a very good one. If you agree, I intend to sue in multiple states and jurisdictions on your behalf for wrongful imprisonment and demand reparations for all the years you have served unjustly."

I said, "We will testify for you. Explain how Soneji framed you, the whole thing, and show them the evidence, including a journal written in his own hand."

"And because of that, you will likely get millions," the attorney said.

"What?" Beech said, stunned.

"True," Sampson said. "You'll be taken care of for the rest of your life, Mr. Beech."

CHAPTER

100

ON THE FIVE-HOUR DRIVE home, John and I felt a lot better than we had coming down that morning. It was terrible that Harold Beech had spent decades behind bars for crimes he didn't commit. But we were putting an end to his incarceration.

We decided that, while we could never forgive ourselves for our role in Eamon Diggs's imprisonment and violent death, we would be men enough to travel to Pittsburgh, see Diggs's family, explain what had happened, and recommend they sue as well.

As we neared my home, Sampson said, "It does make you wonder, though."

"Wonder what?"

"How things would have been different if Soneji had been

caught at the beginning, after Joyce Adams and before Conrad Talbot."

"Whole lot fewer people dying needlessly," I said, sighing and feeling the guilt of that. "Soneji was a rabid dog, and he was in front of us from early on. I mean, he was right there in the Charles School faculty meeting the day after he shot Conrad Talbot."

"And at Washington Day after the computer science teacher and her husband and baby died on the Beltway after he sabotaged the brake linkage."

"Cold," I said, shaking my head. "And he was right there the whole time when Maggie Rose and Shrimpie were taken. Right under our nose for so long. He was so ordinary, so unremarkable, he was invisible, just like he always wanted to be."

"Remember his wife? Missy?"

"It was years before she knew that he was working part-time at Washington Day. Mr. Secrets, she called him, and she was right."

All of it nagged at me as I trudged up the steps to our house after Sampson dropped me off. Bree wasn't home from work yet. Ali was in his room studying.

I found Nana Mama in the kitchen, getting a leftover casserole out of the refrigerator. "You made good time," she said.

"Yes, ma'am," I said, taking a seat at the kitchen island.

"How'd Harold Beech take it?"

"Angry at life before we told him. Astonished at life by the time we left."

"That must have made you feel good."

I nodded. "It did. But I can't help wondering if it's enough. Honestly, it makes me question if I want to go on being a detective. I mean, my reputation, my career—it was all built on lies, Nana."

My grandmother set the casserole dish down on the stovetop. "First of all, getting Harold Beech out of prison is *not* enough. It's a start, but you'll have to keep at it, doing good deeds in his name and in Eamon Diggs's memory. And second, enough of this woe-is-me stuff. You were born to be a detective, Alex Cross. You were born to right wrongs."

"Even my own?"

"Especially your own," she said. "That's the mark of a real man."

For reasons I couldn't explain, I felt overwhelmed at that. I went to her, leaned over, and hugged her tiny little bird body tight.

"What's this about?" Nana said, sounding baffled and patting me on the back.

"I love you for always setting me straight, for always seeing a smart way forward." I pulled back and looked down at her. "I don't tell you that enough. I don't know what I would have done without you after Maria died. And I don't know what I'd do without you now."

"Well, thank you for all that. My God," she said, wiping tears off her cheeks after I kissed her on the head. "And I love you too, Alex. But I'll have you know, according to my cardiologist, I'm not going anywhere anytime soon."

I thought of everything I'd been through that day and started chuckling.

"What are you laughing at?"

"I don't know. I've spent years going after evil spiders in all sizes and shapes. And here you are, this little old lady in her nineties, and you are the strongest person I've ever known, and you remember everything. You're like...you're like an elephant or something."

Nana Mama laughed. "I'd say I'm more like a tortoise these days. But a lot of them *do* live to be a hundred years old or more."

"I've heard that," I said, hugging her again. "Lucky me."

ABOUT THE AUTHOR

In 1993, James Patterson wrote *Along Came a Spider*, which introduced the world to Alex Cross, a young detective working out of Washington, DC. Since then, every Alex Cross thriller has been an international bestseller. *Return of the Spider* is the thirty-third novel in this extraordinary series.

James Patterson is the author of other bestselling series, including the Women's Murder Club, Michael Bennett and Private novels. James has donated millions in grants to independent bookshops and has been the most borrowed adult author in UK libraries for the past fourteen years in a row. He lives in Florida with his family.

Have you read them all?

ALONG CAME A SPIDER

Alex Cross is working on the high-profile disappearance of two rich kids. But is he facing someone much more dangerous than a callous kidnapper?

KISS THE GIRLS

Cross comes home to discover his niece Naomi is missing. And she's not the only one. Finding the kidnapper won't be easy, especially if he's not working alone . . .

JACK AND JILL

A pair of ice-cold killers are picking off Washington's rich and famous. And they have the ultimate target in their sights.

CAT AND MOUSE

An old enemy is back and wants revenge. Will Alex Cross escape unharmed, or will this be the final showdown?

POP GOES THE WEASEL

Alex Cross faces his most fearsome opponent yet. He calls himself Death. And there are three other 'Horsemen' who compete in his twisted game.

ROSES ARE RED

After a series of fatal bank robberies, Cross must take the ultimate risk when faced with a criminal known as the Mastermind.

VIOLETS ARE BLUE

As Alex Cross edges ever closer to the awful truth about the Mastermind, he comes dangerously close to defeat.

FOUR BLIND MICE

Preparing to resign from the Washington police force, Alex Cross is looking forward to a peaceful life. But he can't stay away for long . . .

THE BIG BAD WOLF

There is a mysterious new mobster in organised crime. The FBI are stumped. Luckily for them, they now have Alex Cross on their team.

LONDON BRIDGES

The stakes have never been higher as Cross pursues two old enemies in an explosive worldwide chase.

MARY, MARY

Hollywood's A-list are being violently killed, one-by-one. Only Alex Cross can put together the clues of this twisted case.

CROSS

Haunted by the murder of his wife thirteen years ago, Cross will stop at nothing to finally avenge her death.

DOUBLE CROSS

Alex Cross is starting to settle down – until he encounters a maniac killer who likes an audience.

CROSS COUNTRY

When an old friend becomes the latest victim of the Tiger, Cross journeys to Africa to stop a terrifying and dangerous warlord.

ALEX CROSS'S TRIAL
(with Richard DiLallo)

In a family story recounted here by Alex Cross, his great-uncle Abraham faces persecution, murder and conspiracy in the era of the Ku Klux Klan.

I, ALEX CROSS

Investigating the violent murder of his niece Caroline, Alex Cross discovers an unimaginable secret that could rock the entire world.

CROSS FIRE

Alex Cross is planning his wedding to Bree, but his nemesis returns to exact revenge.

KILL ALEX CROSS

The President's children have been kidnapped, and DC is hit by a terrorist attack. Cross must make a desperate decision that goes against everything he believes in.

MERRY CHRISTMAS, ALEX CROSS

Robbery, hostages, terrorism – will Alex Cross make it home in time for Christmas . . . alive?

ALEX CROSS, RUN

With his personal life in turmoil, Alex Cross can't afford to let his guard down. Especially with three blood-thirsty killers on the rampage.

CROSS MY HEART

When a dangerous enemy targets Cross and his family, Alex finds himself playing a whole new game of life and death.

HOPE TO DIE

Cross's family are missing, presumed dead. But Alex Cross will not give up hope. In a race against time, he must find his wife, children and grandmother – no matter what it takes.

CROSS JUSTICE
Returning to his North Carolina hometown for the first time in over three decades, Cross unearths a family secret that forces him to question everything he's ever known.

CROSS THE LINE
Cross steps in to investigate a wave of murders erupting across Washington, DC. The victims have one thing in common – they are all criminals.

THE PEOPLE VS. ALEX CROSS
Charged with gunning down followers of his nemesis Gary Soneji in cold blood, Cross must fight for his freedom in the trial of the century.

TARGET: ALEX CROSS
Cross is called on to lead the FBI investigation to find America's most wanted criminal. But what follows will plunge the country into chaos, and draw Cross into the most important case of his life.

CRISS CROSS
When notes signed by 'M' start appearing at homicide scenes across the state, Cross fears he is chasing a ghost.

DEADLY CROSS
A shocking double homicide dominates tabloid headlines. Among the victims is Kay, a glamorous socialite and Cross's former patient – and maybe more. But who would want her dead, and why?

FEAR NO EVIL
Alex Cross ventures into the rugged Montana wilderness where he's attacked by two rival teams of assassins, controlled by the same mastermind who has stalked Alex and his family for years.

TRIPLE CROSS

Hunting an elusive killer who targets families around Washington, DC, Cross must work harder than ever to discover the truth.

ALEX CROSS MUST DIE

An airplane explodes in the sky. A serial murderer is on the loose. With two killers and two different motives, Cross is in a deadly race against time.

THE HOUSE OF CROSS

A serial killer is taking out America's finest legal minds, and Alex Cross is called to investigate. But during a dangerous mission to track down the killer, his loved ones go missing.

Also By James Patterson

ALEX CROSS NOVELS

Along Came a Spider • Kiss the Girls • Jack and Jill • Cat and Mouse • Pop Goes the Weasel • Roses are Red • Violets are Blue • Four Blind Mice • The Big Bad Wolf • London Bridges • Mary, Mary • Cross • Double Cross • Cross Country • Alex Cross's Trial (*with Richard DiLallo*) • I, Alex Cross • Cross Fire • Kill Alex Cross • Merry Christmas, Alex Cross • Alex Cross, Run • Cross My Heart • Hope to Die • Cross Justice • Cross the Line • The People vs. Alex Cross • Target: Alex Cross • Criss Cross • Deadly Cross • Fear No Evil • Triple Cross • Alex Cross Must Die • The House of Cross

THE WOMEN'S MURDER CLUB SERIES

1st to Die (*with Andrew Gross*) • 2nd Chance (*with Andrew Gross*) • 3rd Degree (*with Andrew Gross*) • 4th of July (*with Maxine Paetro*) • The 5th Horseman (*with Maxine Paetro*) • The 6th Target (*with Maxine Paetro*) • 7th Heaven (*with Maxine Paetro*) • 8th Confession (*with Maxine Paetro*) • 9th Judgement (*with Maxine Paetro*) • 10th Anniversary (*with Maxine Paetro*) • 11th Hour (*with Maxine Paetro*) • 12th of Never (*with Maxine Paetro*) • Unlucky 13 (*with Maxine Paetro*) • 14th Deadly Sin (*with Maxine Paetro*) • 15th Affair (*with Maxine Paetro*) • 16th Seduction (*with Maxine Paetro*) • 17th Suspect (*with Maxine Paetro*) • 18th Abduction (*with Maxine Paetro*) • 19th Christmas (*with Maxine Paetro*) • 20th Victim (*with Maxine Paetro*) • 21st Birthday (*with Maxine Paetro*) • 22 Seconds (*with Maxine Paetro*) • 23rd Midnight (*with Maxine Paetro*) • The 24th Hour (*with Maxine Paetro*) • 25 Alive (*with Maxine Paetro*)

DETECTIVE MICHAEL BENNETT SERIES

Step on a Crack (*with Michael Ledwidge*) • Run for Your Life (*with Michael Ledwidge*) • Worst Case (*with Michael Ledwidge*) • Tick Tock (*with Michael Ledwidge*) • I, Michael Bennett (*with Michael Ledwidge*) • Gone (*with Michael Ledwidge*) • Burn (*with Michael Ledwidge*) • Alert (*with Michael Ledwidge*) • Bullseye (*with Michael Ledwidge*) • Haunted (*with James O. Born*) • Ambush (*with James O. Born*) • Blindside (*with James O. Born*) • The Russian (*with James O. Born*) • Shattered (*with James O. Born*) • Obsessed (*with James O. Born*) • Crosshairs (*with James O. Born*) • Paranoia (*with James O. Born*)

PRIVATE NOVELS

Private (*with Maxine Paetro*) • Private London (*with Mark Pearson*) • Private Games (*with Mark Sullivan*) • Private: No. 1 Suspect (*with Maxine Paetro*) • Private Berlin (*with Mark Sullivan*) • Private Down Under (*with Michael White*) • Private L.A. (*with Mark Sullivan*) • Private India (*with Ashwin Sanghi*) • Private Vegas (*with Maxine Paetro*) • Private Sydney (*with Kathryn Fox*) • Private Paris (*with Mark Sullivan*) • The Games (*with Mark Sullivan*) • Private Delhi (*with Ashwin Sanghi*) • Private Princess (*with Rees Jones*) • Private Moscow (*with Adam Hamdy*) • Private Rogue (*with Adam Hamdy*) • Private Beijing (*with Adam Hamdy*) • Private Rome (*with Adam Hamdy*) • Private Monaco (*with Adam Hamdy*)

NYPD RED SERIES

NYPD Red (*with Marshall Karp*) • NYPD Red 2 (*with Marshall Karp*) • NYPD Red 3 (*with Marshall Karp*) • NYPD Red 4 (*with Marshall Karp*) • NYPD Red 5 (*with Marshall Karp*) • NYPD Red 6 (*with Marshall Karp*)

DETECTIVE HARRIET BLUE SERIES

Never Never (*with Candice Fox*) • Fifty Fifty (*with Candice Fox*) • Liar Liar (*with Candice Fox*) • Hush Hush (*with Candice Fox*)

INSTINCT SERIES

Instinct (*with Howard Roughan, previously published as Murder Games*) • Killer Instinct (*with Howard Roughan*) • Steal (*with Howard Roughan*)

THE BLACK BOOK SERIES

The Black Book (*with David Ellis*) • The Red Book (*with David Ellis*) • Escape (*with David Ellis*)

TEXAS RANGER SERIES

Texas Ranger (*with Andrew Bourelle*) • Texas Outlaw (*with Andrew Bourelle*) • The Texas Murders (*with Andrew Bourelle*)

STAND-ALONE THRILLERS

The Thomas Berryman Number • Hide and Seek • Black Market • The Midnight Club • Honeymoon (*with Howard Roughan*) • Sail (*with Howard Roughan*) • Swimsuit (*with Maxine Paetro*) • Don't Blink (*with Howard Roughan*) • Postcard Killers (*with Liza Marklund*) • Toys (*with Neil McMahon*) • Now You See Her (*with Michael Ledwidge*) • Kill Me If You Can (*with Marshall Karp*) • Guilty Wives (*with David Ellis*) • Zoo (*with Michael Ledwidge*) • Second Honeymoon (*with Howard Roughan*) • Mistress (*with David Ellis*) • Invisible (*with David Ellis*) • Truth or Die (*with Howard Roughan*) • Murder House (*with David Ellis*) • The Store (*with Richard DiLallo*) • The President is Missing (*with Bill Clinton*) • Revenge (*with Andrew Holmes*) • Juror No. 3 (*with Nancy Allen*) • The First Lady (*with Brendan DuBois*) • The Chef (*with Max DiLallo*) • Out of Sight (*with Brendan DuBois*) • Unsolved (*with David Ellis*) • The Inn (*with

Candice Fox) • Lost (*with James O. Born*) • The Summer House (*with Brendan DuBois*) • 1st Case (*with Chris Tebbetts*) • Cajun Justice (*with Tucker Axum*)• The Midwife Murders (*with Richard DiLallo*) • The Coast-to-Coast Murders (*with J.D. Barker*) • Three Women Disappear (*with Shan Serafin*) • The President's Daughter (*with Bill Clinton*) • The Shadow (*with Brian Sitts*) • The Noise (*with J.D. Barker*) • 2 Sisters Detective Agency (*with Candice Fox*) • Jailhouse Lawyer (*with Nancy Allen*) • The Horsewoman (*with Mike Lupica*) • Run Rose Run (*with Dolly Parton*) • Death of the Black Widow (*with J.D. Barker*) • The Ninth Month (*with Richard DiLallo*) • The Girl in the Castle (*with Emily Raymond*) • Blowback (*with Brendan DuBois*) • The Twelve Topsy-Turvy, Very Messy Days of Christmas (*with Tad Safran*) • The Perfect Assassin (*with Brian Sitts*) • House of Wolves (*with Mike Lupica*) • Countdown (*with Brendan DuBois*) • Cross Down (*with Brendan DuBois*) • Circle of Death (*with Brian Sitts*) • Lion & Lamb (with *Duane Swierczynski*) • 12 Months to Live (*with Mike Lupica*) • Holmes, Margaret and Poe (*with Brian Sitts*) • The No. 1 Lawyer (*with Nancy Allen*) • Eruption (*with Michael Crichton*) • The Murder Inn (*with Candice Fox*) • Confessions of the Dead (*with J.D. Barker*) • 8 Months Left (*with Mike Lupica*) • Lies He Told Me (*with David Ellis*) • Murder Island (*with Brian Sitts*) • Raised By Wolves (*with Emily Raymond*) • Holmes is Missing (*with Brian Sitts*) • 2 Sisters Murder Investigations (*with Candice Fox*)

NON-FICTION

Torn Apart (*with Hal and Cory Friedman*) • The Murder of King Tut (*with Martin Dugard*) • All-American Murder (*with Alex Abramovich and Mike Harvkey*) • The Kennedy Curse (*with Cynthia Fagen*) • The Last Days of John Lennon (*with Casey Sherman and Dave Wedge*) • Walk in My Combat Boots (*with Matt Eversmann and Chris Mooney*) • ER Nurses (*with Matt Eversmann*) • James Patterson by James Patterson: The Stories of My Life • Diana, William and Harry (*with Chris Mooney*) • American Cops (*with Matt Eversmann*) • What Really Happens in Vegas (*with Mark Seal*) • The Secret Lives of Booksellers and Librarians (*with Matt Eversmann*) • Tiger, Tiger • American Heroes (*with Matt Eversmann*)

MURDER IS FOREVER TRUE CRIME

Murder, Interrupted (*with Alex Abramovich and Christopher Charles*) • Home Sweet Murder (*with Andrew Bourelle and Scott Slaven*) • Murder Beyond the Grave (*with Andrew Bourelle and Christopher Charles*) • Murder Thy Neighbour (*with Andrew Bourelle and Max DiLallo*) • Murder of Innocence (*with Max DiLallo and Andrew Bourelle*) • Till Murder Do Us Part (*with Andrew Bourelle and Max DiLallo*)

COLLECTIONS

Triple Threat (*with Max DiLallo and Andrew Bourelle*) • Kill or Be Killed (*with Maxine Paetro, Rees Jones, Shan Serafin and Emily Raymond*) • The Moores are Missing (*with Loren D. Estleman, Sam Hawken and Ed Chatterton*) • The Family Lawyer (*with Robert Rotstein, Christopher Charles and Rachel Howzell Hall*) • Murder in Paradise (*with Doug Allyn, Connor Hyde and Duane Swierczynski*) • The House Next Door (*with Susan DiLallo, Max DiLallo and Brendan DuBois*) • 13-Minute Murder (*with Shan Serafin, Christopher Farnsworth and Scott Slaven*) • The River Murders (*with James O. Born*) • The Palm Beach Murders (*with James O. Born, Duane Swierczynski and Tim Arnold*) • Paris Detective • 3 Days to Live • 23 ½ Lies (*with Maxine Paetro*)

For more information about James Patterson's novels, visit www.penguin.co.uk.